Praise for *From Shadow's Perspective*

This is the kind of book that sneaks up on you, sniffing around your edges like a curious puppy until you fall in love with it. The characters, even the ghosts, are lively and the adventure of it all: danger, psychic Dobermans, jealous housemates, death, heartbreak and a father's love all carry the reader through to a place that finds redemption. Read this book. You will not regret it.

—Kevin Fisher-Paulson, San Francisco Chronicle columnist,
Author, *A Song for Lost Angels* and *How We Keep Spinning . . .*

A beguiling sequel to *Between Shadow's Eyes*, Jill Hedgecock's *From Shadow's Perspective* has everything you'd want in a weekend page turner: cold cases, complex characters, ghostly intervention, and a fine Doberman who brings out the best in her young owner, too.

—Susannah Charleson, *New York Times* bestselling author of *Scent of the Missing: Love and Partnership with a Search and Rescue Dog*

This sequel to Jill Hedgecock's *Between Shadow's Eyes* picks up where the first novel ends with yet another paranormal thriller. A ghost child appears in a classroom and launches another mystery for teenage orphan Sarah Whitman and her zipper nose, ghost-seeing Doberman. Despite warnings from her ghost of a father that her life is in danger, Sarah's obsession with discovering the truth behind the town's secret of a missing boy threatens her relationships with virtually everyone she knows, as well as sidetracks her emancipation hearing.

Jill Hedgecock is a master at storytelling. She fashions a mystery through subtle clues and lingering characters that converge into a crescendo of surprises and consequences that always seem to climax into a consummate thriller. An entertaining read that you will enjoy, especially after having read *Between Shadow's Eyes*.

—*Diablo Gazette*

Sarah Whitman and her Doberman Shadow are back again in this suspenseful masterpiece that will pull the reader directly into Sarah's world. Author Jill Hedgecock masterfully captures the bond between Sarah and her dog, a Doberman named Shadow as readers follow Sarah's journey to unravel a mystery surrounding the disappearance of a toddler in her small town. This is one of those books that leaves you with no choice but to keep turning the pages until the surprising conclusion.

n Walter, DobermanPlanet.com

Young Sarah Whitman and her beloved rescue Doberman, Shadow, are back in *From Shadow's Perspective,* a riveting sequel to *Between Shadow's Eyes.* Orphaned and living with her kindly guardian next door, Mr. O'Shawnessy, Sarah is fighting for her court-ordered emancipation. She longs to return to her own home and her devoted dog, and to get away from Mr. O'Shawnessy's "mean girl" granddaughter, Margaret. Ostracized at school and tormented at home courtesy of Margaret, and plagued at every turn by the ill-intentioned veterinarian, Dr. Griffin, Sarah fears her plans may be derailed. Add in a romantic triangle, an ugly secret, some characters who are not quite as they seem, and a couple of ghosts, and you have a plot that will keep you twisting and turning unexpectedly until the very end. I loved *Between Shadow's Eyes,* but the sequel is even better! Don't miss it!

—Deb Stevenson, author of award-winning *Soaring Soren: When French Bulldogs Fly*

From Shadow's Perspective is beyond awesome. It kept me riveted until the very end and I still wanted more. There probably wasn't one page in the entire book that didn't leave me wanting me to read more. Nothing was predictable.

—Diane Walsh former board member of the Illinois Doberman Rescue and Owner of East SF Bay's Endless Pawsibilities Pet Services

Writing from passion, Jill Hedgecock plunges the reader into *From Shadow's Perspective,* the story of now-orphaned Sarah, "the one oddball," and her beloved Doberman, Shadow. Guided by her Doberman, ghosts, and her father's copy of Adventures in Wonderland, this worthy sequel to *Between Shadow's Eyes* takes you through a challenging, upside down world to a satisfying and glorious Writing from passion, Jill Hedgecock plunges the reader into *From Shadow's Perspective,* the story of now-orphaned Sarah, "the one oddball," and her beloved Doberman, Shadow. Guided by her Doberman, ghosts, and her father's copy of Adventures in Wonderland, this worthy sequel to *Between Shadow's Eyes* takes you through a challenging, upside down world to a satisfying and glorious conclusion.

—Aline Soules, Author of *Evening Sun*; Emerita Librarian and selector, Juvenile/Young Adult Collections, Cal State East Bay

When orphaned Sarah rubs the spot between her dog's eyes, she sees ghosts. Seriously! You'll love the mysterious, atypical look at a teenager's life and loves, whether you are a current student or reimagining your teen years. Original and creative!

—B. Lynn Goodwin, author of *Never Too Late: From Wannabe to Wife* and *Talent*

FROM SHADOW'S PERSPECTIVE

A SUSPENSE NOVEL

From Shadow's Perspective

Cover Photograph by Charles Lindsey (cskphotography.net)
"Lone Boy" Photograph–John G. van Groos

Ruby, an American red, zipper-nosed Doberman Pinscher is an Instagram sensation.
Follow her at www. instagram.com/rubydooby_do

Cover Design and Interior Typesetting by Melissa Williams Design

Published by Goshawk Press

ISBN: 978-1-7322415-3-4 (paperback)
ISBN: 978-1-7322415-4-1 (eBook)
First Edition

www.jillhedgecock.com

FROM SHADOW'S PERSPECTIVE

—————————— A SUSPENSE NOVEL ——————————

JILL HEDGECOCK

GOSHAWK
P R E S S

Dedicated to all the Doberman Rescues Organizations across the world.

For a list of Doberman Rescues in the United States by state visit:

Doberman Pinscher Club of America (DPCA)

https://www.dpca.org/rescue/by-state.php

CHAPTER ONE

"I can't explain myself, I'm afraid, sir," said Alice,
"because I'm not myself, you see." [1]

More than anything, I wanted to melt into the lawn of Walnut Acres High. Across a wide expanse of green grass from where I sat, boys formed a semi-circle around a cluster of girls in the shade of a giant walnut tree. Other small clusters of girlfriends and separate groups of guys radiated out from that core group. The hum of conversations from various cliques hovered in the air like a dense fog. I might have mustered the courage to ask to eat with a group if it weren't for Margaret who sat in the popular-kid group, surrounded by her squad of six. The Magnificent Seven they called themselves. I imagine they thought of me as The One Oddball.

I plucked a red-and-green Fuji apple from my lunch bag, bringing the fruit to my nose. The scent always made me sad. My father once told me my mother smelled like

---

1—All chapters begin with a Lewis Carroll quote from the 1865 novel *Alice's Adventures in Wonderland*, unless otherwise indicated.

apples. She died as I came into this world, so I have no memory of that. Still, I cling to this detail about her, this apple scent, this one thing, and it transports me into imagining an alternative life, a life I never had—one of soft, cradling hands and lullabies.

My father did his best. But men love children in a different way. He read to me. He tucked me into bed. He kissed my skinned knees and bruised feelings. When he learned his cancer had spread, and he was dying, my father tried to cram a lifetime of advice into the last few months of his life. That was my Dad—trying to shape life's messiness into a neat little box.

His twelve relationship rules spelled out on a laminated card were safely hidden in my backpack. But the advice hasn't helped me win over my legal guardian's granddaughter, Margaret. Last month she threw a rumor mill of poison on the path I walked to transition to this high school. And so no one dared to speak to The Freaky New Girl. Margaret O'Shawnessy continued to make sure of it.

Margaret turned her head and said something to her boyfriend, Paul. He, along with several of her clan, guffawed with laughter. Then the raven-haired beauty with emerald eyes, who was as ugly as a person could be on the inside, stood and zeroed in on me. Margaret took a swig of the soda in her hand as if to throw down a challenge. Her red and manicured nails squeezed the aluminum can so hard I could picture the indentations that formed. She handed her cola to Paul and headed in my direction.

I bit into the waxy skin of the apple. Margaret O'Shawnessy hated me the first day we met. Things only got worse last spring when I moved in with her and her grandfather after the authorities learned I was a sixteen-year-old orphan living alone next door. Whatever compelled my housemate to leave her friends now to come speak to me couldn't be good.

She strode toward me with such purpose I had to suppress an urge to jump to my feet and bolt to my car. But the other kids would think me a coward. And Sarah Whitman was no coward.

When Margaret drew close, I wrinkled my nose at her then stuffed the rest of the apple into my brown paper lunch bag. Lifting my face to the sun, I pretended I was unconcerned with her presence, as if I preferred sitting in the warm rays of this October day by myself to hanging out with other teens. I wouldn't let it show that I longed to join everyone else as they laughed and discussed the latest movie or a hot, boy band. I wouldn't take part when others engaged in mean-girl gossip though. I would not be like Margaret.

"Sarah," Margaret said in the cajoling, whiny voice she only used when she needed something. "Can I see your trig homework?"

My skin prickled. The only reason she wanted to see my math assignment was to copy my work. Cheating could lead to detention or even flunking a class at Walnut Acres High and, if caught, Margaret would say I copied her work.

"I didn't finish it." Hoping to win her over, I added, "If you want something explained, I can try to help."

"Seriously? You expect me to believe Ms. A student, Ms. Perfect, hasn't completed an assignment? I know you have it in your backpack."

Margaret thrust her hand into my open bag. What the hell? I scrambled to stop her, but it was too late. Why hadn't I zipped it up when I put the apple away?

I hopped to my feet and lunged at her as she extracted the organizer that held my homework problems. She was taller than me, and as she waved the black folder above her head, a shiny plastic card tumbled to the grass, landing face up.

No. No, No, NO. My cheeks flamed as we both scrambled for it, but her reflexes were quicker than mine.

"What's this?" Margaret said snatching the card.

Her eyes tracked the words. Then her mouth broke into a huge grin, and she bent over laughing. I wrenched the card from her grasp, but she had read enough of the content to have ammunition to embarrass me for the rest of my life.

"Oh," she giggled. "This is rich." She gasped for breath as moisture slid from her eyes. "This is ... OMG ...

I jammed the laminated card into my backpack. My father's pearls of wisdom were supposed to help me make my interactions with other people positive, but this card had just made my situation worse.

Before he died Dad had gone over his other set of rules with me—the Game Plan Rules—the ones to keep me safe, but he hadn't mentioned that he had written down these relationship rules. Why?

I only discovered the plastic relationship rule card last week when I unpacked old boxes of his belongings looking for my birth certificate. I needed a certified copy for my upcoming emancipation hearing. When I found the card, I obsessed over the rules, searching for hidden meanings, looking for clues about how he treated my mother, but mostly feeling connected to my father once again. I read them so many times that I memorized them. I didn't really need the card anymore. Why hadn't I left it at my own house? What had I been thinking bringing it to school where someone might discover it? Now that I thought about it, I knew the answer. It gave me the illusion that my Dad was near.

Now Margaret had fresh material to ridicule me with. She'll make sure to tell everyone that The Freaky New Girl needs a cheat sheet to figure out how to make friends. Margaret burst into another fit of laughter. I thought over each rule trying to figure out which one Margaret found so funny.

Twelve Relationship Rules

Rule #1: *A successful relationship needs to have balance. Balance of power, balance of respect, and balance of compassion.*

Rule #2: *Be generous.*

Rule #3: *Nobody loves a drama queen. Even if they say they do.*

Rule #4: *Act interested. Be interesting.*

Rule #5: *Always be honest.*

Rule #6: *Never make a promise you don't intend to keep.*

Rule #7: *Run like the wind from possessive guys.*

Rule #8: *Avoid anyone who has no sense of humor.*

Rule #9: *Treat others the way you want to be treated.*

Rule #10: *Never pretend to be something that you're not.*

Rule #11: *Never forsake safety. Keep a cell phone on you. Meet dates in public places, and never, ever, get high or drunk on a date.*

Rule #12: *Love is infinite*

Which one will she blurt out to her Magnificent Seven club? She would probably keep quiet about Rule #3 since she was a Drama Queen. Then again, she probably didn't see herself that way. Rule #7? She could add that I won't ever need that one since no guy would be interested in a loser like me.

Margaret finally regained some self-control. One hand covered her stomach as if she worried her intestines might spill out from the unfamiliar exertion of laughter.

"I can't wait to tell everyone," she said.

"Don't, Margaret. Please."

"I won't if you give me your trig homework."

Yeah, right. She would take my homework then tell everyone about the card anyway.

"It's cheating."

"What about Rule #2? You're supposed to be generous."

How many had she managed to read before I snatched the card from her? Even if she had read Rule #5 regarding being honest, she wouldn't think it applied to her. For a moment, I toyed with the idea of handing over the assignment. Anything to get her to stop bullying me. But I couldn't risk it. An accusation of cheating could jeopardize my emancipation request. If I couldn't move back into my home with my dog, Shadow, and get away from Margaret, I might just lose my mind.

"I can't," I straightened my spine to show her I wasn't afraid of her threat. "It would be better if you kept your mouth shut."

Empty air hung behind my threat. I didn't even know what I meant. Ms. Magnificent got away with nasty pranks by predicting how people would react. She wouldn't expect me to retaliate if she talked smack about me. And she was right. I wouldn't risk causing trouble, and she knew it. Especially not when my court hearing would be scheduled any day now. She held all the power.

"Or what?" Margaret whispered under her breath, "You going to hit me? You know you want to."

She thought I wanted to physically assault her? Really? I despised her, but that didn't mean I would get violent. I fished out my car keys as if nothing had happened. Then I looked into her green eyes and forced a smile.

"Seems to me," I said, "that you and your friends could use some guidance on how to be nicer people. Sometimes that means keeping your thoughts to yourself and walking away."

I slung my backpack over my shoulder, whirled on the ball of one foot and headed for the parking lot. Yesterday my art teacher had given me permission to leave campus to pick up Shadow and bring her to the drawing class. Fridays were always living model assignments. The principal's twenty-minute pass for today gave me enough time to drive home and retrieve Shadow before my final class of the day.

"I'm telling," she shouted as she moved toward her clique. "You can't leave campus."

"Go ahead," I said and kept walking.

Little did she know my backpack held a pass to leave school today.

"Sarah," a male voice called. "Wait."

Over my shoulder, I saw Kyle jogging my way. Kyle who I thought really liked me. But we had met only few times this summer before he left on a prolonged family vacation that extended to the beginning of the school year. He hadn't kept in touch while he was away. Even after he returned last month, he didn't text or call me. He was Paul's best friend, which meant he also hung around Margaret. I assumed she poisoned him against me.

Hearing his voice took me back to the first time I laid eyes on him last spring. His concern for me as I descended a steep trail in the oak-hilled nature park attracted me to this redheaded boy. That, plus the way his curls sprang from his head in haphazard directions. He towered a foot or so over me, which made me feel safe, though I didn't understand why.

I was thrilled when he transferred into my art class last week. As the days stretched and he barely looked at me, much less said a word when he passed by, I knew the romantic spark we once shared had fizzled on his end.

I didn't stop moving toward my car, but I turned and walked backwards until he caught up. Only then did I come to a halt. The air swirling around the lawn at Walnut Acres High seemed to seize up. A quick glance toward the Magnificent Seven confirmed that everyone in Margaret's kingdom had grown silent and now watched us. A nearby group, the Wannabe-Popular crowd, soon followed suit, and then like a domino effect, the world became quiet.

Kyle seemed oblivious to the change in the atmosphere. He shoved his hands in his pants pockets and offered his lopsided grin. He resembled a cute puppy—clumsy and endearing. Hope filled my chest. Maybe it was still possible to blow oxygen on the smoldering kindling and resume where we left off.

"Hey," he said, "don't let Margaret get to you."

I shrugged.

"Um…" he added. "I've been meaning to tell you… um… the still life you did last week in art class was awesome." I hazarded a glance. His blue eyes radiated warmth. "It was so creative. I love metaphorical art."

During our last assignment to draw a bowl of fruit, I made the pear into the head of a Doberman with a long snout. I hadn't meant my drawing to be a metaphor, so I didn't know how to respond, and even if I did, my heart tripped over itself, and my lungs seemed determined not to exhale air and let me speak. I stepped on my foot to jar myself out of my paralysis. Dad's Rule #4 blinked in my brain like a stoplight: Act interested. Be interesting. But how, when I wasn't willing to ask what he meant? My question would probably embarrass both of us. He would think he misread my intent, and I would seem less smart.

When my art teacher had discovered my dog Shadow was my inspiration, she asked if the dog was friendly and well trained. After I said yes to both questions, Mrs. Durgette asked if I would bring her in for our living models lesson.

Kyle tilted his head sideways and chewed on his lower lip as the silence stretched.

Say something. Anything. My tongue unwound. But my brain refused to form a single interesting thought.

"Uh, thanks," I mumbled.

His burgundy T-shirt featured a silk-screened photo of the rapper, Akon, highlighted in white and various shades of gray. I recognized this technique as chiaroscuro, contrasting light and dark to make a three-dimensional image appear.

"Great shirt," I said.

He glanced down at his clothes then back at me. "Yeah?"

I nodded. My limbs felt too long, my blouse gaudy, my jeans too tight. I clutched my car keys to my chest then felt ridiculous, so I dropped my arms.

"I'm sorry I've been out of touch," Kyle said. "Let's go to Starbucks after class and catch up. You don't have a sixth period, right?"

Was it possible that he was still interested in me despite how unpopular I was? Before I recovered from the shock and found my voice, a loud snap crackled through the air. Kyle didn't react. He stood with his head a tad off-kilter. His crumpled brow suggested only that he was awaiting an answer to his question. I've been curious to know if others also heard the loud noise my father's ghost made when he materialized. I didn't expect others to see him. Even I couldn't make out his translucent body, not right now at least. If Shadow was with me, and I put my index and middle fingers together and placed them between her eyes, I could. Without my dog though, it was only possible to feel Dad's presence.

Kyle scuffed the ground with a black, high top shoe. Was he feeling as awkward as I was, or did he wonder why I was taking so long to answer?

"Uh-huh," I stammered. "No sixth period."

By now, most of the kids had lost interest and resumed talking and laughing. Only Margaret kept staring at us as though trying to lip-read our conversation.

A bracelet of warmth encircled my right wrist. Then slight pressure fell across my shoulders as though someone had slung an arm across my neck. A tugging motion pulled me away from Kyle. What the hell was my father doing? He had only materialized once before. Last spring Dad appeared and rescued me when my life was in danger from Dr. Griffin, a wacko veterinarian. So why the sudden reappearance? A strong jerk on my arm nearly sent me toppling.

"Dad!" I blurted in protest.

When I lifted my head, my gaze connected with Margaret's. Could this day get any better for her? My housemate now had juicy new material to ridicule me with.

"Are you okay?" Kyle said.

He looked around then brought his gaze back to me. He didn't seem to notice Margaret's icy stare.

His brow wrinkled further in confusion. Dimples remained even when he wasn't smiling. Freckles tickled his nose. He was so darn cute. Not that it mattered. He must believe I'm a crazy person now. Crap. Thanks a lot, Dad. I imagine the rumors floating through the hallways after lunch. "The new girl was acting so weird on the front lawn. Her arms were all like ... like I don't know, but she was totally cray cray." Margaret must have a bucketload of ideas on how to throw shade my way. I scrambled to formulate a rational explanation for my outburst and apparent clumsiness.

"I planned to visit my dad's grave," I said. "After school, that is."

"Oh," he said looking stricken. "I'm such an idiot. I'd forgotten about your father's passing."

Really? Margaret complained to anyone who would listen how her grandfather felt sorry for me because I was an orphan with no brothers or sisters. Despite Margaret's disapproval, if my neighbor, dear Mr. O'Shawnessy, hadn't taken me in temporarily, Shadow would have been re-homed. I couldn't imagine giving her up. It was hard enough forcing her to live alone next door at my house because of Margaret's "allergies."

My father's plan hadn't fallen into place as he had hoped. His scheme to keep the secret that I was underage and living alone had ultimately failed. To keep me out of foster care, he bought me a house in a new town where no one would know me. After social services discovered my circumstances, I had been lucky when my elderly neighbor

Mr. O'Shawnessy invited me to move in with him and Margaret.

"Tomorrow?" Kyle's brow knitted together the way Shadow's did when I held a treat.

Before I was able to reply, my arm levitated outward as the warm air binding my wrist pulled me toward the parking lot. What was Dad doing? And what did Kyle think now? I was making a spectacle of myself again.

"I have to go," I said over my shoulder, pointing my index fingers so that it would appear my outstretched arm gestured toward my car. "My dog's going to be our living model for our art assignment today. See you in class."

I turned and ran, imagining Margaret with her head tipped back in hysterical laughter. Dad's ethereal pull escorted me all the way to my white Civic. Yanking the driver's side door open, I stumbled inside then slammed the door shut. The warm weight of my father's grip still held my arm.

"Dad," I flicked my arm, trying to extract it from his grasp. "Let go."

My father's hold remained steadfast. I flapped my arms to no avail. Movement in the rearview mirror caught my eye. A sense of being watched filled me with dread. Don't let it be Kyle. Please don't let it be Kyle.

But of course, there he was—the red-haired boy of my dreams. Kyle stood a mere car-length away, frowning. I imagined what he witnessed—me yelling at air as I jerked my arm around like a maniac.

"Now look what you've done," I whispered under my breath.

To my amazement, Kyle saluted me. For a moment I thought he might have missed my outburst. But his fingers wiggled in slow motion. The wave you would give to humor a crazy person because you're afraid of the consequences if you don't. Kyle took giant strides backward, each step putting a greater distance between us.

CHAPTER TWO

"Oh my ears and whiskers. How late it's getting!"

Tension drained from my neck the further I drove from the school. Dad's ghost disappeared as quickly as he had appeared. Why would he sabotage my slim chance of making a new friend? Was he being over-protective of his little girl, afraid I might like the guy, and fall into bed with Kyle after a coffee date? How dumb was that?

My car turned onto Cherryglen Drive. My yellow stucco house with manicured shrubs—the house Dad bought to keep me out of foster care until I turned eighteen—now stood empty most of the time. Only Shadow kept the place lively. I hoped the courts would let me move back home soon.

Mr. O'Shawnessy's brown-shingled house looked drab next to mine, but his cheerful attitude filled the inside with a homey atmosphere—until his granddaughter, oh Magnificent One of the Magnificent Seven, walked in. Then, the air chilled. It was time for me to move back into my house. Leaving was the one thing that Margaret and I agreed on.

My foot hit the brakes as I spotted the yellow VW beetle parked across the street from my house. I knew that car. As I drew closer, a dog footprint decal on the back window eliminated any lingering doubt that this was that whacko veterinarian Dr. Claudia Griffin's vehicle. Like a tourniquet, a cold loop of fear encircled my heart and squeezed hard. What was the crazy animal behaviorist doing on my street now? For five months she had honored our agreement to stay away. It had been our deal. If she left Shadow and me alone, I wouldn't turn the hood ornament over to the authorities. Over twenty years ago she had used the object to harm her prom date and she had taken my threat seriously until now. What changed?

I coasted by her empty car and pulled into my driveway then sat in my Civic afraid to go inside. Dr. Griffin must be after one of two things: the hood ornament or Shadow. As long as I had the silver eagle she had used as a murder weapon all those years ago, I could control her. Well, she wouldn't find her car decoration. That object was stashed in the potted mums I kept next door at Mr. O'Shawnessy's home. Those wilted flowers and her hood ornament would stay there until the court system deemed me competent to care for myself and allowed me to move to my real home.

Had she been feeding Shadow treats through the slats in the backyard fence during school hours? Shadow's doggie door allowed her to go in and out of the house as she pleased. I wasn't supposed to be home yet. Had she been doing this every school day? I wouldn't put it past the woman given her obsession with my dog. If this were her routine, I would never have caught her if I hadn't come home early today.

The cold knot of fear around my heart cinched tighter. What would she do if I surprised her? Calling the cops on her wasn't an option. That might jeopardize the outcome of my emancipation hearing. To go next door and alert my guardian wasn't a good idea either. I suspected he would want to phone the police, and the courts would deem my house unsafe and unfit for a teen girl to live in by herself. Right now, my caseworker seemed confident the court would recommend that I be allowed to return home. But if the court discovered an unstable woman had managed to enter my house, they could deem the neighborhood unsafe for a seventeen-year-old girl living alone.

Crap. Only ten minutes remained to collect Shadow and get back to school. I needed a stellar attendance record until my court date. Crap, crap, crap. My art teacher, Mrs. Durgette, would want to know where I went if I returned to school without Shadow. She would tell the principal, and he would call my social worker. Result: No emancipation.

I swung my legs out and dashed from my white Honda toward the porch. The door didn't show any scratches or other signs of forced entry. The only lock was a deadbolt that must be locked from the outside. Had I forgotten to set the deadbolt this morning? Even though I didn't sleep here, I showered and dressed for school in my own house. It was possible I was careless because I overslept. In my rush to get to school on time, I probably didn't lock up. Now instead of inserting my key, my hand twisted the knob until the latch gave way. I didn't open the door though. What if Dr. Griffin was inside ready to ambush me?

An electric charge of air announced my father's return. A wall of his warm essence blocked the doorway. He didn't want me to enter my house. But wasn't this why he dragged me to the car? I thought he wanted me to get home quickly. But now it seemed he feared what might happen if I went inside.

I nibbled on the fingernail on my right pinky. I didn't really want to go in either, but I needed Shadow. However, I didn't need to enter all the way. My dog always greeted me in the entry. The leash I kept on a peg next to the doorframe was within reach too. My hand snaked around my father's presence and eased the wooden door open a crack. Shadow wasn't waiting near the front door.

"Shadow," I whispered, pushing the door wider. "Shadow, come."

My dog's answering yip sounded as if it came from the backyard. Why didn't she use the doggie door to come greet me? Had the dog door flap in the glass slider insert somehow jammed? Something was definitely wrong. I gathered my courage and barreled my way around my father. After I pulled my cell phone out of my pocket, I tapped the numbers 9-1-1 but did not press send. One more keystroke and help could be on the way if that whacky woman posed a threat.

Shadow barked again. I tiptoed toward the back as my heart hammered so fast I thought I might faint. I eased open the drape that covered the sliding glass door to the backyard. The manual lock that secured the dog door was engaged. Holy crap! Was it possible I stranded her outside this morning? If Dr. Griffin was seeing a client on the block, I might be overreacting. In truth, this morning was a blur.

My red Doberman's brown, expectant eyes sparkled underneath splotches of yellow eyebrows. Her tapered ears perked into ramrod points. Her docked tail vibrated like windshield wipers on overdrive. I heard a clunk come from the back bedroom. Perhaps Dr. Griffin had experienced a rude awakening when she entered my house. Shadow's initial fondness for the woman changed after the events that transpired five months ago. Had the veterinarian forgotten that Shadow growled at her the last time she saw my dog? Perhaps the vet locked her in the backyard today while she looked for the hood ornament. I picture it now. Dr. Griffin luring Shadow onto the patio with a treat then locking her outside.

I let my dog in, patted her head, rubbed her zipper nose, and scanned the room for Dad's ghost. Nothing. I locked the back door then listened for movement in the house. Only silence. Had I imagined a thud?

My inner voice had strong opinions. Go. Now. Take Shadow and leave. Not yet, my rational brain countered.

Find out if Dr. Griffin is in the house. Or see if she is hiding in the back seat of her car. Wait. You don't need to worry. Shadow would be agitated if the woman were here.

My dog pranced down the narrow hallway toward my bedroom. Her footfalls echoed on the hardwood floor. It was my routine to leave the bedroom door open, but it was closed now. Wouldn't Dr. Griffin have left it open to make a quick exit? Shadow looked at me with those bright, intelligent eyes. Surely, she would bark if an intruder were behind the door. She didn't hesitate to let me know when things upset her. I made up my mind. I turned the doorknob.

"Keep the door shut," Dr. Griffin's loud voice commanded from inside my bedroom.

I let go as if I had touched molten lead and stepped backward. Holy Mother. I was hoping I had been wrong. The whacko vet was here, in my bedroom even. Shadow's tail vibrated, but still she didn't bark. She seemed more intrigued than protective.

I sprinted down the hall but hesitated when I reached the living room. Shadow hadn't budged. My bedroom door remained closed. Why hadn't the woman come out after me? Had Shadow scared her, or was she too busy ransacking my room for the hood ornament? Well, she wouldn't find it. I didn't have any blackmail-worthy objects in there either. No bongs, no funny white powder, no papers, or tests emblazoned with giant red "Fs."

"Shadow, come," I called.

My dog didn't even look in my direction. She inclined her head and sniffed at the bottom of the door. What was the woman doing in there?

My breath became ragged as fear morphed to anger. How dare this woman tell me to keep MY bedroom door shut? I should order her to leave. Dr. Griffin had no right to be in my house. Besides, my father wasn't interfering, so she must not pose an immediate threat. I strode down the passageway gripping my cell phone and holding it out before me like a cross that would ward off a vampire. Grabbing Shadow by the collar, I awkwardly turned the knob with my phone in hand and thrust the door open with my elbow.

Dr. Griffin lay prostrate on the carpet peering under my bed. She wore blue jeans and a hooded sweatshirt, a surprisingly normal outfit for someone who preferred saris and activist T-shirts. The woman lifted her head in my direction. Her blonde hair fell over her face. Turquoise, horn-rimmed-style glasses sat askew on her face.

"Oh no. No, no, no. Get Shadow out of here, quick."

Shadow's body tensed. Her growl sounded menacing. Good girl.

"You get out, or I'll let her go," I shouted.

Shadow must have sensed my fear. She lunged toward the bed, and I lost my grip. To my surprise, my dog ignored Dr. Griffin. Shadow's head disappeared under the box springs, but she was too big to wiggle underneath. Dr. Griffin screeched, and her face disappeared too.

"Get the hell out of my house. Right now. Before I call the police."

"He's under here," her muffled voice emanated from beneath the bed.

Who was the "he" she referred to? My dad's ghost? The space was too small for a person to crawl under. Whining, Shadow clawed at the carpet. Dr. Griffin's presence upset my dog. Enough already. This was my house. MY home.

"Last chance." My finger hovered over the call button. "I'm calling 9-1-1."

"No, wait."

Shadow grew more frantic. Pant. Wiggle. Pant. Her feet took her nowhere fast. I clenched and unclenched my fists. Crap. I didn't want to call. I couldn't call.

Anxiety and frustration intensified my anger. I raised my arm to throw my cell phone at her, but then the hood of her sweatshirt moved and a whiskered, gray snout followed by two beady, pink eyes popped into view.

I had always wanted a pet rat almost as much as a puppy. Dad refused to let me keep any animals because we moved so much due to his job. If my father hadn't died of cancer, I wouldn't have been in the shelter parking lot and agreed to take Shadow from the woman begging me to give the stray she had found a home.

The rat's nose twitched then retreated into the gray material like a tortoise head tucking inside its shell. Could that animal be what Dr. Griffin searched for? The woman was clueless enough that she might not even feel the creature in her hood. Good grief. Why had she brought a rat into my house?

"Uh," I blurted. "If you are looking for a gray rat, it's on your back."

"Yes, of course." Dr. Griffin said with exasperation. "Austen is right where I put him. It's Mansfield, the black and white one, that has escaped. He's under your bed."

What? But before I puzzled out how these two rodents landed in my house, I must get control of my dog. Shadow went berserk as her anxiety to get to the loose rat increased. I took a deep breath intending to call Shadow off. Instead I yelped as the black-and-white creature emerged. It streaked past me into the hallway causing me to jump back.

"There he goes," I shouted.

Shadow backed her head and shoulders out from under the bed and tore after the rat. I tried to snatch her collar, but she was too quick. Regardless of how I dealt with Dr. Griffin, one thing was for sure: I did not want Shadow to hurt the animal, nor did I want my dog to suffer a rat bite. I raced into the living room and saw Mansfield's scaly, pink tail disappear underneath the couch. A millisecond later my crazed barking and whining dog slid on the slick hardwood floor crashing into the upholstered furniture. I lunged for Shadow but she eluded my grasp again.

"Is he... Did Shadow get him?" Dr. Griffin asked, breathless from behind me.

"The rat's fine. He's under there." I pointed at the sofa.

I clutched my cell phone tighter in case she decided to pull something. But I didn't think she would. My father would be trying to force me outside if he sensed I was in danger. It would be better to help her catch the rat. I needed to get back to school.

Shadow danced next to the sofa. She couldn't even wedge her muzzle in the narrow space where Mansfield-the-rat hid. The skittering of rat claws under the couch sent Shadow into a frenzy. She flattened her body and shoved her nose into the narrow crevice. I don't think Dr. Griffin's presence registered with my dog. I removed Shadow's blue vinyl lead from a peg by the door and snapped it on her. If Mansfield decided to emerge, I now had control. But I wasn't going to put Shadow outside. I felt safer with my dog by my side.

The rat didn't seem inclined to leave though. Should I call pest control? A humane one that set live traps. What other choice did I have? The couch must weigh over a hundred pounds—too heavy to lift. I doubted that even together Dr. Griffin and I had sufficient strength to move it.

Dr. Griffin wasn't able to reach underneath, but she fell to her knees to peek under the furniture.

"He's wedged in the corner," she announced. "There's no way I can catch him. Now what am I going to tell Mrs. Bellweather?"

Mrs. Bellweather? These rats belonged to her? I would have never thought the old woman who lived across the street would keep rodents as pets. But what did I know?

Her house lay at the end of the narrow lane and I seldom saw or encountered her. If she housed a menagerie of pets back there, I would not have a clue. Dr. Griffin lifted her head. "I'm supposed to be training her two rats to stop fighting. The woman is very opinionated and doesn't think her precious babies will sleep well in unfamiliar surroundings, so I couldn't keep them overnight."

I rolled my eyes. As usual, Dr. Griffin, animal behaviorist extraordinaire, wasn't making any sense. If Mrs. Bellweather only knew how unfamiliar Mansfield's surroundings were now.

Rats, Mrs. Bellweather, Shadow, and Dr. Griffin. The pieces fell together. Dr. Griffin had come to my neighborhood on business. The temptation to retrieve the hood ornament must have been too great. I imagined her knocking on the door. Receiving no answer, she tried the knob, found it open, and entered. Shadow is outside. Griffin locked her out or maybe she lured my dog to the backyard with a bone. But the presence of rats still baffled me.

Wait, where was Austen? Pink nostrils twitched from Claudia's hood then his whole head poked out from the folds of gray fabric. Whew. Austen had somehow clung to Dr. Griffin during the pursuit. Fortunately, Shadow hadn't noticed that animal's presence. Behind the coffee table on the floor hid an open rat cage that I had missed seeing before.

The little guy ventured further out of his hiding place, revealing a black splotch that mimicked an ink dot on his gray rump. I didn't need two wayward creatures in my house. No, three counting Dr. Griffin. Worse, Shadow might spot Austen at any moment. That probably wouldn't end well.

Years ago I had a friend who kept a pet rat, so I understood how to handle them. I had fallen in love with the species and spent a lot of time with hers. I plucked Austen out of the hood with my free hand, curled my fingers around his ribcage, deposited him inside his home, latched the door, and put the cage on top of my bookcase out of Shadow's reach.

"Austen's secure in the cage," I announced.

"Oh," she murmured, turning to look in my direction. "Thanks."

I glanced at my phone. It was almost time for the ten-minute bell. I needed to remove her from my house and head off to school with Shadow. But I wanted an explanation first.

"Now. What the hell are you doing in my house?"

"I can explain." Panic entered her voice. Her eyes suddenly riveted on the phone in my hand. "I swear once I get Mansfield, I'll leave. I'll never venture into your house again. I only wanted to see Shadow, and the front door was unlocked, and I didn't want to leave the rats in the hot car, so I brought them inside. They started fighting, and when I opened the cage to intervene, Mansfield jumped out. I put

Shadow out, and ... and ... It was stupid, I know. I promise it won't happen again."

Was it possible her version of events held truth? Shadow didn't seem bothered by her presence. Her laser-focus remained fixed on Mansfield. I didn't have time to press her and noodle out the holes in her story.

"I want you to leave. Now. Or do I call the police?" Dr. Griffin raised her head. I waved the phone at her. I wanted her to believe I would dial.

"Okay, okay." Dr. Griffin said as she rose to her feet. "Just help me get the rat first."

"There isn't time. I have to get back to school. I'm taking Shadow with me so the rat will be safe. I'll catch Mansfield when I get home then I'll call you when the cage is out on the porch. And if you ever come near me or my house or Shadow again, I will call the police. Now get out."

A loud snap charged through the air. Dad. I smiled. I knew Dr. Griffin saw ghosts. She had been the one who figured out that spirits had caused Shadow's barking problem last spring. Warmth settled on the nape of my neck as if Dad rested his hand there. The woman's eyes widened.

"Let me guess," I said. "Tall, bearded man in a hospital gown, right?"

Dr. Griffin's chin mimicked a bobble head. The movement righted her eyeglasses. I imagined she had a better view of Dad's knobby knees now.

"That would be my father. He wants you to leave, too."

The imposing form of Dad ought to get her moving. He had been intimidating in real life. As a ghost he must be twice as scary. The clock on the wall showed a few minutes until the bell. If I left now, I would only arrive five minutes late to class. The other students will have their drawing pads placed on easels. Entering while they assembled supplies wouldn't be so bad.

"Look, you can come back for Mansfield in a few hours. But right now you have to leave," I said in a firm voice. When she didn't move to the door, I added. "When I call the police, I have a silver object that might interest them."

A wild look entered Dr. Griffin's eyes like a horse that's encountered a snake. I remembered her mood swings when I had first known her. I suspected she suffered from some form of mental illness

"Oh holy whiskers," she said in a high-pitched voice, her gaze fixed on the wall clock. "It's so late!"

This woman definitely had a few screws loose. She dropped to the floor, made a few kissy noises, and crooned to the rat how Auntie Claudia wanted to help, so could Mansfield please, please, please come out of his hidey-hole.

My gaze fell on the fire poker—the one that she had whacked me on the head with last spring, even though she claimed the ghost of her boyfriend had done it. Her grasp on reality was tenuous, so I needed to be careful.

"Time to go," I said in a calm voice.

"I can't leave Mansfield," she whined. "There are only a few hours to catch him before I'm supposed to return him to Mrs. Bellweather."

"Dad will make sure he doesn't go anywhere," I said in a steady voice, knowing full well my father probably couldn't stick around in this realm long. "I'll come straight home after class then I'll flush him out from under the couch. Now, are you going to leave or shall I call the police?"

The warm presence at my shoulder disappeared. Dr. Griffin scrambled backward like a crab. She stared at something invisible to me. Did Dad now tower over her and give her "the look?"

"Okay, okay," she said. "I'll meet you back here in an hour. Shall we say 3:00?"

"Yeah," I said, pointing at the front door.

After she left, I turned to where I guessed my father still stood and whispered, "Thanks, Dad."

Then I rushed out the door with Shadow in tow and locked up. I imagined my classmates settled in front of their easels, scanning the room for the assigned subject to draw. If I got lucky and hit green traffic lights, Shadow would make a regal appearance, and my teacher would overlook that we were late.

CHAPTER THREE

*"How cheerfully he seems to grin, how neatly
spreads his claws.
And welcomes little fishes in, with gently smiling jaws."*

Shadow's nails clicked on the cement walkway that led to the number 500 wing at the rear of the high school. Even with my dog at my side, walking the halls after the class bell rang felt ominous. I strode to Room 507 and pushed open the door. Eighteen heads swiveled to watch my late entry. Only one student hadn't turned. With his chin tucked to his chest and his back to me, Kyle's attention remained focused on a set of pencils on his desk. He selected one and examined the pointy black tip.

Mrs. Durgette also ignored my entrance. She strutted back and forth at the front of the room in an oversized, white, chef's coat splattered in blue and red paint at the sleeves. The front was stained black from splotches of charcoal dust. I respected the passion she showed in her work, but sometimes her enthusiasm for demonstrating and explaining technique consumed the whole period, and we students never had a chance to practice what we learned. Now engrossed in a drawing lesson on anatomy, she seemed oblivious to the students.

"Each part of the human body can be drawn in terms of shapes," Mrs. Durgette gestured at the human mannequin near her desk. "Arms and fingers as cylinders, faces and heads as ovals."

Shadow pulled at the leash, her shortened tail held high. Her red coat shone golden under the muted fluorescent light. Her mouth hung open in an enthusiastic pant. If only I could bottle my dog's excitement at being in school and sell it to the fourth years plagued by senioritis. Shadow's gaze seemed to ask what came next.

"Oh, what a beautiful animal," Jessica Winters whispered. She frowned at me. "Poor dog."

Harvey Bolland occupied my usual seat at the back of the class. The only open easel was in the center aisle in the front row—the seat next to Kyle. Running the gauntlet of students and further disrupting the class seemed a formidable task. Better to wait until Mrs. Durgette finished. But I soon questioned my strategy as she soldiered on in her lecture, ignoring the fidgeting students. Shadow sat then leaned against my leg from where I stood near the wall by the door. Finally, the teacher's gaze travelled the room until they rested on my face.

"Well, Sarah," Mrs. Durgette said. Her stern voice announced her displeasure at my late arrival. "At last. I see you brought our drawing subject." She lifted the plastic human form and moved it into a corner behind her desk. "Well, come on up. You should sit near your dog for this lesson."

I guided Shadow around Paul Marks' legs. Jerk-face didn't have the decency to pull his feet out of the aisle. He and Margaret were perfect for each other. Both were inconsiderate, though Paul lacked Margaret's vindictiveness. Paul had been nice to me the first time I met him and Kyle back in April when I had just moved to town. But after five months of Margaret spewing poison at the mention of my name, it appeared Paul bought into her viewpoint. Why would Kyle befriend this guy much less consider him his best friend?

I slunk into my seat, using a hand signal to position Shadow by my side. I pulled my collection of charcoal pencils from my backpack. After I set them on my easel, Shadow's pink tongue snaked out to lick my fingers.

Mrs. Durgette returned to teaching mode. I stroked my dog's sleek coat. Her calming presence reduced my stress level.

"Capturing a living creature is about perspective," Mrs. Durgette continued. "An artist must not only draw what he or she sees; they must bring themselves into the work. For instance, they might depict their opinion of the person they are painting by capturing a facet of their personality. Say, a woman is flirtatious. The artist might accentuate the eyelashes, make the head incline, the eyes bigger, so the person appears to bat her eyes."

I zoned out the rest. Shadow's attention kept gravitating to an empty corner. She tended to move her eyes rather than rotating her head. From my research, this was distinctive of the Doberman breed. What was she looking at? I nudged her, and she tipped her head then stole a kiss.

"Sarah," Mrs. Durgette said. "Tell us something unique about Shadow."

I hated being called on in class. My brain always seemed to freeze. Even if I knew an answer to a question, I struggled to find the right words to articulate it. I hadn't been paying attention either. Wait. Hadn't she been discussing how to capture personality in images? Yes. She had asked what made Shadow special. It should be an easy question, but my thoughts couldn't settle on a single thing.

"Uh," I said, scrambling for some tidbit other than that my dog could see ghosts. Despite my efforts, my mind couldn't grasp any other information.

"Tell us the first thing that pops into your head," she persisted.

"Um, well." I studied Shadow's pointy ears, her cropped tail, her muscled body. Nothing about my dog's personality surfaced as a cohesive thought. She lifted a paw to shake hands, and a lightbulb flickered in my brain. "Um ... Oh yes. Sometimes she stacks her front paws on top of each other when she lies down."

That was lame. Shadow nudged my hand with her nose—something she often did when she wanted to be petted, but a lot of dogs do that.

"No, Sarah, I mean her personality. What makes her special?"

The only thing I could think to add was the way I can put my fingers in the space between her eyes, and ghosts become visible to me. No way would I reveal that secret.

Mrs. Durgette moved to stand before me. A splotch of gray hair at her temple caught my attention. My brain refused to focus. She wanted an answer. A correct answer.

"Tell us something she does well. Does she play fetch?"

Shadow showed zero interest in chasing balls. I patted her head and she leaned against me. I needed to say something.

"She enjoys being pet in the space between her eyes," I blurted, before I could stop myself.

"O-kay." Her pale lips drooped in displeasure. "But that's not something easily captured in a portrait, is it?"

Mrs. Durgette surveyed the students. She focused like a fighter pilot finding a target, zooming in on some poor sap behind me.

"Daniel, what do you see when you look at Sarah's dog?"

With the attention shifted to another student, Shadow's many special qualities bounced through my brain. At this moment she leaned against my leg to show her affectionate and loyal side. When she wanted me to chase her around the yard, she dipped her head and gazed up at me so the white below her lids showed. Her playful nature was something that could be drawn.

"Um, she seems curious," Daniel mumbled. "Maybe I'd tilt her head?"

"Excellent. And Mr. Marks," Mrs. Durgette said turning to Margaret's boyfriend, "can you give us an example of how you might capture personality in your portrait?"

Had Paul noticed the "mister" or understood its significance? Mrs. Durgette only used such formalities for the discipline-problem students. I turned in my seat. Paul leaned back in his chair, shoving his legs further into the aisle while tapping the eraser of his pencil in rapid succession against his drawing pad.

"Uh, yeah." He gave her a smart-aleck look. "For a certain kind of girl. With, you know, like she has a reputation for, well, you know. Yeah. I'd show lots of her … Well, you know." He cupped his hands in front of his chest to convey his meaning.

The class erupted in laughter. Paul shifted position to sit tall in his seat. His grin declared how pleased he was with himself. Mrs. Durgette dropped her chin and gave him the we-both-know-you're-a-wise-guy look, but she half-smiled and turned away without sending him off to the principal's office.

I imagined Dad with an I-told-you-so look on his face. He hated low-cut blouses and forbade me to wear any form of skimpy clothing.

"Glad to see *you've* been paying attention," Mrs. Durgette said.

Her mud-brown eyes fell on me once again, emphasizing her comment was directed at me.

"Sarah, and how would you portray Mr. Mark's personality?"

Was she kidding? I imagined the shade of on red my face must be close to magenta. Even the tips of my ears burned. How could she have selected him of all people? This was Margaret's boyfriend. He was one of the most popular guys in the school. No matter what I said, I would be ridiculed. Worse, people would repeat my description to Margaret.

Lawyers could talk their way out of situations through careful word choices. Maybe I could do the same. I turned in my seat to study my blond-haired, green-eyed classmate. Paul was a class clown who enjoyed strutting his stuff. He lived and breathed football. The jerk smirked at me as if whatever artistic interpretation I concocted wouldn't do him justice. Dad's voice filled my brain as he spouted off Relationship Rule #2: Be generous. Perhaps my dad was right. Maybe flattery was my best option.

"Well," I said. "That depends on the background setting. If the backdrop were outside, say on the football field, I would draw his jaw squared with fierce determination, his shoulders thrust forward." I warmed to the vision. I put my hands atop my shoulders. "I'd focus the portrait from here and higher. I would draw him leaning forward like he was in a start position, staring straight out of the picture. But if he were in the classroom . . . if he were in school, maybe the opposite? I might show him reclined in his desk chair, his gaze directed off the page, grinning at a private joke."

Silence descended in the room. This and the shocked expression on Jessica Winters' face revealed my answer had gone too far. Shadow nudged my hand to be petted, but I was afraid to move. Mrs. Durgette puckered her lips and nodded approval. Her head tilted as she scrutinized me. I prayed she wouldn't gush over me as though I were her new favorite student. Only after she cleared her throat and walked to her desk did my knotted shoulders relax.

I stole a glance at Paul. His chin rested on his fist; his lips curled into a smile when our eyes met. The smitten expression on his face sent a chill along my spine. Had he misinterpreted my words? Did he think I *liked* him? His grin was so lecherous I expected his fingers to sprout claws.

Two seats over, Cyndi Marshall pulled her iPhone from her jeans pocket. With her hand out of sight of Mrs. Durgette, her fingers flew across the keys. Cyndi was one of the Magnificent Seven. No doubt she was texting Margaret what I said about Paul.

I twisted my head to see Kyle's reaction, but his attention remained on Mrs. Durgette. His upper body stiffened, as if he sensed my scrutiny. Waves of angry energy seemed to ooze from him.

What was his problem? He had avoided making eye contact since I entered the room. Was it because I declined his coffee invitation?

"Well, that was a great segue," Mrs. Durgette said, drawing my attention back to the front of the room, "because I've borrowed a prop from the drama department that will be the backdrop for this exercise." She glanced at the clock on the wall. "Oh dear. Only fifteen minutes left? Guess we better start drawing."

Mrs. Durgette wrestled a large piece of folded cardboard from behind her desk. The creased brown surface depicted a fireplace hearth with logs ablaze in yellow and orange flames.

"Now class, I want you to note how the bricks are just a series of staggered rectangles. Each one is exactly the same size ...

Not another lecture. Would we even have a chance to sketch Shadow? My sweet pup shifted her weight and placed her chin on my thigh. She sucked in a breath and sighed. I, too, wished Mrs. Durgette would stop pointing out the obvious.

I stroked Shadow's head. She lifted her nose, encouraging me to rub the space between her eyes. As much as she loved it, I rarely indulged her. The last time my fingers lingered there too long, she collapsed and landed in an emergency vet clinic. Triggering her ghost-seeing ability for extended periods caused her physical harm. Still, she was being such a good pup. Surely, a few quick strokes were harmless. As the tips of my fingers landed square between her eyes, an image flickered behind Mrs. Durgette.

What the…? My father's ghost in technicolor, clad in his dingy, blue-gray hospital gown, marched behind my teacher, mimicking her movements. When she paused in her incessant back and forth pacing and placed her hand on one hip, my father followed suit.

I bit my lip to hide my chuckle. Dad had been a bit of a clown. But what was he doing here and why? Was this part of his daily routine to follow me around school? Now, my amusement morphed into annoyance. We were going to have to discuss respecting my privacy if this were to be his usual behavior, but today a more urgent issue must be addressed. He wasn't watching over Mansfield-the-rat like he promised. I raised my eyebrows and inclined my head forward. As if understanding my question, he put both his hands together as if in prayer then placed them against his cheek—the universal sign for sleeping. Still, what if the rat awoke? Keeping tabs on the animal was way more important than making fun of my teacher.

When Mrs. Durgette resumed pacing, Dad followed her step for step, making ludicrous faces with each foot placement. His eyes flicked to the corner of the room. I was sitting at an angle with a full classroom view, so my attention shifted to follow his gaze.

On the floor behind Mrs. Durgette's desk sat a chubby, translucent little boy. A toddler ghost probably no more than two years old. Tears stained his reddened cheeks. But he wasn't crying anymore, he was watching my father with great interest.

What were this child and Dad doing in my art class? Who might the little ghost boy belong to? Mrs. Durgette?

I should remove my hand. The longer I held my fingers between Shadow's eyes, the greater the risk to her health. Yet, something about the boy felt wrong. Dad pointed at the ghost child then gestured in my general direction. What was that supposed to mean? Was this a brother who died before I was born? A deceased nephew I never knew existed? Maybe he was a distant cousin.

I turned back to the child. His round cheeks and pug nose didn't resemble either Dad's or my features. As far as I knew red hair was not a family trait. My Dad's ghost wore the outfit he had on when he died. This little boy wasn't in hospital garb as though he had been sick or in pajamas, which might have meant he died in his sleep. The small, red-collared shirt he wore suggested he passed away during the day and not in a hospital. Perhaps, in the fall season since long sleeves covered his elbows and lower arms. Blue jeans and tennis shoes completed his outfit. He appeared to be a normal kid, dressed to go outside and play in cool weather. His haircut showed a precision that suggested his family took him to a professional salon. They must have loved him. So why was he dead?

CHAPTER FOUR

The Duchess: "Tut, tut, child!"

The area at the front of Room 507 rose a foot or so higher than the rest of the room. Mrs. Durgette's wooden desk and black swivel chair were the only pieces of furniture up there along with a few props. This elevated design enabled the teacher to better display objects for drawing assignments. I settled Shadow into a sitting position in front of the cardboard fireplace backdrop on this raised structure. Staggered easels through the classroom allowed even the students in the back a clear view of my dog.

I gave Shadow a hand-signal to stay and took two steps away from her to make sure she didn't move. My gaze swept over the room, getting Mrs. Durgette's perspective of her students. Most busied themselves by selecting drawing tools. Paul leaned out into the aisle and grinned at me, but I pretended not to notice.

Kyle sat unmoving, eyes studying his lap. I left Shadow on stage to take my seat next to him. I cleared my throat hoping to show him a sad puppy dog expression and melt his heart, but he turned his face away. His rejection felt like the time I did a face plant while trying to steal a soccer ball. Moisture pooled under my lids. The reminder of my days playing soccer also brought the memory of my father cheering me on from the sidelines, the smell of grass, and the way my cleats pinched my toes.

"Go, Sarah, go," Dad's voice filled my head.

Was it real or a memory? Was he warning me to leave the room? Maybe carbon monoxide gas had once filled this room and killed the toddler boy, and it was happening again. No, Dad would have pointed at the door, and he would have been agitated. Were my Dad and the little ghost boy still here?

I tilted my head listening for more, but the only sound in the art room was the scritch-scratch of pencils and charcoal sticks against paper. Mrs. Durgette demanded silence from her students while they drew. Shadow used to bark at ghosts, but she had shown no objection to my ethereal father or the spirit of the child. The only way to know if the boy's spirit was still here required placing my fingers between my dog's eyes, but with Shadow on display about ten feet away, that wasn't possible.

Hopefully Dad had returned to my house to check on Mansfield. During my father's final days in the hospital, I was certain I would be able to feel his essence watching over me sometimes because of our special bond, but that hadn't happened. More tangible things like the crackle of his arrival and the warmth of his touch alerted me that he was around.

Mrs. Durgette cleared her throat, reminding me to focus on the assignment. Shadow was a consummate professional. My pooch sat motionless. She didn't even track Mrs. Durgette's movements as the woman strolled the room. My pet's attention remained riveted on me, waiting for my release command from the "sit-stay" I had given earlier.

"Nice," Mrs. Durgette said as she passed by Jessica's creation.

"Remember what I taught you about body parts and shapes," my teacher grumbled at Harvey. Poor guy. Mrs. Durgette had used his drawings twice now as examples of what not to do. His acne seemed to have flared to new levels these last few weeks.

My paper remained blank and she was headed down my row. As Mrs. Durgette paused one seat away to examine Kyle's work. I scrambled to outline Shadow's basic form.

"Excellent improvisation," she whispered to Kyle. "I like the way you altered the bricks."

Mrs. Durgette walked by my sketch without comment. A pang of disappointment coursed through me. My efforts had incorporated her lesson. Shadow's form was well-proportioned, which I accomplished by measuring her body parts against certain features. Her head was approximately a third the length of her back, her front legs measured the same size as the distance from her nose to ears. Through Mrs. Durgette's words, my dog appeared as shapes. Shadow's ears resembled triangles, her eyes, circles. Her long, pointy nose was nothing more than a cone. When put in perspective, Shadow became easy to draw.

I peeked at Kyle's sketch. The image of the fireplace occupied most of the page. Four of the bricks above Shadow's outlined form had been altered. The thick charcoal marks and indentations where he pressed hard seemed odd. Was there a message in those bricks? The mortar was blackened around the first brick in the shape of an "L." Next to it, the far-right cement shading resembled a capital "I."

Kyle studied me for a reaction. His movements had been jerky ever since he retrieved his pencil. I frowned. On the third brick, black outlines occurred on all sides except the bottom and it had a vertical slash drawn across the middle. An "A". The letter hidden in the last brick was an "R." LIAR.

I had lied. How did he know? Had Margaret told him my father's grave required a two-hour drive? Until today, I avoided violating Dad's Relationship Rule #5 with Kyle: Be honest at all times—though he did caveat it with "unless the truth damaged the person." Because my ghost-father had flustered me, I had lapsed. Perhaps I could reveal a snippet of truth now and explain later. I decided to scrawl a few words on my sketchpad.

I lifted the right corner of my pad to the blank sheet underneath. I kept my movements slow so as not to alert Mrs. Durgette. My cryptic note of "loose rat" should be enough for now. Surely, it was an odd enough note to pique his curiosity, and he would allow me time after class to clarify its meaning. Kyle pretended to examine Shadow, but his eyes slanted in my direction.

The teacher had progressed one row over, but she would backtrack past me soon. Private discussions during drawing time broke Mrs. D's class rules, so I needed to act fast. I scribbled quickly. Footsteps approached. I dropped the paper and resumed work on an outline of Shadow's tail. Mrs. Durgette hovered over my shoulder. My hand trembled, and my pencil fell to the floor. She breathed out a huff of disapproval. Crap, crap, crap.

The imposing form of my teacher reached over my shoulder. My whole body tensed. Then Mrs. Durgette's hand lifted the page. Oh no. Oh no. The words on the page. That wasn't what I meant to write. In my rush not to be caught I forgot an "o." Worse, I only scribbled the letter "r" of the word rat and failed to put much space between the words. Scrawled on the page was the word "loser." Beside me, Kyle pressed the charcoal so hard it snapped in two.

Mrs. Durgette stiffened and turned to the class.

I wanted to disappear. For once, I wished Shadow wasn't well trained. Stand. I tried to will her to her feet with my thoughts. Give me an excuse to rush you out of the room for a potty break. But my dog sat on in her regal pose.

"May I have your attention," our teacher said

This was our clue to stop drawing and turn to face her. She remained silent until all students were listening. I stared at my charcoal pencil on the floor, mortified by what she might say or do. I imagined her asking me to stand and reveal my horrid note.

I straightened my spine and lifted my gaze, trying to appear brave. Everyone had stopped work. Even Paul leaned forward with interest.

"Can someone tell me," she said in a tight voice that communicated the full extent of her disdain, "the consequences of belittling someone's artwork in this class?"

As usual, Cyndi, the class suck-up, shot her arm into the air. Mrs. Durgette nodded for her to speak.

"The offending party," she said in a prim voice, "is to be docked a full letter grade."

"That's correct. I will not tolerate harsh criticism. Art is a form of self-expression, and this room is a safe place." She turned to frown at me and repeated, "a full letter grade."

The bell spared me further humiliation. Shadow jumped to her feet, and I rushed to attach my dog's leash. I turned to ask Kyle to give me a chance to explain, but he had already collected his things and disappeared.

Shadow's laser focus awaited my release command.

"Ms. Whitman," Mrs. Durgette squawked. "I need to speak with you."

Ms. Whitman? Great. Now she considered me a discipline problem. As much as I wanted to defend myself to Mrs. Durgette, I needed to get home. Now I wouldn't even have time to find Kyle and apologize either. I gathered my art supplies, not bothering to pack them inside my backpack, reminded Shadow to remain in her stay, and walked to my teacher's desk.

"Here," she said. "I'll need you to bring in Shadow into class all next week." She handed me a fistful of pink passes similar to the one I used today. These five slips of paper granted me permission to leave the school premises each day. "I'm surprised and disappointed. Very disappointed."

"It's not what you think," I said.

"Tut, tut," she said, raising her palm to stop my explanation. "I'll hear no excuses. I'll see you on Monday."

I nodded, collected Shadow, and rushed through the doorway with my dog at my heel. As I cleared the doorframe, my body collided with Paul's. Charcoal pencils flew in all directions. My sketchpad tumbled to the ground. At least it hadn't landed open to the page with the word "loser" scrawled on it.

"Sit," I told Shadow, and she did.

As I scrambled to retrieve my art materials, Paul squatted next to me to help collect the pencils. At least Jessica Winters wasn't around. I imagined a Snapchat of Paul sidled up next to me making its way into Margaret's cell phone.

"Sarah. Uh... I wanted... that was great what you said about me. I mean... it's like weird, I mean like, cool, like you know me. I mean like we've never really talked or anything."

Paul handed me a fistful of pencils and his hand lingered on mine. Wow. Was this really happening? I had no interest in this guy. None.

Yet, his touch felt good, and I didn't immediately pull my hand away. I hadn't had physical contact with a human being for months. Mr. O'Shawnessy, my legal guardian, probably feared even a chaste hug might be misinterpreted by social services. It was also possible the old man sensed any inkling of affection toward me would irritate Margaret.

"Paul!" I heard the screech of outrage from down the hall.

Speak of the devil. I didn't have to turn my head to feel the wrath of Margaret descend upon us. Great. Now I had actually given my nemesis a legitimate reason to continue to harbor a grudge against me. I had inadvertently been the cause of her and Paul breaking up last April. They had resolved their problems over the summer. I had suspected her reconciliation with him had been nothing more than vacation entertainment, but here it was October, and they were still together.

I tried to pull from his grasp, but Paul held tight. I tugged harder and freed my hand. The pencils went airborne once again. Shadow bristled at Margaret when she clutched Paul by the elbow and dragged him toward the student lockers.

"Hey," he called, not resisting Margaret, but also not the least concerned by her reaction. "See ya later."

This guy was dumber than dumb. He had no idea the storm of jealousy his actions had just triggered. Easy for him to be nonchalant. He didn't have to live in the same house with Margaret.

CHAPTER FIVE

Caterpillar: "Who are you?"

Poor Shadow. Everyone in the school wanted to pet her. We ran a gauntlet of reaching hands through the hallways until at last we emerged into the open air of the parking lot.

"Hey, Sarah," a male voice called. "Wait up."

My heart lifted. Kyle? At last a chance to explain. When I turned though, a guy sporting red hair run amok didn't greet me. Instead, the burly form of blond-haired Paul approached at a full jog. Not Margaret's boyfriend again. Didn't he realize his girlfriend would resent his contact with me? She was nowhere in sight, but a handful of witnesses, including two of the Magnificent Seven, lingered near their cars. I ducked behind a truck, closing the distance to my Civic. He caught up to me as I reached my car. Dang it.

"Hey," he said. "Want to go over to Safeway for a cappuccino and a bag of potato chips? We could sit outside with your dog."

Was he kidding? Were there two more unsuitable food groups? What was it with guys and coffee dates? At Safeway no less. Wow. What did Margaret see in him? Sure, he was handsome and a rising star on the football team, but I had never been one to be attracted to the outer shell. Well, dimples were a plus. But mostly, it was personality that drew me in.

Shadow looked up at him and gave her tail a dismissive wave. She wasn't impressed, but she wasn't agitated either. This guy might not be bright, but he was probably harmless.

"I can't. I'm going home."

"Great," he said nodding. His eyes bulged as though he scored a winning touchdown. "Let's go."

Was he dense or a brute who wouldn't take no for an answer? And he hadn't thought this through. I lived with Margaret. And even if he presumed I referred to the house next door where Shadow lived as "home," how long before his girlfriend discovered his infidelity when only a driveway separated the two structures?

Paul opened the passenger door of my car and grinned. Unbelievable. He needed to get a grip. I was about to protest when I noticed his biceps spilling out from his short-sleeved tee. It wouldn't be a bad idea to have him nearby when I met Dr. Griffin. Besides, this guy could lift my hide-a-bed with one hand. He offered a solution to the logistical problem of extracting the rat from under the couch, assuming Mansfield hadn't budged from his spot. Margaret was already pissed off at me. Why not let Paul pay some restitution for complicating my life?

"Get in," I said.

I opened the rear door, tossed in my backpack, and guided Shadow onto the seat behind the driver. Paul's arms were empty. No books, no papers. Apparently, he didn't plan to do homework over the weekend. He slid inside and buckled up without further comment. As I backed the car out, he turned in his seat to face me.

"This is the greatest day of my life," he gushed. "I mean, meeting you, the things you said about me. Who are you?"

Who was I, indeed? His ramblings were making me nervous. He had not only misinterpreted my "invitation," but also now he had assumed my classroom statements showed I was interested in pursuing a relationship. I had to set him straight.

"Paul—"

"I can't believe how right you were. It's like you saw inside me. And now we're going to your place."

Going to my place? What exactly did he think we would do? Good grief. This guy moved fast. I didn't think subtlety was an option. I needed to be blunt.

"Paul, I'm not having sex with you."

"Well, I'd hoped . . . Paul slumped back into the seat. "I mean, you'd be surprised. That's what a lot of girls want from me. But that's okay. You are so different. And I really feel like I can talk to you. I mean you don't understand what it's like to be me. Playing high school ball is everything, well almost—"

"Paul—"

"—like, I'm not sure I want to go to college. I mean, my family went to Carlsbad Caverns on vacation and we went caving. What's the word? It starts with an "s."

"Spelunking. But Paul—"

"Yeah, spelunking. It's what I want to do. I don't need to go to no college and take hard classes if I want to be a tour guide . . ."

I tuned Paul out as he spewed information about stalagmites. The car rolled to a stop at a red light, and I turned to see what Shadow was doing while Paul rambled on. My tuckered pooch had curled up on the back seat and dozed off.

I was already having second thoughts. This was stupid. I considered turning at this intersection to loop back toward the school. Besides, I was dragging Paul to my house under false pretenses. For the second time today, I had violated Dad's Relationship Rule #5 about being honest. I hadn't told him why I had invited him to come home with me. If only he would stop jabbering for a second.

"Paul."

" . . . and so I've decided to do my senior project on spelunking and, you know—"

"PAUL," I yelled.

This finally stopped him. I didn't take the time to apologize. He might interject an in-depth account of his summer cave experience if I took a breath. "We're going to my house so you can lift a couch."

"Err . . . what?"

"There's a pet rat loose in my living room. It's under the sofa, and I need you to lift it so I can capture it. Will you help me?"

Paul leaned back in the seat. His eyebrows crinkled together as he processed this information. No wonder this guy liked caves; he must be genetically similar to Neanderthals. It took a moment then he shrugged.

"Okay," he said.

The light turned green. I pressed the accelerator and guided the car toward my house. Poor guy looked so dejected that I felt terrible. I had to give him credit for agreeing to help me. The least I could do was switch over to his favorite topic to cheer him up.

"You know what is cool about caves? Scientists are still finding new species in the deepest parts. Weird creatures. Some don't even have any pigment."

"You mean they're clear?" he said, sitting up straight.

"More like opaque. But what if you studied biology in college? You could be one of those guys out there finding new species."

"Cool. That'd be like the best job ever. And I could be famous." Then he deflated once more. "I don't know.

I'm retaking biology 'cause I failed it the first time. It's interesting and all, but I'm not good at the tests."

No big surprise there. Biology was no cakewalk, especially if the teacher was lame. The high school had two biology teachers. The male teacher didn't linger after school hours so I had met with the woman, Mrs. Confetti, one time because I had a few questions about practice SAT questions. Once was enough.

"Do you have Mrs. Confetti?" I asked.

"Yeah," he said. "I had her the first time, too."

"I'm sorry. She's awful. I'm taking biology as one of my SAT subject tests. I asked her a question on genetics after school last week. I needed a simple yes or no, but she spent a half hour explaining how plant cells made energy from sunlight. Her response had absolutely nothing to do with my question. Maybe it's not you. Maybe it's the teacher."

He shrugged. "Did you really only ask me to come to lift a couch?"

"Yes. I wouldn't want to come between you and Margaret."

"Yeah, well, I can't talk to her like I can talk to you, but she's all right. Anyway, I'm pretty good at ghosting people. Hey, what'd you do to Margaret anyway? She sure hates you."

I was having trouble keeping up with his ramblings. He must be missing brain cells if he thought it possible to ghost Margaret and the other Magnificent Six? And how had he forgotten about prom night?

"Uh, if you recall, you broke up with her on prom night last spring because you got mad that she refused my offer to look after her grandfather while you two went to the dance. You stormed off when she wouldn't leave her granddad home alone. Then she blamed me for offering a solution in front of you. Sound familiar?"

"Oh, that. I sort of over-reacted. But it was prom, and she was being ridiculous. And we worked it out. It still makes me mad that I missed prom because of her."

Well, on that point we agreed. Margaret should have gone to the dance.

"That incident wasn't the only issue," I added. "Her dislike was instantaneous. Before social services discovered that I was underage, I lived alone in the house next door to Margaret. When I first moved there, Shadow barked a lot. Margaret thought the noise damaged her grandfather's health."

"Really?" Paul glanced at my dog in the back seat. "She's so sweet and quiet."

"Anyway," I said. "When Mr. O'Shawnessy let me move in with them so I didn't have to go into foster care, Margaret blew a gasket."

Paul whistled through his teeth. "Wait. What? She's never said anything. Seriously? You live with her? I mean she never invites me inside, but how come I've never seen your car parked there?"

"I spend most of my time at my own house next door."

I was tempted to say more. I could tell him how she hid my car keys on the first day of school to make me late. How she had ripped my math homework into tiny pieces out of spite. How she spilled milk over the drawing I made for her grandfather for his birthday. But I refused to stoop to her level, so I held my tongue.

Margaret's beat-up old car was parked in front of the house next door to mine. Paul frowned.

"You know, if you and I aren't happening…" He scrunched down in his seat. "Can you take me back to school? Margaret was pretty upset that I was nice to you after art class."

Did this doofus think I would bring him home with me if Margaret were next door? She had carpooled to school this morning with one of her friends, and she had a sixth period. Really? He didn't know his girlfriend's class schedule?

"Don't worry," I said. "Margaret has a sixth period, remember? She got a ride to school. That's why her car is there."

"Err…" Paul said. "You don't know how mad she can get."

Good grief. I lived with her. Nitroglycerine ran in her blood. Besides, the damage had been done the moment he showed interest in me. Anyway, I couldn't let him back out now. Dr. Griffin and I couldn't lift the couch without his help.

"I can't take you back now," I said. "But if you help me, I can get you to school before sixth period gets out."

"I don't know ..."

Paul slunk lower in the seat. In my mind, I flicked through Dad's relationship rules and landed on Rule #6: Be generous. Problem was, I needed him to be generous. Wait. Maybe there was something. It wouldn't sit well with Margaret, but ...

"I'll make you a deal," I said. "You help me catch the rat, and I'll help you review the material for your next test in biology."

"You would do that?"

"Sure," I said. "As long as you understand this is a business arrangement. Nothing more."

"You really think I'm having trouble because the teacher is bad?"

Probably not. Though she wasn't helping the situation. The guy wasn't the brightest bulb. But for the third time today, I violated Relationship Rule #5 and lied.

"Absolutely," I said as I swung into my driveway.

CHAPTER SIX

"What a curious plan!" exclaimed Alice.

I cut the ignition. Dr. Griffin sat on the porch, leaning against the wall by my front door. Her arm rested on Austen's rat cage with her chin tucked against her chest. She appeared to be asleep.

"Who's that?" Paul asked.

"Dr. Griffin," I said. "The loose rat is her... patient. She's an animal behaviorist. She'll help us."

I didn't want to take the time to explain why the rat was in my house. I wasn't even sure if I could. To my relief, Paul shrugged as if this made perfect sense.

I looked closer. Dr. Griffin's mouth hung open; she was definitely taking an afternoon siesta. I rolled down each of the four windows of my car a few inches before cutting the engine, so Shadow wouldn't get too warm in the Civic while we caught the rat. I got out of the car and Paul followed.

"So this is your home, huh?" Paul said. "Nice. Nicer yard than Margaret's. And good paint job."

The yellow stucco and white trim on the one-story rancher did feel inviting. Dad and I had moved around enough that I knew this was an ordinary tract home, except for the yard. The front was landscaped with tall plants designed for homeowner privacy and to give the impression of a high-end home. The yard work kept me busy, but I didn't mind. What a contrast to Mr. O'Shawnessy's weedy lawn and bedraggled shrubs.

I looked around to see if anyone was watching. The quiet, safe neighborhood and privacy had enticed Dad to buy it. He snapped up the property after his terminal cancer diagnosis. I wondered if he was disappointed that his strategy to buy this home for me to keep me out of foster care had failed, or if he was happy that Mr. O'Shawnessy had become my legal guardian.

"Where do you live?" I asked Paul as we approached Dr. Griffin's hunched form.

"East end of town," he said, lowering his head. "By Wal-Mart. Uh ... my dad works there."

Apartments made up most of that neighborhood. No wonder this house impressed him. Margaret seemed so superficial. I was surprised she would hang out with a guy with blue-collar roots. Then again, Paul's future looked bright. Margaret often bragged that he was eighth in the list of top ten high school football players in California. A full scholarship to a prestigious college was within his grasp. Just last week, I had overheard someone say that the head coach at Cal Berkeley had called him.

Paul lingered, while I stepped around Dr. Griffin and inserted my house key and twisted the lock, keeping the door closed in case Mansfield lurked on the other side. I thought the noise would wake the woman, but she was out cold. I nudged her with the toe of my sandal. She awoke with a start. She squinted up at me then staggered to her feet.

"Sarah," Dr. Griffin said, stretching her arms over her head and yawning. "I must have dozed off. What took you so long?"

"Doesn't matter, I'm here now. And I've brought Paul to help lift the couch." I pointed at the bulky football star.

"Paul?" Her head swiveled in his direction then back to me.

He moved close, towering above her. He probably outweighed her by at least a hundred pounds.

"Paul," I said in an overly cheerful voice. "This is Dr. Claudia Griffin."

"Hello, Dr. Griffin," Paul said, offering his hand.

Given how surly he acted in class, his manners surprised me.

"Nice to meet you, Paul," she said, giving his hand a cursory shake with her fingertips while her eyes were anything but welcoming.

Fortunately, her rudeness was lost on Paul. I didn't know if she resented his presence because she didn't want a witness to her mistake, or if during my absence, she concocted something more sinister to keep me quiet after capturing the rat. Maybe she planned to use the fire poker to bash in my head. Finish the job she didn't complete last time.

I pushed open the front door and motioned for Paul to follow, making my way through the hall and into the main room. Dr. Griffin picked up the wire cage and followed us into the living room behind us. She set the rat enclosure on the floor next to the sofa bed and dropped to the ground to peek underneath.

"Yep, yep, yep," she said. "You were right, Sarah. He's still under here. Your dad's ghost must have kept his word."

I cringed. Would Paul talk to Kyle about ghosts and Dr. Griffin? Could news of this bizarre situation somehow slide through the high school rumor mill and spew out into the ears of inquiring social workers?

Dr. Griffin glanced around the room. "It appears Papa left. Wouldn't have thought him to be shy around strangers."

Paul looked from me to Dr. Griffin. A wrinkle had formed in the space between his eyes, and his head lilted at an odd angle. Poor guy. His first taste of the vet's weirdness seemed to confuse him. This was typical of her. She wasn't "all there" whenever she was under stress.

"Never mind," I said to Paul.

"I must say," the vet said, lifting her head, but remaining prostrate on the ground. "You and Paul make a cute couple."

"Yeah?" Paul said. A big grin spread across his face.

Crap. I had finally convinced Paul a romantic relationship wasn't happening, and now Dr. Griffin was giving him ideas. She looked at me and nodded encouragement.

"We're not together," I said.

I imagined Margaret standing on her front porch next door watching Paul walk up the driveway with a fistful of flowers, only they would be for me, not her. Paul had to leave before Dr. Griffin put thoughts into Paul's head.

"You and Sarah should come to dinner tonight at my house."

What? Had the woman lost her mind? Memories of the last dinner flooded back. Shadow's collapse, the trip to the emergency vet. David-the-Ghost showing up in my house. Me getting whacked on the head with a poker after I fled home.

"No." I said before Paul could respond, leaving no question that I meant it. "You have gotten the wrong idea. Paul has a girlfriend and I have homework."

"Homework?" Paul said. "But it's Friday."

I glared bullets at Dr. Griffin. Paul resembled a cat ready to pounce. He was all over this idea. I had to put an end to this fast.

"And anyway," I blurted, "I don't think my boyfriend, Kyle, would want me to go out with Paul."

"No way!" Paul said, punching my shoulder. "Cool. You and Kyle? Since when?"

"Never mind," I said.

The way Dr. Griffin raised her eyebrows put me on edge. I could almost see her brain processing this new information and strategizing how to use it.

Paul frowned. It would be best for all of us if we caught Mansfield and everyone left. The last thing I needed was for this to drag on and have Margaret catch Paul inside my house.

"Dr. Griffin," I said, pointing at the far corner of the couch across from where Dr. Griffin lay on the ground. "Is Mansfield still on that side?"

She nodded. "He hasn't moved."

"Okay then," I said. "Paul, you lift this edge where the rat is. Dr. Griffin, you stay where you are. I'll try to get Mansfield where he's hiding. If I miss, Dr. Griffin, you can snag him when he runs toward you."

I squatted next to the corner near Paul. His fingers curled under the bottom of the sofa. We were side-by-side, so close the heat of his body warmed me. He glanced over and smiled.

"Count of three," I said. "One, two … three."

The couch lifted about six inches. I lunged for the little black and white body. His fur was surprisingly smooth and slick. I had him. And then I didn't. His lean body and pink tail slipped through my fingers. The little guy was wicked fast. He scurried straight toward the vet. But she seemed too startled to move.

"Get him," I yelled.

The vet's fingers reached into the shallow gap, but Paul held up the corner opposite from her end, and she couldn't reach her hand through. Mansfield turned and headed for a wider gap between couch and floor. Beside me, Paul's muscles bulged.

"Hold on," I said.

I jumped to my feet and circled around to the side of the couch in time to see Mansfield's pink nose and white snout appear near Dr. Griffin's head. In a flash, the little devil had wiggled his sleek body free. I lunged and grabbed Mansfield as his back legs cleared the couch. He squealed, but I held fast.

"Got him."

Paul eased the couch down. Dr. Griffin rose to her feet and jumped up and down clapping. Paul grinned a big Cheshire cat smile.

"My prayers have been answered," the vet said, raising her arms into a "V."

Warm liquid spread across my cupped hands. Gross. Mansfield had peed. I looked down. Disgust turned to horror. His little body had gone limp. Pink, glassy eyes shone vacant and unseeing. I didn't need a degree in veterinary medicine to diagnosis the problem. Mansfield was dead.

His glossy fur suggested he had spent a lot of time grooming himself. His white face shone as bright as my dentist's teeth. He had been a beautiful animal, pure white, except for a small patch of black on his rump. Even his pink tail lacked the scaly look of older rats. This was an animal that had taken care of himself, probably because his owner loved him dearly.

Dr. Griffin and Paul still hadn't noticed what happened. The vet twirled around the room like a ballerina while Paul hooted encouragement. I wanted them to stop celebrating.

The woman sashayed to stand before me with her hands outstretched. Her vibrant blue eyes twinkled with relief and happiness. I couldn't find the words to tell her, so I handed over the limp form.

"Ooh, you silly rat," Dr. Griffin crooned. "You had us all—"

Mansfield's head lolled to the side. The vet frowned at the motionless body. Her lips parted as her eyebrows rounded into an expression of fear and disbelief. She cupped Mansfield to her chest, rocking him back and forth like a baby.

"Oh," she said. "Oh, no, oh, no."

Paul's mouth dropped open. His gaze darted from Dr. Griffin to the lifeless rat to me.

"Holy crap," Paul said. "Is it dead?"

His burly shoulders slouched forward. He turned away, shaking his bowed head.

What had gone wrong? Was the stress of being free too much for the old guy? Had I been too rough when I grabbed him?

This disaster was all my fault. If only I had shut the bedroom door as Dr. Griffin asked me to, if only I hadn't rushed off to class leaving Mansfield alone in an unfamiliar environment for more than an hour then Mrs. Bellweather's precious pet would still be alive.

CHAPTER SEVEN

Alice: "Now what am I going to do?"

D r. Griffin collapsed on the couch, cradling the dead rat. I stared at the yellow fluid pooled on my hand. It emitted an earthy, organic smell. I shuddered. Over and over again I wiped the rat urine on the seat of my jeans, trying to hide the evidence. I felt as if the equivalent of blood stained my hands. A living creature died because of me.

I didn't know what to say. Not that it mattered. A lump the size of Mount Vesuvius had invaded my throat and taken away my voice.

My eyes tracked from Paul to Dr. Griffin. The vet stroked Mansfield's sleek fur. Paul leaned against the living room wall. His face drooped like a bloodhound's jowls. Neither of them looked at me, the way you ignore someone who ripped a loud fart. But I hadn't contaminated the room with a vile odor where all you needed to do was open a window to solve the problem. Death is permanent. A fog of despair appeared to have descended on the three of us.

"Man," Paul said. "I never seen nothin' die before."

"Don't just stand there," Dr. Griffin whacked her palm on the side of her head then added, "do something."

Dr. Griffin's jaw's muscles clenched. She flipped over the limp rat. With its belly exposed on her hand, she fused her index and middle fingers together and pressed up and down on Mansfield's chest in rapid succession. She grimaced, placed her lips over the rat's snout, and blew. Mansfield's ribcage expanded.

CPR for rats? Did they teach this skill in vet school or was she improvising? Please work. This has to work. I crossed my fingers, something I hadn't done since I was a child.

Dr. Griffin depressed Mansfield's tiny chest and puffed air into his lungs again and again. She paused at every fifth compression to see if the rat had recovered. Time seemed to have stopped. Pressure built behind my eyelids. My fingernails dug into my palms as I held my breath. Surely, if I didn't breathe, the rat could. Please Mansfield. Please come back. My chest tightened, hoping for a miracle. Moments passed, and the little furry body remained still. Mansfield was gone. My body demanded air, and at last, I inhaled, even though the small, furred creature hadn't.

"It's done." My clean hand covered Dr. Griffin's fingers to still her efforts. "It can't be fixed."

The woman's lip quivered. Her blue eyes seemed to darken a shade. She continued to press and release, press and release. A droplet rolled down the bridge of her nose followed by another.

Paul patted the vet's shoulder. I had to give the big oaf credit. He had a kind heart.

"I'm really sorry," he whispered, "but Sarah's right. It's time to stop."

Dr. Griffin sniffled and nodded. The vet smoothed Mansfield's fur as if he were still alive, as if he still enjoyed the attention. She shook her head then straightened.

"Mrs. Bellweather adored this animal," Dr. Griffin said. "What am I going to tell her?"

The full magnitude of what I had done descended. Did the old woman love Mansfield as much as I loved Shadow? If so, she will be devastated. A tear traced the side of my face.

"I'll come with you," I said, my voice cracked with the pain I felt. "I'll explain to Mrs. Bellweather how this was all my fault—"

"No," Paul said to me. "You didn't do nothin' to the rat. It just kinda ... died."

A twinge of guilt flitted through me. Here he was defending me and trying to make me feel better. Perhaps I had been too quick in my judgement of Paul. There was a charming sweetness about him.

"Thanks, Sarah," Dr. Griffin said. "But I'll take care of this."

I wiped at my face and nodded.

"Can we go now?" Paul said. "I need to get back."

I glanced at the wall clock. Twenty minutes until sixth period let out. Margaret will hunt for Paul when her class ends. There was still plenty of time to drop off Paul before the bell rang. Margaret's spies had probably already discovered her boyfriend had helped me. But so what? The witch's temper will flare, but what else was new?

Then a horrible thought took hold. Did Mansfield die because of bad karma? If Paul hadn't come, I might have coaxed the rat out with cheese instead of gripping him too tightly, and he would still be alive.

"Of course, she can take you back to school," Dr. Griffin answered for me. "I'm going into the office and get some brochures on pet bereavement before I break the news to Mrs. Bellweather."

Pet bereavement. Such a tame way to describe the devastation over losing your furry friend. Did they have a brochure for how to cope if you killed a person's pet?

I looked at my palms. No blood. Why weren't they bloody? My thoughts slipped through the crevices of my brain like an undulating eel.

"Sarah?" Paul said. "Are you okay?"

I shook my head no then nodded yes. I thought again how I would feel if Shadow died. Shadow. She was still in the car. The windows were all partially open, but still, I shouldn't leave her there much longer.

"Um, let me wash my hands first." My voice seemed to come from very far away.

It was as if I had stepped into another realm as I handed Dr. Griffin the rat cage. Austen sniffed the air. Did he know I killed Mansfield? They had been fighting. Was he glad? Or did they engage in sibling fights but underneath the squabbling really loved each other?

Dr. Griffin walked to the front door with Paul close on her heels. I stumbled to the kitchen sink where I scrubbed and scrubbed under warm, then hot, then scalding water, as if it were possible to wash away my guilt. From the window I could see the dejected veterinarian descended my driveway. Sympathy for the woman replaced my annoyance. It must be the hardest thing in the world to tell someone their beloved pet had died.

Paul suddenly appeared at my side. "Let's go."

He turned off the tap and handed me a dishtowel. My hands should hurt, but I felt nothing. Would my reddened skin serve as a scarlet letter? Paul took my elbow, and my feet took me to the front door. I fumbled with the key as I tried to lock up. When I turned, Paul blocked my path to the car.

"You okay?" He placed a hand on my shoulder. I leaned into his chest. When he wrapped his arms around me, I shifted onto my tippy toes to receive his embrace.

Just then the door to Mr. O'Shawnessy's house opened. Over Paul's shoulder, I watched the frail old man poke his head out and peer across the driveway. I pushed Paul away.

"I thought I heard voices," my guardian called in his strange mixed accent of Irish and Scottish brogue. "Hey. You, lad. Best you be leaving."

"Yes, sir. But Sarah offered to drive me back to school. I have football practice."

The big oaf stared at his feet, waved, and strode to the car.

"He doesn't have another way to get there," I said to Mr. O'Shawnessy. "I'm going to drop him off and I'll be right back."

At least Margaret had never brought Paul home to meet her grandpa. He couldn't know this was his granddaughter's boyfriend. What would he think of me if he did? He might throw me out. Why had I allowed Paul to hug me? What was wrong with me?

"Everything's bonny then," my guardian said.

"Yes," I said, rushing to the driver's side of the car. "Shadow's coming along for the ride. It's all good."

He nodded and disappeared into his house. But nothing was good. Nothing at all. An animal had died in my hands today and it was my fault.

* * *

My Civic pulled into the high school parking lot before the final school bell. Dozens of cars cluttered the asphalt stalls. Most were older. A mass exodus of humanity would soon depart in a cloud of exhaust fumes.

Shadow lay in the back curled up. A somber mood permeated the car. Even the air seemed thick. Paul hadn't uttered a word since we left my house. What a change from the drive there when he rambled on non-stop. I expected him to dwell on how strange Dr. Griffin was. Who in their right mind gave CPR to a rat? But he said nothing.

"You all right?" I asked.

"Yeah," he pursed his lips. "Do you think Margaret's grandfather will tell her about what he saw on the porch?"

Ah. That's what troubled him. Mr. O'Shawnessy didn't know Paul was seeing his granddaughter. Margaret probably failed to mention to her boyfriend that she wasn't supposed to be dating, so she always snuck out to see Paul. Well, I wasn't going to enlighten him.

"No. Mr. O'Shawnessy's cool. Plus, he didn't recognize you."

Paul nodded, but his lip remained puckered in a pout.

"You and Kyle, huh?"

I lied to Dr. Griffin about Kyle. But why fess up? If Paul thought I was involved with someone else, he would return his attention to Margaret and forget I existed. I smiled and shrugged which seemed enough of an answer.

"Can you stop here?" Paul pointed to a vintage Chevy truck. "I need to get my shoes for practice."

The rear bumper of the vehicle was dented and the right taillight broken. The scraped white paint had rusted, so the truck hadn't been in a recent crash. I pulled the Civic into the empty slot next to his beater.

I half expected him to bolt from my car, rush to Margaret, and tell her what warped things he witnessed this afternoon. Paul's hand rested on the door handle, but he made no move to exit. His head was bowed as if in prayer. He turned sad, green eyes in my direction.

"That's deep," he mumbled. "I've never seen an animal die. But it was way cool what the vet did, trying to save the rat's life."

I had to make him understand he needed to stay silent. If it leaked to social services that Dr. Griffin had broken into my house, no way would the courts agree to let me live in my home without adult supervision. And then there was the wrath of Margaret. His blabbing could threaten both of us.

"You know you have to keep quiet about what happened. You can't tell anyone you were inside my house or what you witnessed. You know how Margaret will react."

Paul frowned and scratched his chin. "I don't care if she gets mad. You still going to help me with biology though?"

What a bargain he got. Less than five minutes of lifting the end of a couch in exchange for hours of free tutoring. Yet, Dad's Relationship Rule #6 came to mind: Never make a promise you don't intend to keep. I was honor-bound. And if I agreed he might agree not to tell his girlfriend about helping me.

"A deal's a deal," I said.

A lopsided smile formed on his face. But it wasn't relief I glimpsed in his eyes; his expression was one of a smitten lover. I shook my head no. I had to set him straight. Fast.

"Three sessions," I said. "Maybe Kyle can join us too."

Paul's smile evaporated. Good. For now at least, it seemed any romantic notions had been laid to rest. But it was only a matter of time before he would learn Kyle wanted nothing to do with me. One problem solved for now.

I glanced around the parking lot. No witnesses at the moment, but a whole different scenario might arise if we were spotted studying together. Where could we go? Tutoring at my house was out of the question, not with Margaret right next door and the possibility that Mr. O'Shawnessy might see Paul go inside. Most after-school help was offered in the library, but the odds of meeting Paul there without the event becoming a viral text were slim. A diner, or a coffee shop, or any public place for that matter held risk too. This small town didn't have room for secrets.

"My next test is Tuesday," he said. "Can we meet at my house on Saturday afternoon at one? But no Kyle. I want your full attention. Tomorrow afternoon at one?"

This time a full grin spread across his face and reached his green eyes. Dimples formed in his cheeks. Not quite as spectacular as Kyle's, but close. His mussed hair gave him a boyish charm. He reminded me of a giant teddy bear.

His house? As long as his mother was home, this did seem the best option. But not at 1:00 p.m.

"I can't do it. Shadow and I take a dog agility class then."

"That sounds cool. Taking a class with your dog. But Shadow is already so well trained. I can't believe how she held so still during art class."

"She's amazing," I gushed. Nothing made me as happy as when people raved about my sweet girl. "But she's smart and needs activities to keep her busy and happy. We're learning how to sequence jumps, complete the dog walk, and how to jump through a tire. It's super fun."

"Can I come watch?"

Ugh. Spending more time with Paul was a bad idea.

"It's too distracting for the dogs," I said, which was partially true at least. "Let's focus on finding a time for your tutoring."

Paul nodded. "Hey, how about Monday after school? Monday is perfect. Mom always has chocolate chip cookies warm out of the oven. She says it's a great way to start the week."

"How can I refuse cookies?" I said. "But I'll need to swing by home to check on Shadow and take her on a quick walk. How about four o'clock?"

"Yeah. That works. You're a nice person. No matter what Margaret says."

If Margaret learned of this arrangement, my home life would resemble ground zero. I didn't trust Paul's ability to keep our sessions secret. Paul should tell her about the sessions before she found out from someone else.

"You'll eventually have to tell Margaret I'm tutoring you. She's not going to like it. But why don't you wait until tomorrow when she's more likely to be in a good mood."

"Well," he said, "that might take a while, and she's gonna be pissed all over again when I tell her. But she'll have to suck it up. Even if I don't decide to study biology in college, I have to pass this class or I don't graduate."

He frowned then nodded.

"I'll tell her before our first session. You're right. People will talk."

Shadow stirred in the back seat. At least I managed to keep one secret from this small community. I didn't want to imagine the consequences if Shadow's and my ghost-seeing abilities were revealed.

Ghosts. The ethereal image of the little boy popped into my head. In this small town, it should be easy to find out who the little guy was. The bell rang, and Paul unbuckled his seat belt.

"Paul, did a little boy die around here recently?"

Paul frowned. He tugged on the handle, opened the door, and stepped out. His fingers tapped on the roof of the car before he poked his head back inside.

"Not that I know of," he said.

"You sure? A redheaded boy. Three years old or so?"

Paul shrugged. "Don't think so. Not much happens in this town. Besides, I'm sure my mom would've helped out with meals for the family. Anytime somethun' happens to a child, Mom's too busy to cook for us. She's making casseroles for everyone else—a kid's family, firefighters, doctors, you name it. We don't have home-cooked dinners for days, sometimes weeks. So I'd have remembered if a kid died. Anyway, see you Monday."

The car door clicked shut. Maybe the boy wasn't from here. Or maybe... I hadn't asked about lost children. Perhaps, the little ghost boy was still listed as missing, but people had given up looking for him because it happened too many years ago. I pondered my father's description of the blurred, grainy faces that used to be displayed on milk cartons. Could this toddler be one of them?

CHAPTER EIGHT

"That's very curious!" she thought. "But everything is curious today."

Shadow stayed curled in the back seat on the return drive home. Was she tired from modeling in art class? Or is her lethargy a symptom of something worse? Once when I used my dog to see ghosts, she collapsed and went into a coma. But that happened after I conversed with a ghost multiple times and kept my fingers between her eyes for far too long. Today I channeled through her for less than a minute. Surely, the brief ghost viewing of my Dad and the little boy hadn't hurt Shadow.

I turned onto our street. Dr. Griffin's car was gone. She hadn't returned from her vet office with the bereavement pamphlets yet, so Mrs. Bellweather was likely ignorant of Mansfield's fate. I pulled into the driveway.

My sweet pup stood and yawned. Her taut muscles rippled as she extended her forelegs in a full body stretch. When her four paws were once again squared under her body, she shook from head to rear as if she emerged from a bath. A shower of red fur wafted into the air. She shoved her head into the front seat and gazed at me with bright, brown eyes.

So many bad things happened today. When given in advance, metronidazole eliminated any lasting neurological effects to my dog when I used Shadow for her ghost-seeing abilities. Would it work after the event too? Even though she seemed fine, why tempt fate?

I got out of the car, and with leash in hand, trudged to my porch. Shadow pranced by my side. After I entered the house and secured the latch behind me, I headed to the cupboard where Shadow's food and emergency medicines were stored. I struggled with the white, childproof cap on the amber container then extracted a small white capsule.

Five more days with Shadow in the art room. What if Dad wanted me to investigate the little ghost boy's disappearance? What if this toddler needed my help? I shouldn't, but the temptation to use Shadow as my medium might be too great. If I stashed a few doses in my backpack, I would have them handy to prevent any ill effects. One for now, five on standby. Five on stand-by to use only if necessary. A dose of metronidazole, a harmless drug usually prescribed for diarrhea, might cause constipation but without the medicine, she could die. Taking precautions was a no-brainer.

I rummaged through the fridge and pulled out Shadow's open can of dog food. I pinched a bit of mushy food and crammed the medicine into the center of the tidbit. Shadow danced around at my feet until I offered the morsel which she gobbled pill and all. I placed the other doses in a plastic bag and stowed them in the bottom of my backpack. I made a mental note to pack string cheese in my lunch every day to trick Shadow into swallowing the pills.

I spotted the milk carton as I put away the dog food. Although I ate dinner at Mr. O'Shawnessy's house, it was more convenient to inhale a bowl of cereal at my house for breakfast on school mornings while I fed Shadow, so I kept a few groceries on hand.

I lifted out the quart of milk. Black and white Holstein cows in a grassy field covered the front, nutritional information listed on the side. I twisted the container to view the other side. My Dad once told me they put missing children's pictures on the cartons. Too bad they stopped doing that. Perhaps those blurry pictures had been deemed ineffective compared to the clear images broadcast online these days.

I replaced the milk container and shut the fridge. Time for some research. I extracted my laptop from my backpack. When it came to my Internet use, I proceeded carefully. The caseloads of social workers were probably too heavy to spy on foster kids for inappropriate web surfing, but why give the authorities a reason to deny my petition for independent living? No Facebook account for me—not that I had any friends anyway. Well, there was Tess. But even my long-distance best friend could post something the courts found objectionable, so why take a chance?

I settled into the desk chair in my living room where I often did my homework. Shadow came to me and pressed her forehead to my leg, a signal she wanted a neck rub. My hands massaged her muscled shoulders for a moment. Alert canine eyes pleaded for more. I rubbed her neck and she groaned, soaking up the pleasure. Curiosity got cats in trouble, but a little investigation on the computer from the safety of my home would be harmless.

I opened a browser and typed in "missing children." Two promising websites appeared: klaaskids.org and missingchild.com. I clicked on the klaaskids link. The words at the top of the page stated that a child can disappear as fast as a mile a minute which sent chills across my skin. Below was a slew of kidnapping statistics.

I clicked on website after website. Facts whirled on each page. Three distinct types of kidnapping were identified. A bit less than a half of all abductions were by a relative of the victim, another third by acquaintances, and only a quarter by a stranger. Another staggering statistic blared from a website that looked old and hadn't been updated in a long time. The number of police reports of missing juveniles increased 470% between 1982 and 2000. I stared at the numbers quoted for the year 2000: 876,200. How was it possible that in a single year more than three-quarters of a million young people either vanished completely or disappeared long enough to warrant a call to the authorities?

That was interesting, but I wanted to see photographs of missing three- or four-year-old children.

I double-clicked on the beyondmissing.com link and scrolled to: "What to do if your child disappears." This website allowed law enforcement agencies to create and distribute Amber Alert flyers via email, fax, and text to a database of missing children agencies within a 200-mile radius of the abduction. Not what I hoped for.

I returned to the original search and noticed the National Center for Missing and Exploited Children link. I clicked on www.ncmec.org and hit the jackpot. This site was structured to perform searches of missing children, by location, date of disappearance, and gender. Problem was, I didn't have all the information needed to do a search. The ghost was a boy, but what should I input for year missing? Could I assume he lived here in California? I selected CA, since a local crime seemed like a good guess. Now for the year. This was tricky since my experience with ghosts suggest they don't age. The kidnapping might have happened ten years ago, and he would look the same. I tried 2 in the *Missing for ___ Years* field and hit submit. Thirty-three records appeared. Most were teen or pre-teen boys, ranging from eight to sixteen years-old. A single three-year-old, and a total of two four-year-olds were also listed. None of the younger boys had red hair or the ghost child's vivid blue eyes and chubby cheeks. I plugged in a 3 for years missing field then tried a 4. No match. I sighed and closed the webpage.

Finding out the identity of the little ghost boy would take a lot of research. Too much homework required my attention plus I needed time to study for the SATs, fill out college applications, and now I had to fit time in to tutor Paul too. An idea formed. I hadn't picked a senior project topic yet. What if I selected missing children as my subject matter? Figuring out who the boy was could be part of my research.

But did I want to look into this? The information might be disturbing. Even this little bit of searching on kidnapping set my nerves on edge. If Dr. Griffin wanted to get rid of me, it seems abduction was easy.

I needed to start my calculus problems before I forgot the lesson, and there was another, more pressing issue: Margaret. Dad's Relationship Rule #2 said to be generous, and I intended to follow his advice. I would make her favorite dessert: brownies.

I washed my hands again and again, thinking of the rat pee and feeling unable to get clean. Finally, I forced myself to stop.

With the oven set to 350 degrees, I stirred oil and water into the brownie mix in a stainless bowl, poured the concoction into a pan, and placed it in the pre-heated oven.

I lost myself in logarithmic differentiation problems not even noticing the sweet aroma of hot cocoa until the oven timer buzzed. Shadow followed on my heels as I dashed into the kitchen to check on the brownies. Warm chocolate-scented air washed my face as I opened the oven door but the center hadn't set.

I glanced out the kitchen window facing the street. Dr. Griffin's yellow bug pulled up on the far side of the road. I froze. Poor Claudia. Time to break the news to Mrs. Bellweather. My chafed hands burned, but I turned on the tap and washed them again just thinking of Mansfield.

At the sound of a car door slamming, Shadow scrambled to the front door and let out an excited yip. Dr. Griffin walked around her vehicle to the trunk. Why would she have placed bereavement pamphlets in there? And indeed she hadn't. She hefted a heavy bag of dog food and headed toward my house. I turned off the water, dried my hands, and contemplated hiding. In the end, when she knocked, I cracked the door wide enough to have a conversation, but not enough to imply she was welcome to enter. Shadow barked and tried to sneak out, but I blocked her path with my leg.

Dr. Griffin didn't waste time with pleasantries. "I feel so bad about what happened. I bought some stuff for Shadow. Please accept this food and a few dog toys. I have a few more things in the car."

Her legs bowed under the weight of the dog food. I shook my head no. Whatever she touched became tainted.

"Please, Sarah."

The brand of kibble wasn't one I knew. Red Rhino. The words "organic" and "all-natural" peppered the shiny exterior. The image of a transparent rhino set against an orange sunset on the packaging suggested the food was high-end. I recalled the circle of rhinos surrounding the hood ornament on Dr. Griffin's coffee table. She would buy this label. She believed rhinos were her spirit animal.

Her blue eyes pleaded behind her thick-rimmed glasses. Be generous. I heard Dad's rule in my head.

"If it makes you feel better, you can leave it on the porch. But you are not to step foot inside this house. There will be consequences. Do you understand?"

"I know, I know," she said, dropping the bag.

I shut the door and twisted the lock, not even bothering to watch her unload the other gifts from her car. Instead, I returned to my calculus. Shadow yipped once more and I heard the rustle of plastic, but I did not go to the front door. The latch was engaged. The woman couldn't get in. What an idiot I had been to run out of the house without locking the door this morning—or had I? I kept a spare key under a rock in the landscaping next to the porch. What if she had poked around and found the mother lode—a shiny object that allowed her easy access to the inside of my house?

I rushed to the oven to take out the brownies then went to look through the peephole to confirm Dr. Griffin had gone before stepping outside. In addition to the forty-pound bag of dog food, plastic bags bearing logos for Critter Country, Petland, and Simon's Feed Store were piled next to it. The crazy vet stood beside her car with her back to me.

As she lifted something from the rear seat, I quickly lifted the rock where I stashed the key. It was gone.

That lying witch. She hadn't found my door unlocked. She had broken into my house. Worse, now she had easy access, coming and going as she pleased. She was probably only after the hood ornament, but with this cray cray woman, who knew? I retreated inside leaving the dog gifts untouched. I secured the door behind me, not that it mattered if she had a key. For the first time, I was glad I was still living next door.

I needed to change my locks, but it was after business hours. Too late to call today. I usually stored my laptop computer here, and even though I didn't think Dr. Griffin would steal it, I decided to take it next door for now. I was confident she wouldn't mess with Shadow as long as I had the hood ornament. Wait. What if social services discovered I called a locksmith? Explaining the missing key would make me appear irresponsible. The locks would have to wait until after my hearing.

The best thing for me to do now was finish my homework. After reading a mind-numbing equation, I rolled back in my chair. I couldn't concentrate. Dr. Griffin's actions nagged at me. None of the stores where the vet purchased gifts for Shadow were particularly close to her office or my house. Each of these pet stores sold small pets, including rodents. Had she found a rat resembling Mansfield and substituted him?

I rushed to my kitchen window. Across the street I saw Dr. Griffin extract a cage from the back seat of her car and set it on the ground. I did not see a separate bag or box with Mansfield's remains, nor did I see any bereavement pamphlets. Dearest Dr. Griffin, I'm afraid I smell a rat.

CHAPTER NINE

*"—so long as I get SOMEWHERE," added Alice as
an explanation.*

As I processed the possibility of Dr. Griffin's plan to
deceive Mrs. Bellweather, the oven timer buzzed
making me jump. I must have accidentally reset it. I
silenced the ring, but when I returned to the window,
Dr. Griffin was no longer in sight. I opened my calculus
textbook, but my mind kept drifting to our neighbor
across the street who lost her beloved pet rat. The more I
processed the idea, the more I realized Dr. Griffin couldn't
have located a substitute rat for Mansfield. Not with those
unique markings. Was she breaking the news to the poor
old woman at this very moment?

I didn't feel right about Dr. Griffin taking all the blame.
Maybe I should walk over to Mrs. Bellweather's and explain
my role in Mansfield's death. Dad's Relationship Rule #9
was to treat others the way you want to be treated. I would
want to know the full truth of what had happened. Almost

forty minutes passed since I spotted Dr. Griffin across the street. Mrs. Bellweather must have recovered from the initial shock and would be ready to hear the full story. I decided to do the honorable thing and go apologize.

Shadow stood from her post under the table and arched her back into a stretch.

"No," I said. "You stay here."

When I cracked the door open, I recoiled. Dr. Griffin sat on my porch next to her pet store purchases. I expected blood-shot eyes, a tear-stained face. Dr. Griffin, despite her weirdness, did care deeply for animals. But she seemed fine. Even her blue eyes held a twinge of satisfaction.

"What are you doing here?"

OMG. What had she said to the elderly woman? That she was keeping Mansfield overnight? I wish Dr. Griffin had stayed away from me. I wanted no part of this. I was about to slam the door, but Shadow slipped past, planted her feet, and barked at the woman.

"There she is," Dr. Griffin said.

The veterinarian tossed a handful of dog biscuits, and Shadow scrambled for the treats. Some watchdog.

"Uh, Sarah . . . I was hoping you'd come out soon. I'm afraid I forgot my cell phone."

Yeah, right. Why hadn't she knocked? This smelled like another ploy. Why couldn't she leave me alone? I wished Paul were still here. I'd feel safer. I couldn't close and lock the door, not with Shadow out on the porch. And I suspected she had a key anyway. Crap, crap, crap. I pretended nonchalance, but what I wanted most was to put distance between Dr. Griffin and my dog.

"Shadow," I called.

Dr. Griffin opened her palm to reveal a fistful of soft treats. Shadow either forgot her training or lost her hearing and gobbled the treats.

"Please call the number," she said. "If the phone doesn't ring I'll know I left it elsewhere, and you can have Shadow."

I bristled at her tactics, but I whipped my cell out of my pocket anyway. I still had her contact information in my phone from last spring when she had treated Shadow for her barking problem. I punched the number. The faint sound of the theme of the movie, *Ghostbusters*, filtered in from the living room. I almost chuckled at the ringtone she had selected for me.

"Stop feeding my dog," I said, "and I'll get your phone."

She closed the treat bag and Shadow came to me. I shut and locked the door then redialed. I walked toward the sound and found her cell on my couch. Well, well. It must have fallen out of her pocket when she collapsed on the sofa after she discovered Mansfield had died.

As I headed for my front door, the shrill ring of the telephone in my hand startled me. Caller ID revealed the person on the other line was none other than E. Bellweather. I didn't answer. I opened the door and showed the device to Dr. Griffin who had risen to her feet.

Her eyes studied the thin black letters announcing who was on the other end. The vet's body went still. I jabbed the phone in her direction as the object continued its demand for attention. She must have done something she shouldn't have. The phone fell silent.

"You didn't."

"Didn't what?" Dr. Griffin said, twitching like a nervous bird that spotted a hawk overhead.

"Substitute a rat with Mansfield's markings," I said, pointing at the pet store bags. "That's why she's calling, isn't it? She has noticed the difference. And that's why you don't want to answer the phone."

Dr. Griffin studied her feet. Her cheeks flamed pink.

"No," she said without looking up. "Though I admit I tried, but I couldn't find an older rat, much less a black and white one with a distinctive dark patch on its rump."

I nodded. This part rang true, but had she told all?

"So how did Mrs. Bellweather handle the news?" I asked.

"Actually … quite well." Dr. Griffin's fingers fluttered to her face.

"Really? What did she say?" I pressed.

The phone in my hand started to ring again. Caller ID once again indicated it was Mrs. Bellweather.

I offered the phone to Dr. Griffin. When she refused to take it, I hit the answer button. The phone's incessant ring quieted. Dr. Griffin's alarmed eyes held mine.

"Hello, Dr. Griffin's office," I said.

The woman on the other end sniffled and blubbered something unintelligible.

"Sorry?"

"I think Mansfield's dead," she said. "I must speak to the doctor immediately. Maybe he can still be saved."

Holy crap. I pictured Dr. Griffin curling the dead rat into a ball as if it were asleep and delivering him to her client as though nothing had happened. This scenario explained the lack of brochures. I glared at the woman on my porch.

"Of course," I said.

This time I threw the phone toward Dr. Griffin. Her trembling hand caught the black object midair then placed it next to her ear.

"Dr. Griffin speaking." After listening for a moment, her face blanched "I'm across the street with another client. I'll be right there."

Her index finger, pale and thin as rat bones, pushed the off button. The woman's blue eyes held mine as though daring me to say something. I opened my mouth, but the screen door across the driveway creaked open, and for the second time today, my guardian poked his head out his front door.

"Aye, Sarah, there ye be. Mrs. Wright rang 'bout Monday's emancipation hearing. She be wantin' ye to call."

Double crap. I wish he would keep his voice down. The last thing I wanted was for Dr. Griffin to know my court date. Still, it was a relief to know when it was happening.

And so soon! If things went as planned, I could move back home as early as next week. No more Margaret. Sleeping in my own bed with Shadow at my side sounded like heaven.

"Okay," I said to Mr. O'Shawnessy. "Now, please go sit. I don't want you to become overtired."

"Aw, ye worry too much. Such a sweet lass, ye are." But he waved and closed the door, just the same.

"So your emancipation hearing is on Monday, is it?" Dr. Griffin said. Her eyes gleamed like a lioness' on a weakened antelope. "It would be a shame if I came and testified how you brought Paul home with you. What would social services think of a young girl who invited boys into her home?"

Blood rose to my cheeks. I bit my lower lip. Paul was in my house to help fix her mess. How dare she threaten to use this against me?

"Don't you need to go save Mansfield?" I spat. "He only died moments ago, didn't he?"

"Now, now. Don't get too riled," she continued. "I promise to keep my mouth shut about how you brought your boyfriend home after school, if you keep quiet about Mansfield. Deal?"

I considered dim-witted Paul being called to the stand. He might say he went inside my house and forget to mention all he had done was lift a couch. I cringed at the image of life with the wrath of Margaret for another year if they denied my petition. What would happen to Shadow if the authorities deemed me too irresponsible to care for a pet? My independence and Shadow's fate depended on my actions. I couldn't let this woman ruin the image of self-sufficiency and maturity I have worked so hard to attain.

I half nodded, though I wasn't certain. She smiled, taking it as agreement.

"I have to go," she said. "Don't even think about contacting Mrs. Bellweather with any wild stories, got it?"

The woman didn't wait for a response. She sprinted down my driveway, across the street and rocketed across the long, narrow driveway leading to Mrs. Bellweather's house. I shut my front door and crouched to gather Shadow into my arms.

"I think I just made a big mistake," I said to my dog.

What was I thinking? I should have marched over and told Mrs. Bellweather the truth. I should have never agreed to Dr. Griffin's blackmail. What did my actions say about me? I was as culpable as that rat of a vet. I had made a deal with the devil.

I sighed and rose to my full height. The stuff on my front porch needed to be moved. As I stepped outside, Margaret's car pulled into the driveway next door. Her green eyes shot darts across the expanse of air separating us. One look at her smoldering face confirmed not even brownies would temper her anger. In her twisted mind, my offering of her favorite dessert represented an admission that I encouraged Paul's advances. Why else would I be nice to her? She stormed to the front door of her house, her black hair swaying, while anger emanated from her in waves.

I gathered the plastic bags filled with dog treats and toys. I had no intention of keeping any of this ill-begotten loot. Dr. Griffin's empty yellow VW bug gleamed bright across the street. She had no business driving a cheery-colored car. Red, the warning color of a female black widow suited her better.

Wait. I had leverage. What was I thinking? I still had her murder weapon. I could still tell Mrs. Bellweather the truth. And maybe I would... eventually. But this didn't change the reality of Mansfield's death. Dr. Griffin could ruin my court hearing out of spite, even if it meant risking the revelation of her secrets. The woman was unbalanced.

I plunked the gifts for Shadow into the trunk of my car along with the bag of dog food—all of these items soon to be delivered to the local animal shelter. I didn't want these reminders of Dr. Griffin in my house. Except that wasn't the whole truth. The woman's gift would trigger a memory of Mansfield too.

A few months before he died, Dad discovered I had read the CliffsNotes for a test on The Grapes of Wrath. He said nothing good ever comes of shortcuts. But back then I had a good reason to take the easy way out—wanting to spend more time with my dying father at the hospital. Dad wouldn't have approved of my agreeing to Dr. Griffin's terms now. I had no good excuse for taking a shortcut by not going over to Mrs. Belweather's house right and making sure Dr. Griffin explained exactly how her rat died and that I was responsible. Instead, I returned to my house and closed the door, fully aware that I was not doing the right thing.

CHAPTER TEN

"Now, I give you fair warning," shouted the Queen...

I placed the dog food bowl in front of Shadow right on schedule: dinner at 4:30 p.m. Even after all the biscuits and treats, my pooch dove into her food without hesitation. Oh, to be a dog! No moral dilemmas.

I still couldn't get the image of poor dead Mansfield from my head. My Brazil nut outer shell that kept my emotions under control had developed fissures. I sank into a chair at my dining room table and took a deep breath. Shadow inhaled the rest of her food then came to my side and placed her head on my leg. That pure sweet act, that selfless love brought my grief to the surface. I bit my lip to stop the tears.

I needed to pull myself together. I should call Tess. I fished my cell from the bottom of my backpack and turned notification off vibrate. Three voicemail messages had arrived, all from the same familiar number. Mrs. Wright rarely called. Three messages meant a problem. Crap. Mr.

O'Shawnessy told me this morning my social worker had phoned him the day before trying to reach me. Yesterday, my phone battery had died. And he had reminded me just now too. How could I have forgotten such an important thing?

My hearing started at 8:00 a.m. Monday, and now it was almost the end of Mrs. Wright's Friday workday. She was sympathetic to my predicament, but she expected me to be responsible. Her support could vanish over something like this. I took a deep breath and dialed her number. She answered on the first ring.

"Oh, thank goodness you called back," she gushed. "The judge hearing your case has asked you to bring two character witnesses besides Mr. O'Shawnessy to the hearing. There's not much notice. I can ask for a delay, but I wanted to speak to you first."

Delay? No way. Margaret would make my life miserable thanks to Paul. I couldn't fathom having to suffer her drama and mean-spirited pranks for weeks or months. Problem was who would speak on my behalf? Well, I would think of someone.

"No, don't postpone. Don't worry. I'll find two people."

"I'm giving you fair warning, Sarah. This judge is err... thorough. They will have to be credible. Ideally, a teacher from school who could attest to how well you've transitioned. I know that's a tall order though given the hearing is during work hours and this is last minute."

Someone from school? Mrs. Durgette would have been a logical choice, but even if I convinced her to speak on my behalf, she might mention I called a fellow student a loser. I couldn't risk it. There wasn't time to ask any of my teachers at this late date anyway. Who else? Other than Mr. O'Shawnessy, I had no friends in this town. That wasn't going to stop me though.

"Okay, I know the perfect people."

A lie. Another shortcut. But my determination would prevail. I either had to solve this problem or face Margaret's nuclear reaction if I didn't move out soon. She asked me daily when I would leave.

"Do you want me to contact them for you?" she asked.

"Uh, no," I stammered.

"Okay. If you're sure you can get them there. But I'll need their names."

Triple crap. The only person who showed me any kindness at the school was Paul.

"Paul ... Paul Marks."

I scrambled for a second name, but the only other person who came to mind was Dr. Griffin. No way. My mind went blank. I heard a beep, indicating another call on Mrs. Wright's phone.

"Great, Paul and Mark," she said. "I look forward to meeting them on Monday. They have to show, Sarah. Trust me. You don't want to anger this judge."

Fate had spared me concocting a second name, and I grabbed the brass ring.

"They'll be there." The confidence in my voice startled me.

A dial tone filled my ears. There was no going back. I didn't know anyone named Mark. I wondered if Paul would say something to ruin my chances of gaining my independence. Or would Paul even agree to come? I considered looking up his phone number and texting him, but what if he didn't delete it, and Margaret snooped on his phone and saw the message? Even a text as innocuous as "call me" would send Margaret into a jealous rage. Besides, he was still at pre-game football practice. It would be better to wait until I could speak to him.

Then I remembered he would need a note from his mom to be excused from school. Should I call her and introduce myself, or should I wait until I confirmed with Paul that he could come? I should phone her anyway. I would be at her house to tutor Paul on Monday afternoon. It would not surprise me if the big oaf forgot to tell her. I envisioned an awkward moment when I appeared on her doorstep with no notice.

I had ordered a copy of the school directory when I registered for school, so I extracted it from under a stack of Spanish homework. Paul Marks was the second name on the "M" page. Sadie and Richard Marks were listed as his parents. To call or not to call?

I riffled through Dad's relationship rules and landed on Relationship Rule #9: Treat others the way you want to be treated. But depending on whose perspective I chose, a different answer arose. If I were Paul, I would want to be the one to tell my parent I needed a tutor to help me pass biology. Her expression when I delivered the news might be important. But Paul's mom might want to meet the person who would be tutoring her son. Who was she inviting into her home? Hell, he had a football game tonight. He might even forget to tell his mother about the tutoring, whether his team won, and he was happy, or they lost, and he was bummed.

What was the rush anyway? My dilemma could wait until tomorrow after Paul had a chance to tell his parents about the tutoring. I fingered the directory. This would make a good temporary hiding place for Dad's relationship rules card. I would move it to Dad's favorite book later. I pulled it out of my backpack and stuck it under the front cover. One less thing to worry about, but there were plenty of other problems to take its place.

I pulled out a dining room chair and sank into it. I laid my head on the cold tabletop. Shadow moved to my side and nudged my hand as if to say, "Pet me and forget your troubles." Sweet, sweet, Shadow. She knew how to make me feel better.

How had things gone so bad so quickly? Dad. That's how. Because of him, I lied to Kyle—a guy I liked—and then inadvertently insulted him because Dr. Griffin allowed a rat to escape in my house which led me to break classroom rules which caused Mrs. Durgette's annoyance with me which led her to drop my grade. And now it seemed, there was no stopping the avalanche of unfortunate events. So much had gone wrong. But the worst thing was that Mansfield died, and Dr. Griffin tricked a client into believing her dead pet had been sleeping.

Now I wished Dad would come back. He must have appeared this afternoon because of Dr. Griffin when he believed my life was in jeopardy. Had he been around all along, watching over me? Maybe he had only let his presence be known when I was in trouble.

"Daddy? Are you here?"

I lifted my head from the table.

"Dad. I need your help."

An electric shock buzzed my hand, traveled through my arm and neck, and tingled across my brain. I wasn't frightened. I felt my father's presence in the energy. Then a warm tube of air encapsulated my forearm, a comforting sensation of love.

"Sarah."

My dad's voice vibrated in my head. Was this a thought, or was my father inside my brain?

"No, Sarah," Dad said. The words formed as thoughts not a voice speaking outside me. "You're fine. Listen to me. I can only do the mind bind once. There isn't much time. I have so much to tell you. Please, may I have your permission to complete the process?"

Mind bind? What did "complete the process" mean? Completely inhabit my brain? An underlying urgency penetrated Dad's words or my thoughts or whatever this connection was. Should I agree? What if he found my ugly, selfish thoughts and unkind acts? He would be so disappointed in me.

"Don't worry," he said. "My love for you is unconditional. I would never ask this of you if it wasn't important."

Yet I hesitated. What if the mind meld damaged my brain? Or I collapsed as Shadow had when David-the-Ghost had conversed with me through my dog?

"Think about Relationship Rule #12." Dad's voice persisted. "But I'm leaving now. So you can make the decision by yourself."

Cool air flowed over my arm, and an emptiness filled my chest. For the second time today, my eyes filled. Not because he trusted me to make the right decision, but because of Rule #12. The memory of Thanksgiving Day when Dad had presented the final rule swelled in my mind. The smell of turkey and sizzling butter from the kitchen, the underlying scent of the yellow and orange carnations Dad had bought for a table centerpiece. Burning wood crackled and popped in the hearth, creating warm air that embraced the two of us in our cozy home. That was the day he tucked a five-by-seven index card into my napkin. The three black words loaded with meaning. *Love is infinite.* Had he decided that day to make this phrase Relationship Rule #12 or had the decision come later?

Dad hadn't yet told me his cancer had spread and the diagnosis was terminal. Or that he had three to six months.

He had wanted me to know that the time he had left in this world didn't matter. His love was infinite. So why doubt him now?

"Yes. Come back, Dad. You have my permission."

A swirl of warm air covered me from head to toe. I leaned back in my seat, tense, not sure what would happen next. My entire body went rigid. My scalp—oh God, the sensation was like ice water had been poured on top of my head, and cold rivulets now trickled into every hair follicle. I gulped air until warmth filled me. Every muscle melted as though I had received a full body massage. I felt sleepy, so sleepy. My eyes closed.

Yikes. I transformed into a weightless substance. A state of floating with my mind whole and functional. Yet, I existed without arms or legs, no skull, not even a mouth. I morphed into a blob who experienced movement in slow motion.

My vision was overtaken by my favorite colors, turquoise and plum which danced in a psychedelic pattern. This was like the kaleidoscope scene in the movie, *Across the Universe*. The sixties. Was this what a drug-induced trip was like? My being, or whatever I had become, collided with a squishy mass. The unpleasant sensation of fingers massaging my brain sent a shudder through my floating oasis.

"Sarah? Is that you, Pumpkin?"

Dad's voice wasn't in my head anymore. He fused with me, like interwoven muscle fibers. A wave of sweetness filled me. A sense of utter completeness and joy slid through me.

"Am I dead?"

"Not exactly," Dad thought. "You are in-between. Our minds have melded."

A dozen questions scrambled my brain. I tried to sort through my jumbled thoughts. Why had he appeared today? Who was the ghost boy?

"Hold on there, Sweetie," Dad thought. "One question at a time. "I'm here because you are in danger and because I need your help. I made a big mistake. You weren't supposed to get involved in the little ghost boy's disappearance. Forget you saw him in the art classroom. Don't try to find out who he is."

"Why?" I said. "Who is he?"

"Sweetie," he thought, but I heard his words in his baritone voice as if he spoke them. "There are rules. I can't explain. I should never have ... involved you. And the second thing: I can't cross over until you do something for me."

"Cross over?" I said. "Like through the white light?"

"Yes. Shush. We can only talk this way just this once. I need you to let go. Oh no. I thought there would be more time. No. Not yet. I can't even tell you exactly what ... Pumpkin, please, you're in danger. Stay away from—"

A terrible pain seized my head as if I had eaten ice cream too fast. In the distance, there was loud knocking.

Dad's thoughts untangled from mine. His presence catapulted away. I shuddered, jarred to the bone from the sudden departure of half of me. A heart-thundering shock wave coursed through my body as I became whole.

"Daddy," I cried aloud. "Daddy, don't go."

My head rested on the table when I regained awareness of my body. Shadow whined at the back entrance asking to go out. Strange. She usually used her doggie door. My legs took me to her side. What the heck? The lock was engaged. Dad must have secured it. I released the latch to the dog door and she bolted outside.

The pale-yellow sky suggested it was late. I whirled around to check the time. The wall clock showed it was after six. How long had I been in an altered state?

I hoped Mr. O'Shawnessy wasn't worried. I usually didn't linger at my house after school on Fridays, because it was my night to cook dinner. I needed to have the food on the table early so Margaret could watch Paul play football. She was probably even more furious with me now, if that were possible.

I returned to the kitchen to slice the cooled brownies and put them on a plate. Shadow burst inside and I kissed her head.

"I'll be back in time to give you a biscuit before bed," I promised her.

After I hoisted my backpack onto my shoulders, I crossed the driveway to face Margaret. I felt defeated. Nothing would ever make her like me.

And anyway, I had more pressing worries. Would I be able to get Paul's parents to agree to let their son skip morning classes to testify on my behalf? And I had to find a second character witness, preferably someone named Mark. Then there was Dad's warning. Who had Dad wanted me to stay away from? If I had helped him cross over, would I ever see him again? And why should I stop trying to find out the identity of the little ghost boy? One thing I knew for certain, my encounter with Dad, whether real or imagined had left me with more questions than answers.

CHAPTER ELEVEN

"Well! I've often seen a cat without a grin," thought Alice; "but a grin without a cat! It's the most curious thing I ever saw in my life!"

As I reached the porch of my guardian's house, the door flung open. Margaret loomed large on the threshold, her raven hair framing her face like a lion's mane. Green eyes the color of emeralds bored into me.

I squared my shoulders, garnering courage. I hadn't wronged my guardian's granddaughter. It was Paul who had crossed the line. Then I remembered the gift in my hands.

"I made your favorite," I said, offering the plate of brownies.

She pushed the dessert back in my direction. She inherited both an Irish temper and fortitude from her family roots. Refusal of chocolate was a bad sign. Brown, gooey sweets and her love for her grandpa were Margaret's only two real weaknesses. If brownies wouldn't pacify her, I was sunk.

"Stay away from Paul," she hissed under her breath.

"Sarah?" Mr. O'Shawnessy called from the living room. "Can you come in here a moment?"

I smiled at Margaret and shrugged my shoulders with the palm of my free hand facing skyward, knowing my temporary guardian had spared me from an unpleasant scene. Margaret rolled her eyes and stepped aside. I slipped around, careful not to let even a single strand of my brown hair brush against her. After setting the brownies on the kitchen table, I let my backpack slide from my shoulder. It landed on the kitchen floor with a thud.

The entry to Mr. O'Shawnessy's house opened into one giant room, the kitchen and dining area to the left of the front door, a living room to the right. I smiled at my guardian, giving Margaret a wide berth where she stood by the entry.

"Margaret," Mr. O'Shawnessy said. "Be a good lass and take Sarah's backpack to her room."

Great. Another reason for Margaret to resent me.

"I've got it." I took a few strides backward and lunged for the bag.

"Nay," Mr. O'Shawnessy's voice held an edge I hadn't heard before. "Margaret will do it."

His tone left no room for negotiation. My guardian had never said a harsh word to me. I was in trouble. Margaret's upper lip curled into a half-smile as she half-dragged, half-carried my heavy backpack from the room and down the main hallway that led to the three bedrooms, grumbling about over-achievers and their books. My guardian waited for Margaret to disappear before he spoke.

"Sarah," he said, shaking his head. "I may be a gaffer, but I still know what's going on. Do you take me for a cleg? A gump?"

Mr. O'Shawnessy's mix of Irish and Scottish terms charmed me. He loved languages, and so he often threw in a bit of British dialect he picked up from watching shows on the BBC channel. Gaffer, I learned in a previous conversation, was an old man. What did cleg or gump mean anyway? From his tone, neither were terms he wanted to be called. In the months I lived here, his sweet nature and kind heart had kept a relative harmony in the household despite Margaret's attitude toward my presence. He liked to say his motto was, "That's nothing to get your feathers ruffled over."

What had I done to upset him? Had, my art teacher, Mrs. Durgette called and told him about my "loser" reference? Was he annoyed I hadn't come home tonight when expected?

"I would never think of you as a cleg or a gump," I said.

Margaret should have reappeared by now, but only a slant of yellow light shone through the open door to my room down the hall. Of course, she would leave the door open to eavesdrop. She wanted to hear the dirt so she could tell the whole school.

"Then why did you disobey me, lass?"

"I'm sorry," I said. "I'm not sure what I've done."

"Never thought you would be dodgy. Ye be having guests and all when ye know it's forbidden. Who be the young lad ye be sidling up against?"

Oh, crap. He was worried about Paul. But I couldn't answer his question, not with Margaret listening.

"He's nobody to me," I whispered. "Just a boy who needs a tutor for biology. He helped me move a piece of furniture today."

Mr. O'Shawnessy's eyebrows bunched together. He looked even more distressed. Was it the tutoring? Did he think I was hedging the truth by saying we were "studying" biology?

If he became upset at a simple hug, I would hate to see how furious and disappointed he became if he were aware of what his granddaughter was up to with this boy every Friday night after the football game. Margaret may be popular, but she wasn't above school gossip. She wasn't supposed to be dating until she turned eighteen according to my guardian. But I wasn't about to be the one to devastate this sweet old man.

"Me eyes don't lie. That boy be havin' his own ideas about ye."

Margaret poked her head out of the door to my room sporting a Cheshire-Cat grin so wide her white teeth almost encompassed her entire face. Her friends must not have mentioned seeing me drive away with Paul or drop him off at school this afternoon. Otherwise, her face would be as red as a tomato right now.

"He's involved with someone else," I said with conviction. After all, it was the truth. "I'm not even interested in him. P... er... my classmate needed help. We'll study...elsewhere. Don't worry. He won't be coming by my house again, I promise."

Margaret stormed into the living room. She probably wanted the guy's name to convince him to avoid me. She-Devil threw her arms around me like we were BFFs. I cringed at her touch, but I kept my face neutral since Mr. O'Shawnessy seemed pleased at this development.

"Sarah," Margaret gushed. "Who is it? His name starts with a P. You almost let it slip. I betcha it's the shy, short boy with the glasses. Percy. Am I right?"

Percy? Yeah, right. The guy had the worst acne, and he was afraid of girls. But maybe I should to tell her about the tutoring now. If Paul said something after the game, she would be twice as mad that I hadn't told her about my plan.

"Uh—" I began.

"Nay," Mr. O'Shawnessy interrupted, "the lad who gave Sarah a hug on her front porch this afternoon he be a strapping brute."

Good grief. I hadn't encouraged Paul's stupid embrace, but even so, his intentions had been honorable. He had just been trying to be nice because I was upset about Mansfield's death.

"Blond?" Margaret asked, stepping away from me.

"Aye. Ye know this boy?"

Margaret's head nodded; her face frozen with an expression of disbelief. Her hands clenched into fists. I pictured her mind flashing back to Paul helping me pick up my pencils that spilled in the hallway after art class. She must think I'm plotting to steal her boyfriend. I had to put what happened into proper perspective.

"The hug meant nothing," I stammered. "I ... I was upset ... one of Dr. Griffin's patients died. Paul's hug was an act of pity. Nothing more."

Margaret's eyes rolled skyward. Then her green eyes morphed into black orbs. They were as dark and shiny as obsidian. Rage radiated off her in icy waves.

Did Mr. O'Shawnessy sense the room temperature drop to the chill factor of an Alaskan winter? Did he notice how Margaret's fingers curled and uncurled? She wanted to slap me, but she didn't dare. Her grandfather had no idea of her relationship with Paul. She loved her Grandpa too much to reveal how much she hated me, knowing that our mutual dislike of each other would upset him.

"Aye, then," Mr. O'Shawnessy said, "it would seem I got myself in a bother over nothing. Sarah's a good lass. She wouldn't lie."

I cringed. It seemed as if all I had done today was lie and withhold the truth which is another form of lying. I wasn't worthy of his confidence.

"Yes, Paul is quite smitten with another girl." I steeled myself and locked eyes with Margaret.

A flicker of uncertainty shone through Margaret's hatred. It must have registered that I could rat her out, but she also understood I was as protective of her grandfather as she was. The old man relaxed and leaned back into the couch. His faded blue eyes held relief.

"I'm sorry," I said to my guardian. "I should have told you where I was, who I was with, and what I was doing. It won't happen again."

The cuckoo clock in the living room sounded seven times. Margaret had missed the opening kickoff. She glanced at the front door. Her grandfather nodded.

"Run along," Mr. O'Shawnessy said to Margaret, "you'd best be off to the football game. No doubt your girlfriends be expecting you."

"I already made dinner," Margaret said over her shoulder, "since you are so late."

Well she was justified in her anger on that count. I would be mad too if she flaked out on her turn to cook. At least this was fixable.

"I'm sorry," I said, "I fell asleep doing calculus at my kitchen table. I'll take your Sunday cooking duty."

She left. I turned to apologize once more to my guardian and explain about the need for two witnesses on Monday, but his eyes were closed.

Good thing Paul was out on the football field already. Margaret might calm down enough not to kill him by the end of the game. I should warn him Margaret had learned about the hug on the porch, but what good would that do at this point?

My stomach grumbled for food so I went into the kitchen to microwave leftovers. I headed to my bedroom with a steaming plate of spaghetti. The smell of garlic and oregano drifted to my nose. While I ate, I read a chapter in the biology book I borrowed from the school library last week to prepare for the SAT subject test. With Paul's first tutoring session scheduled for Monday afternoon, refreshing myself on the material had become necessary.

A sense of relief swept through me as I finished my dinner. In a few short days I could be sleeping next door in my own house. No more walking on eggshells around Margaret. I would miss Mr. O'Shawnessy's cheerful company, but I could still visit him on football game nights without worrying about his granddaughter resenting my presence.

I leaned back in my chair and looked around. Mr. O'Shawnessy had tried to make the room seem welcoming. A giant pink teddy bear lay on the twin bed. He cleaned out the antique dresser he had used for fishing gear. The four drawers of the box-shaped bureau smelled like mothballs, but I kept most of my clothes next door anyway. A small desk and chair completed the furnishings. The floral comforter Dad had given me two years ago for Christmas brightened the barren, cream-colored walls. I hadn't bothered to put up pictures since I had always assumed my time here would be short-lived. It was a depressing space. Even the potted mums I brought home from the hospital last spring had mostly brown, dried-up petals and yellowed leaves.

The plant wouldn't survive the winter, which was disappointing since it remained the safest location to keep Dr. Griffin's hood ornament. My online searches to extend the plant's life revealed that mums grown in greenhouses, and sold as indoor plants, produced few, if any, underground stolons, which are needed to survive cold weather. I would either have to buy a new one soon or find a new hiding spot for the hood ornament.

I sighed. Another problem to solve after my hearing on Monday. For now, I had more urgent problems, like finding two witnesses.

I went to my backpack to find a chapter in my biology book on plant cells to read while I ate. The pack was unzipped. I knew how that happened. Margaret. Had she stolen my homework or ripped up an English essay again?

I rummaged through the bag. At least the laminated card was safe in the directory next door. Nothing was missing—even Shadow's pills remained untouched. Maybe the news about a boy on my porch had pulled her away before she sabotaged my schoolwork.

I set *Modern Biology* on my desk, picked up my fork, and flipped open to Chapter 1, steeling myself for a long night. The only thing to look forward to this evening was my trek next door to give Shadow her evening dog bone before bed.

My backpack drew my gaze. Had Margaret been after my relationship rules or something else?

CHAPTER TWELVE

"Begin at the beginning," the King said gravely, "and go on till you come to the end: then stop."

On Saturday morning, I got up early, threw on a pair of blue jeans, went next door to feed Shadow, and returned to my guardian's house. I made Mr. O'Shawnessy's usual: fresh-squeezed orange juice and toast. Cereal and milk for me. Margaret seldom made an appearance before noon, so sharing the weekend morning meal with my guardian had been my favorite part of living here. The two of us dined together either making small talk or in companionable silence.

Today we discussed the hearing on Monday. I decided not to tell him about my need for two more people to vouch for me until I had firm commitments from the new character witnesses. Surely, Paul would be able to get an excuse to miss school. But who should I ask to be the second person? Tess couldn't speak to my transition into a new school. I didn't want to involve Mr. O'Shawnessy yet. This was my problem.

Escaping the house before Margaret emerged from her beauty sleep seemed like a good idea. I told my guardian that after I walked Shadow, I planned to go to the mall to buy a new outfit for Monday's appearance. I could leave Shadow in the car in this cool weather, so I would take her along, because our agility class took place near the mall.

* * *

Orange and black streamers, skeletons, and pumpkins crowded store windows at the shopping center. Witches suspended from ceilings cackled when I walked by. Several stores offered free candy from bowls beside their cash registers. Halloween was upon us in a few days. I didn't need any reminders. Holiday or not, ghosts had already invaded my world—my dad and a little boy.

The new clothes folded neatly in the shopping bags hadn't lifted my spirits. The navy blazer and matching dress pants, the white, collared shirt, and dark blue pumps with sensible heels transformed me into a mature, responsible adult. An expensive ticket to get back home, but well worth the investment if it worked.

Now that I had what I needed, I rushed to escape the maze of stores. I hadn't meant to leave Shadow in the car so long. Besides, Mansfield's death seemed to trail me in this place. Rats were a common theme in the window displays.

These reminders also made me feel awful for not marching across the street this morning to Mrs. Bellweather and confessing the truth about what happened yesterday.

I hadn't made progress on securing two character witnesses either. No one knew me well enough. I hadn't even had the courage to call Paul. I should have done that earlier when Margaret was asleep, but truth be told, I was afraid. Margaret would have lit into him about our hug, and Paul would be furious with me for telling her about the tutoring. And hadn't I reassured him that Mr. O'Shawnessy wouldn't tell Margaret about the hug on the porch? And then I admitted it in front of Margaret. Now, there might not be any witnesses for Monday.

Would I ever escape the bowels of this mega-complex? A few girls from the high school shopped in Forever 21. Flashes of recognition crossed their faces before they turned their backs. It wouldn't have been as hurtful if these girls were in Margaret's clique, but they were cheerleader wannabes, girls too plump or awkward to meet her approval. Kindred outcasts. Yet even they didn't nod or wave. Probably they still clung to the hope that Margaret might someday let them into her inner circle—such was the power of a queen bee.

The mall environment conjured memories of Tess and me giggling while trying on goofy hats or slinky bras. Instead of cheering me up, today's outing reminded me of better times when I had friends to hang out with.

All around me, mothers scolded whiney toddlers. Old men with bored expressions followed their wives from store to store. Middle-schoolers sniggered behind cupped hands at images of big-breasted women in revealing outfits on the costume packages in the transient Halloween Superstore. A gray-haired man bumped into me and muttered an apology as he rushed into the Apple store. How could I feel so alone amidst all these people?

Up ahead at the entrance to Macy's, a raven-haired beauty stood next to the familiar, brawny shoulders used to lift my couch. Margaret and Paul.

Margaret hung on his arm as if it was a life preserver. I couldn't read his body language. He wasn't gripping her hand or leaning close, but he didn't seem bothered by her touch either. Paul must have convinced her the hug meant nothing. Maybe they came to buy matching Halloween outfits. Whatever the reason for their presence, I should have come to the mall a half-hour later because they stood between me and the path to my car. And now they walked toward me, oblivious that we were on a collision course.

I couldn't face them, so I ducked into the nearest store entrance. At the back of the store, I ran my fingertips along a rack of colorful baby clothes. Of all the possible stores, of course, I escaped into a Baby Gap. If anyone from school spotted me, rumors would probably fly that I was pregnant.

A blonde clerk with a perky smile approached. She was college age and looked familiar. Was she an older sibling to someone in one of my classes? My mind scrambled for any excuse to explain my presence.

"Hi," I said. "Just looking for a gift for my nephew. I'll let you know if I need help."

She nodded and turned on her heel. I tucked my chin and flipped through a row of clearance items, pulling out a pair of blue-striped overalls to lend credibility to my story. Had enough time elapsed for Margaret and Paul to pass by? I replaced the hanger and froze as I spotted a little red polo shirt with gray sleeves—the same one the little ghost boy had been wearing, except this shirt had a turtle logo on it. I pulled the shirt from the rack and fingered the emblem. Dad had warned me not to investigate the ghost boy's identity.

Blondie emerged from behind the counter. "Do you like it? I mean, like, that's a steal at six bucks. Like, they don't make those anymore."

Leave it alone, my mind screamed. Put the shirt away and walk out of the store. Margaret and Paul must be long gone.

"That's okay," I said, replacing the item. "Err, uh, I . . . I forgot his size."

"Well, like, maybe call your aunt," she suggested. "I mean these went for twenty-five dollars last year. Like, they've done four versions so far. The first run didn't have any logo, then a kangaroo logo was added, then came the turtle, and the dog logo came out this fall. The new line that's due to be released in January will have a shark."

I couldn't resist. I shouldn't ask, but the question popped out.

"So the logo-free shirts came out five years ago?"

She looked confused then smiled.

"I guess. I mean we don't have any of the original line. We had a store closure in Nevada, and they had a bunch of old inventory, like, that's why we have this one. So, like, can I ring that one up for you? You can bring it back if it doesn't fit."

Could the shirt hold other clues? I almost said yes, but that would be silly. It was not as if this brand-new shirt would hold any DNA evidence.

"Err, no thanks."

Looking out the glass entrance, the crowd had thinned. A few women passed, pushing baby strollers. A boy strutted by with his baseball cap on backward. Good. No sign of Margaret or Paul.

I pushed open the door and froze. Kyle sat on a bench not five feet away. My heart raced. His wild, red locks were combed off his forehead. Even the profile of his nose with its tiny upward tilt added to his handsomeness. A green T-shirt from The Not So Silent Night concert complemented his khaki pants in a casual, yet sensual way. He didn't need to dress up to be drop-dead gorgeous.

His head swiveled in my direction. Those dreamy blue eyes met mine, flashed recognition, then clouded with anger. I would be mad too if someone had called me a loser.

"Kyle," I said, taking a few tentative steps closer. "It's not what you think."

"It never is," he said then stood and stormed away.

I sank down onto the bench. The seat he vacated still felt warm, yet I felt chilled. His words stung. If I had been honest, I never would have mentioned my dad yesterday. If I hadn't been trying to sneak him a note in art class, I could be sipping coffee and getting to know him better right this very moment.

Shoppers' conversations around me buzzed about Halloween costumes and the Fall Harvest Dance. Excited chatter described the new strapless dress styles as wicked sexy and debated whether a witch costume was too cliché. People passed me by in droves now. Shadow was probably asleep in the back seat, but I should check on her, and I wanted to arrive at agility class early so I could potty her.

As I shifted my feet under me to stand, the bench shuddered as a guy sat next to me. He was too old to be a student. He was too busy texting to notice my scrutiny. It would be a stretch to call him good-looking. Everything about him was ordinary—from the mousy brown hair to the slight hook of his nose. The man cleared his throat. Had he seen me checking him out? Mortified, I stood to leave. When I turned to collect my bags, I offered an apologetic smile for my rudeness. Recognition sparked in his eyes at the same moment I realized where we had met.

"Hey," he said. "You're Shadow's owner. Wait ... it'll come to me. I'm terrible with names."

"Sarah. It's Sarah Whitman. Nice to see you, Dr. Pullman."

"Please, call me Mark."

Mark? This couldn't be a coincidence. My brain synapses went into overdrive. He would be perfect. He could describe me as a responsible pet owner. And he was an emergency vet who worked odd hours. He might even be free on Monday morning. But my elation withered. Would he consider my request? We had only met twice. I smiled at him, but I shouldn't blurt out such a big favor. It would be too pushy without first engaging in small talk.

"How's Shadow doing?" he asked.

I sat back onto the bench, arranging the packages by my feet and placing my purse on my lap. I had liked the man the first time we met. He seemed to be the kind of person who might be willing to help a damsel in distress.

"She'd had some sort of head trauma if I recall," Dr. Pullman said. "That's the most dissatisfying thing about being an emergency veterinarian. A lot of times owners will take the animal to their regular vet for follow up visits, so I never know if there are long term issues."

"Shadow's great. Thanks for helping her."

I tried to think of something to add. Good grief. Why was I always so tongue-tied around adults? Dr. Pullman straightened his shoulders and situated his feet as if he planned to stand. Panic set in. I had to remind him what a responsible person I was and convince him to vouch for me at my hearing. The bookstore logo on his bag indicated he had bought a book.

"Hey, what are you reading—uh—if you don't mind my asking?" I said.

Dr. Pullman's face colored a pale shade of rose. Crap. What did he have in there? Some kind of chick lit? Pornography? Whatever it was, I had made him uncomfortable. The opposite of my intentions.

"Let me guess," I added quickly, "*Marley and Me*. It's one of my all-time favorite dog stories. Did you see the movie?"

Dr. Pullman smiled and leaned back on the bench.

"I did. Jennifer Aniston did a great job, but Marley stole the show. There's nothing like the goofy face of a yellow lab to steal your heart."

The night I had taken Shadow into the vet clinic, a yellow lab with a gunshot wound had come in. Brutus. That was his name. The image of the poor dog's bloody hip had been hard to get out of my mind.

"Um," I said. "How's Brutus? Did he recover from surgery okay?"

Dr. Pullman nodded. "Physically, yes. But I ended up calling in Dr. Griffin to address some of Brutus' behavioral issues."

Dr. Griffin? I examined my packages so the man wouldn't see my dismay. These two people's paths had crossed because of me. What had I done? I hoped Dr.

Pullman's contact with her had been limited to a single phone call regarding his client.

Now to steer the conversation so my request to have him come to my hearing would seem natural. I composed myself and raised my eyes. Dr. Pullman's gaze focused on his purchase. He smoothed the creases from the tan plastic bag with the green logo.

"In fact," he said in a sheepish voice. "I was here running an errand for Claudia."

Claudia? He was on a first name basis with Dr. Griffin? He was doing favors for her? Was he dating her? That would explain the reddening of his cheeks.

"She asked me to pick up a copy of Jane Austen's *Mansfield Park*. It seems one of her clients is a big fan of this author—names all her rats with some association with the author. The poor woman just lost her beloved Mansfield yesterday. Isn't that thoughtful? A book to comfort someone in their time of loss?"

"Yes." My voice came out as a squeak. "I met Mansfield. His owner lives across the street. Small world, isn't it?"

"Yes," he said and stood. "Well, I'd better go."

No. Not yet. Adrenaline coursed through my veins. At roughly six feet, Dr. Pullman towered over me. He seemed even bigger because he had the potential to change the course of my life. It was now or never. I stood to face him.

"Um, I have a favor to ask." The words flooded out, and I couldn't stop. "I know this will seem odd, but I am new to this town, and I don't know many people, and I need someone to come to my emancipation hearing on Monday, and, well, I thought, maybe if you weren't working on Monday morning, it's at eight, you could say how responsible I was for bringing Shadow into your clinic, and how I paid the bill on time. Please? Will you come?"

Dr. Pullman took a step backward. He didn't seem put-upon nor did he wear the hangdog expression of someone who felt obligated to help even though he didn't want to. Still, I thought he might turn on his heel without responding. I conjured up my best puppy-dog eyes. I must have reached the soft part of him that had led him into a career where his primary responsibility was to help injured animals, because his shoulders relaxed and he eased himself back onto the bench, gesturing for me to take a seat beside him.

"Begin at the beginning," he said.

So I did. I told him how my father had died, how he had been abused in foster care, how the secret that I lived on my own had been discovered in the hospital after intruders had broken into my house and hit me on the head with a fire poker. I concluded my story and added that my current living situation wasn't ideal for Shadow or for me, that my social worker supported my desire to return to my house, and that I learned only yesterday that the judge had decided that I needed to bring two people to the hearing on Monday, and could he please come and support me?

Dr. Pullman chewed on the side of his lip. His face was slightly pocked. He must have had a bad case of zits at my age. He looked at me askance.

Did he sense I had withheld information? Should I have confessed Dr. Griffin's role in the revelation to the authorities that I was underage? Should I have told him about my suspicion that she was the one who swung the poker?

"Err—I really don't know you very well, Sarah. I would think that Claudia, I mean, Dr. Griffin, would be more credible. She often speaks of you."

What had Dr. Griffin said? She was a loaded gun. She spoke of me "often," which probably meant he was seeing her. So I couldn't tell him that what he suggested was out of the question.

"Actually," I hedged. "She knows of the hearing ... but it's not going to work for her to come."

A partial truth. It wouldn't work because I hadn't asked her.

"I just don't know." Dr. Pullman rubbed his forehead. "I'm not sure I know you well enough."

I sighed. My whole body felt deflated.

"Hang on." He shook his head then squared his shoulders. "Will you excuse me a moment while I make a quick call?"

I nodded. He got up and walked across the noisy mall, punching numbers as he strode out of earshot. Who was he phoning? As far as I knew, he didn't have Mr. O'Shawnessy's or my social worker's phone numbers.

Duh, of course! He was probably calling Dr. Griffin to ask why she wasn't going to the hearing. Or maybe he was asking her about me and if he should help. Oh no. She would either tell him I never asked her or say she'll come too. I was toast.

My hopes drained from my heart down to my toes. I stood and gathered my packages. I might as well leave. Dr. Pullman waved and jogged toward me. Ugh. I readied myself to accept the "good news" that Dr. Griffin was available to come to my hearing. Dr. Pullman added a jubilant bounce to his step as he approached.

"I've found a solution," he said, offering a wide grin. "I just spoke with Claudia. She confirmed what you said, that she can't come to the hearing."

I wasn't sure I heard, right. Had she backed up my story because she was afraid I would tell Dr. Pullman what really happened to Mansfield, or had visions of the hood ornament danced in her head? No matter what persuaded her, if she declined, it meant Dr. Pullman decided he could vouch for me.

"So you'll come to the hearing?"

"I think so," he hesitated. "On one condition—one I hope you'll find easy to fulfill."

I couldn't imagine what he wanted me to do. I held my breath.

"Here's the deal. Claudia's cooking dinner tonight and she has invited both of us over. That way I can get to know you a little better. What do you say?"

Ugh. Did I have a choice? If I declined, Dr. Pullman wouldn't act as my witness

If I spoke, my tone would reveal my reluctance, so I forced a smile and nodded.

"Six o'clock. She said to bring Shadow so I can take a look at her and testify you are a responsible pet owner. She also said you already have the address. Is that right?"

Again, I nodded. That clever woman. She got her coveted dinner company and railroaded me into bringing Shadow. I'm sure she was happy. So was he. Poor sap couldn't contain his grin. He looked like a bear that discovered a beehive laden with honey. But where Dr. Griffin was concerned, anything sweet was bound to be followed by a venomous sting.

CHAPTER THIRTEEN

"If everybody minded their own business, the world would go around a great deal faster than it does."

Shadow yipped as I turned onto the narrow lane that led to the agility center. Her tail thumped against the side door. The training fields lay next to a livestock pasture, and I suspected that the odor of cow manure tipped her off.

Next to her twice-daily walks, Shadow loved her agility class. She was wicked smart and mastered each new piece of equipment quickly. My handling skills remained on a steep learning curve though. This team sport depends on both members understanding their roles: I teach Shadow patience, and Shadow teaches me how to move my body in dog language.

Whompa, whompa, whompa. If she kept this up, her tail would bruise.

"Okay, okay," I said, laughing. "Settle down. We're almost there."

Enrolling her in dog agility had been a good decision. Mrs. Wright explained the sport to me one day during one of her social services home visits after I confessed that I worried about how much time Shadow spent alone because of my summer job and living situation. She thought it would be a good activity for both of us. After she described how dogs are guided by their owners through obstacles such as tunnels, jumps and weave poles, I knew I wanted to try it. I found a Saturday class that fit my schedule. When the first six-week session ended, and the trainer praised Shadow's progress and recommended we advance to the next level, I was hooked. Shadow and I were now in Beginners II.

Carolyn, our instructor, used a method of common-sense instruction. I appreciated that the other dog-and-handler pairs were as crazy in love with their dogs as I was with Shadow. They celebrated when their pets overcame equipment or behavior challenges. Praise flowed even when their pets made mistakes. There was one bad apple in the group though—a fifty-something woman named Faye.

Faye owned a one-year-old goofball Irish setter-shepherd mix named Madeline. "Maddie" radiated joy, but her boundless energy stunted her progress. Faye had frizzy red hair that matched the color of her dog's fur. And Faye had a temper.

Agility is run with the dogs off-leash. Unfortunately, once unclipped from her lead, Maddie ignored Faye's commands. We spent a great deal of class time watching a flash of sleek, red fur zoom around the training field.

Carolyn had repeatedly asked Faye to tie a lightweight ribbon on the dog's collar so she could be caught, and the training exercise could resume, but Faye insisted Maddie listened better when she was free. So instead of using a training device to teach her dog impulse control, Faye's voice grew hoarse as she screeched commands while Maddie circled the obstacle course. The red dog sometimes took a tunnel or jump but she usually raced along the fenced perimeter. Side conversations among the students when Faye's turn came around revealed how annoyed everyone was, not only because of her high-pitched squawking, but because her refusal to follow Carolyn's request ate into the other student's training time.

When I pulled into the parking lot, Faye and Maddie occupied an area of wood chips outside the training ring. This unfenced yard served as the designated dog relief area. Carolyn had asked us to arrive early and potty our dogs to avoid accidents in the training ring. Fouling the ring during competition meant an automatic non-qualifying score. I didn't care about running Shadow in competitive agility trials, but I didn't want my dog messing up the training ring.

I took the opposite corner from the one Maddie occupied to keep Shadow away from the red ball of energy. My dog became over-excited around high-energy pups. Shadow focused better in a calm environment. Also, since Faye spoke on the phone, the polite thing to do was to give her privacy. Dad would be proud that I followed

Relationship Rule #9: Treat others the way you want to be treated.

Shadow explored at her leisure as we waited for the prior class to finish. About thirty feet away, Faye paced back and forth talking in hushed whispers. As time stretched, the woman grew more and more agitated.

A silver RAV4 arrived. Chelsea, the Maltese, and her owner, Matthew, exited the small SUV and took the central portion of wood chips.

"What?" Faye screeched into the telephone.

I cringed. Shadow startled. Poor Chelsea tugged against the leash trying to get back to the safety of her car. Maddie, though, continued sniffing the wood chips, her whole body vibrating with the adventure of it all. These outbursts must be normal for her.

Matthew waved. His quiet nature reminded me of my father. He said he had a daughter at home who shared my spunky attitude. Matthew and I had become instant friends on the first day of class despite our difference in age. He moved away from Faye and drew closer to me. Chelsea quivered with excitement and wagged her tail. The little, white, fluffy ball and Shadow had a long distance friendship because two-person teams were formed when we did foundational work such as walking on a two-by-four board, a precursor to the dog walk. For safety reasons, certain behaviors were trained prior to introducing a dog to the dog walk: a piece of equipment that required the dog to climb up a slanted board, traverse a narrow, flat expanse of the obstacle elevated four feet above the ground, before descending to the ground. Even though we weren't allowed to let our dogs socialize, our two pups had bonded.

Matthew was the oldest class member with salt and pepper hair and a neatly trimmed, gray beard. I was the youngest. His small dog jumped bars set at eight inches; my much taller Shadow jumped twenty inches. Chelsea's white coat often turned brown from the mulched surface of the training arena, the dark particles didn't stick to Shadow. She left class sporting the same red color as when she arrived. We were the epitome of opposites.

"It's not going to be a good day for Maddie," Matthew said when I was within hearing distance.

He glanced over at Faye whose stiff back faced us. With one ear glued to the phone, she continued to pace with muscles flexed as tight as a ball of twine.

"It's not going to be a good day for any of us," I agreed. "Why doesn't Carolyn give her an ultimatum? Use the ribbon or you don't get to run."

"Faye gets a lot of slack in this town," he said.

Before I could ask why, the gate squeaked open and the participants in the class before us filed out with their dogs at their sides.

I returned to my car to retrieve Shadow's treat bag. She pranced at my side with her mouth open in a happy pant as we entered the arena.

"Sarah," Carolyn said. "Shadow sure is enthusiastic today."

Several other dog-human pairs arrived: Carl and Fitz, the schnauzer mix, Jordan and Flash, the border collie, and Katrina and Chops, the French bulldog.

I guided Shadow into one of the larger crates lining the side of the fenced area. When Faye and Maddie entered the arena, Carolyn pulled them aside. I hoped she would send them home, but after a short exchange of words, Faye placed Maddie in the crate next to Shadow and joined the semicircle of students.

We had a briefing before each class when Carolyn explained the exercises for the day. I glanced at the arrangement of equipment and grinned. We were doing our longest sequence yet. I marveled at how much I had learned. Over the summer, I had devoured agility training videos on YouTube. It helped me understand the end goal of an exercise. Today, the equipment had numbered cones next to them to show the order to take the obstacles. Today we would take a jump, followed by a tunnel, jump, turn the dog, and go back through the tunnel and over the jump we started with. Easy, but fun. Shadow and I loved running short courses together.

"Only one dog at a time out on the field today," Carolyn instructed as she finished her debriefing. "We'll start with big dogs."

Shadow and Maddie would run first. Carolyn let her students decide whose turn it was, but I wished she would call out the run order. I always wanted to go before Maddie, because sometimes Maddie's frenetic zoomies riled Shadow, and she lost focus. I wasn't fast enough today. Faye rushed and reached Maddie's crate first. I took one of the folded sheets on top of Shadow's enclosure and hid my dog's view of the course. Blocking the visual stimulation helped some, but Maddie's barking was sure to energize Shadow.

I nodded at Sylvia who had arrived late with her golden-colored cocker spaniel named Josh. The pair stood next to Sadie, whose Italian greyhound looked too fragile for the rigors of the equipment but rose to the challenge and excelled at "bang game." This exercise involved instructing the dogs to jump onto a slightly elevated part of the teeterboard, walking them to the end to feel how the surface tips and accustoming them to the feel when it clunks to the ground with their body weight. Matthew stood next to the small crates where Chelsea scratched to escape. I moved closer, still curious about what he knew of Faye.

"Chelsea is sure eager for her turn," I said, nodding at the little dog's animated digging at one corner of her enclosure.

"Well, this will take a while," he said, nodding to the starting jump where Maddie refused to sit.

A start line was a critical skill. Maddie usually remained calm long enough to be successful at this task, but today she was unusually exuberant.

"Sit," Faye commanded. "Sit, Maddie. SIT!"

At last Maddie dropped her rump to the ground.

"Wait," Faye said as she took one step away.

But Maddie lost focus. When Faye moved, Maddie launched over the jump and ran off on a zoomie bender. Faye's face blossomed red with frustration. But her dog vocalized her joy as she zipped around the arena.

"What did you mean about Faye getting special treatment?" I asked a little too loudly.

He looked at me askance. It was then I realized that Maddie no longer barked. Faye had stopped moving and stood about fifteen feet away, staring at Matthew and me. The air in the arena seemed to drop several degrees.

Maddie continue to circumvent the perimeter of the ring. My heart revved up several RPMs like it always did when I did something wrong. Matthew and I had been caught gossiping. Faye's blue eyes shot needles at us. Maddie suddenly crashed into the wing of a jump, toppling the obstacle and breaking the spell.

"Call your dog," Carolyn said.

Our instructor, who never seemed frustrated when dogs ran their own courses, had raised her voice several octaves. Even clueless Faye heard Carolyn's displeasure and shifted her attention to Maddie.

"Better get ready," Matthew mumbled. "Shadow's up next."

He was right. I shouldn't poke into Faye's private affairs. Still I puzzled over why the people in this town would give this woman special treatment. Was she a city councilmember? Was she wealthy and therefore powerful and untouchable?

As I returned to Shadow's crate, I noticed sunlight glinting off Faye's fiery locks. The same color hair as the ghost boy's. Not many people have vibrant carrot tops. In such a small town, the chances they were related skyrocketed. And a woman who had tragically lost her son or maybe a nephew would receive special treatment. Most people would bend over backwards to keep from deepening her sadness.

But for every kindness offered, others would have been cruel. I had watched enough crime shows to know when children were victims, the nastiness in people emerged too. I bet the vigilantes poured out of the crevices accusing her of killing the child. Dad had wanted me to stop investigating what happened to the redheaded toddler, yet I seemed to be on a collision course with uncovering the truth.

"Shadow's turn," Carolyn chirped.

Faye had Maddie by the collar and guided her in jerky movements toward the crate, not bothering to leash her. The woman's face was pinched tight. Maddie entered the crate without a fuss. Even so, Faye slammed the metal door shut. The noise probably reached the main street entrance.

When I lifted the sheet covering Shadow's enclosure, she cowered against one side of the crate, shaking. I came here to give my dog a positive experience. Shadow was sensitive to the moods of others and didn't like loud noises. She didn't deserve to be stuck in an environment with cranky people who frightened her.

"Hey, Shaddie," I said. "Hey, sweet girl, are you ready to have some fun?"

Usually, Shadow exited her crate, ears tipped forward, eager to tackle the challenge ahead. Today, she wouldn't budge. I had to reach inside the crate, take ahold of her lead, and give it a gentle tug. That worked.

Once outside the toxic cloud of negative energy surrounding Faye, Shadow regained her chipper self. She sat on command, waited until I had traveled halfway between the first jump and tunnel.

"Reward your dog," Carolyn said.

I returned to Shadow, gave her a piece of cheese, and led out again. This time I released her with an "okay" command. She rocketed over the jump bar and tucked her head to run through the tunnel. Just like in the videos I had watched. I sprinted to the other end so I could direct her to take the next jump, but she anticipated my next direction, and her feet left the ground to soar over the final jump. Seeing me positioned beside the tunnel, she wrapped around the jump wing and headed back to the tunnel. I ran straight, glancing over my shoulder to connect with her. My belly button faced the same direction as the final jump, the way Carolyn had directed. Shadow took the cue. I tossed a chunk of string cheese beyond the jump to keep my dog from turning into me for her reward as my instructor recommended. All this took place in seconds, but even as I gasped for breath, I felt exhilarated by our achievement.

Shadow often didn't keep her rear feet high and knocked down the crossbars, but today she had been perfect.

"Well done," Carolyn said with a grin. "You've got a champion in the rough."

I already knew that. Shadow's shortened tail stood erect. Her red fur shone under the afternoon sun on the crisp, fall afternoon. For a moment, my life felt perfect. I leashed up Shadow and she trotted back toward her crate.

"Dobermans are easy to train," Faye snapped as I passed by.

I stopped short. My bubble of happiness slipped into the ether. I had the sense this woman was used to getting away with snotty comments like this, but her comment was unjust. How dare she diminish our hard work? Shadow rocked that course because we had practiced in the backyard between lessons, and I studied up on training techniques.

I stared straight into Faye's blue eyes. They were the same cornflower color as the ghost boy's. My anger lessened when I noticed the lines of worry around her eyes, the dejected slump of her shoulders. Losing a child or nephew could make anyone bitter. The end of Dad's Relationship Rule #1 required compassion. I dug deep, swallowed my snarky response, and shrugged. But she wasn't finished with me. She touched my elbow and drew her face close.

"If everyone minded their own business," Faye said, "the world would be a better place."

I shrank away from her. Was that a warning? A plea? I placed Shadow one crate over so an empty enclosure separated Maddie from my dog. I kept my attention on the field and avoided eye contact with anyone.

Shadow rocked the next training exercise too, but after Faye's comment, I didn't get as much pleasure from my dog's success. I kept to myself the rest of the session and rushed to the car when class ended. Too much pain surrounded the events that caused the ghost boy's death. Dad and Faye wanted me to mind my own business. It was time to let this go.

CHAPTER FOURTEEN

*Alice: It would be so nice if something made
sense for a change.*

It felt surreal walking through Dr. Griffin's front door
with Shadow at my side. My sweet pooch held none of
my reservations. She danced at my feet, clearly pleased to
be by my side, wherever that took her. I had expected her
to balk at going inside a house she had good reason to want
to avoid. The last time she was here, she had to be rushed to
the emergency veterinary clinic. My fault for using her as a
vehicle to see David-the-Ghost. Maybe my dog had blocked
the memory. She didn't seem bothered by Dr. Griffin either.

I nodded at Claudia but declined when she asked to
take my sweater. My car keys, driver's license, and cell
phone were in the pockets and I wanted them close in case
the evening turned weird.

"Sarah," Dr. Pullman said. He grinned as he entered
the room carrying a glass of red wine. He was dressed

in tan khakis and a cream-colored polo shirt. His smile broadened as he added, "And Shadow too."

Dr. Pullman sidled up to my dog, bending down close so that his hand brushed Dr. Griffin's bare knee then proceeded to scratch behind my dog's ears as if that was his only intention. I looked away, embarrassed.

"It's so great to have Shadow here," Dr. Griffin crooned. "Isn't it, Mark?"

The mention of only Shadow was not lost on me. Dr. Griffin smiled, but her hand clenched the door so tightly her knuckles shone white. Was she angry because I was an imposition on her romantic life this evening? Except I had come at her invitation. Did she know I had lied and said she couldn't be a witness? Or was she on edge because she feared I might tell her boyfriend what really happened to Mansfield? She didn't stoop to pet Shadow either. A wise move since my dog had growled at her when she was at my house.

The woman wore a white, long-sleeved dress with a low-cut neckline. A swirl of turquoise flowers the same blue as her eye color started at the right shoulder and flowed down to the knee-length hemline. Her flat, white sandals were a perfect choice. Her blonde hair had been pulled back into a ponytail, except for a few tendrils framing her face. She must have switched to contact lenses. Gone were the funky, blue-rimmed eyeglasses. Her slim figure and tasteful dress was very different from her usual style. The black widow was weaving her web for Dr. Pullman.

My white top was only partially visible. I had chosen a bulky, gray sweater with tapered points at the hem. A pair of black pants completed my outfit. My look felt too casual. I must have changed three times before settling on this combination. I wanted my clothes to communicate sophistication and maturity. Next to Dr. Griffin I looked like a drab female bird.

After Dr. Griffin closed the door, I bent down and unclipped Shadow's leash. She wiggled and groveled at the woman's feet. Apparently all those treats had won Shadow over. The aroma of garlic and thyme filled my nose.

The house looked as I remembered. The framed poster of Seurat's *A Sunday Afternoon on the Island of La Grande Jatte* still hung above the couch. The same cinderblock bookshelf, same colorless walls, the same coffee table with a circle of rhino figures in all shapes and colors. No hood ornament in the center though. That object was in my possession now. In the next room, a dog clock barked six times, announcing the hour.

Dr. Pullman bent down and fussed over my dog, but his head was lifted and he remained staring up at Claudia moon-eyed. I cleared my throat.

"Oh, my. I better check the steaks," Dr. Griffin said. "May I get you a soda or sparkling cider, Sarah?"

She was all sweetness with Dr. Pullman around. The woman was like a chameleon. She constantly changed her colors.

"Just water, thanks." I said, wondering if she might put a sedative in a flavored drink so that I would nod off at dinner and she would have an excuse to force me to spend the night.

I meandered over to the bookshelf as Dr. Griffin disappeared into the kitchen. A single book lay on the top: *Mansfield Park*. The purchase from Dr. Pullman's trip to the mall. The cover showed a pale, ghost-like woman with dark hair and a puffy, full-length pink dress. Dr. Pullman moved to my side as I picked up the book. I flipped it open and read the words inscribed inside the cover:

In Memory of Mansfield.

Deepest Condolences,
Dr. Claudia Griffin.

"Such a considerate gesture, don't you think?" he said. "Apparently Mrs. Bellweather named her previous pet rat Mr. Darcy. She has a dedicated memorial bookshelf. This will be a nice addition to her collection."

I closed the book and mumbled agreement.

"Dinner is ready," Dr. Griffin announced in a formal voice when she returned with my glass of ice water. "Please, make your way to the dining room."

Oh brother. I forced myself not to roll my eyes as I took the seven or eight steps through an arched doorway into the next room. Didn't Dr. Pullman think her pretentious?

"Sarah," Dr. Griffin said. "You will sit at the head of the table."

Really? Adults were supposed to occupy that spot. She was the host. It was her house. Was she intentionally trying to make me uncomfortable?

I slid into the seat facing her living room as directed. Behind me was a blank wall. Dr. Pullman took the chair to my right, Dr. Griffin on my left, near the kitchen.

The table setting consisted of the same informal, Scotty-dog plates I remembered. Dr. Pullman took his thumb and ran it along the matching salad dinnerware as if the ceramic were etched in gold.

"Lovely. Simply beautiful," he whispered in awe, but he wasn't looking at the plate; he stared at Dr. Griffin.

* * *

Over dinner I outlined to Dr. Pullman why I was responsible enough to live on my own, how I paid bills and cooked healthy meals. Then I talked about the consequences for Shadow if I had to continue to live with Mr. O'Shawnessy. Dr. Pullman nodded, but still didn't commit to attending my hearing.

Dr. Griffin, whenever she wasn't shuffling plates or breadbaskets, changed the subject. She seemed determined to sabotage my efforts.

"Sarah, why don't you tell Dr. Pullman your astrological sign?"

She knew I was a Libra. Had she brought my sign up because she wanted to point out people born under this sign were headstrong and born procrastinators? Well, Libras had good attributes, too.

"I'm a Libra," I said. "Did you know that we are known for our attention to detail, being diplomatic, and are described as natural thought-leaders?"

Had Dr. Pullman heard a word I said? Since Dr. Griffin wouldn't sit down, he acted like a spectator at a tennis match; his head twisted to follow her every movement. No small feat since she flitted around the table like a hummingbird, placing clean forks, removing salad plates. Even Shadow grew weary of keeping up with her activities. She collapsed under the table and let out a deep sigh.

The few times Claudia occupied a chair, she stared at the empty space over my shoulder and commented on the weather or the candidates running for mayor. David-the-Ghost no longer lived here. What captured her interest?

If Dr. Pullman noticed this odd behavior, he overlooked it. Watching him reminded me of a sappy, black-and-white romance movie. The man's brown eyes drank in her every move. He sat on the edge of his seat as though poised to fill her water glass should she actually sit down long enough to take a sip. He flashed a crooked grin at her then smiled some more. Would he be so enamored with her if he knew her deceitful side—how she rolled a dead rat into a ball as if he was sleeping to fool her client into thinking the animal still lived? Was it her guilty conscience that kept her circling the table like a tornado?

"Dr. Griffin," I said. "Please. Sit down and relax."

"Yes," Mark agreed.

"Well," she said to me. "I will if you promise to call me Claudia."

"And you must call me Mark," Dr. Pullman added.

I would have said yes to almost anything to get on with the meal and get Dr. Pullman's promise to attend my hearing. Calling them by their first names seemed easy enough.

"Okay, Claudia."

She set down the water pitcher and took her place. She selected a fork and speared a few green beans. The fork hovered near her mouth as her intense gaze zeroed in on me like a cobra. The vegetables returned to her plate uneaten.

"Sarah," Dr. Griffin said in a sickly-sweet voice. If she added a cackle, she could be cast as the Wicked Witch of the West. "Why don't you tell Mark about your father's illness?"

What? Was she trying to upset me? Besides, why would he want to hear about his cancer? Mark flashed an indulgent smile in her direction. He would probably agree with anything she said. If she suggested we all stay inside the house while it burnt down, he was so far gone that he would think it was a fabulous plan.

"Good idea." Mark plucked his napkin from his lap, "but I ... uh ... need the ... facilities."

"Of course," Claudia said.

Shadow followed Mark out of the room as if it was her job to escort guests to the restroom. Claudia's focus was again beyond my shoulder. She flicked her hand a few times. As soon as I heard the bathroom door click shut, the woman reached out and grasped my forearm.

"Oh Sarah," she whispered. "Can you please make your father leave? He's been hovering behind you all night."

Dad was here? That's what held her attention. I wasn't really surprised. Last night he said I was in danger. But I hadn't thought my father meant to warn me against Claudia. A twinge of jealousy flickered. I wish I could see ghosts without Shadow like Claudia. The woman twisted her cloth napkin into a pencil shape then wrapped it around her knuckles like a fighter. I shrugged.

"My father doesn't take orders from me," I said.

"Please, Sarah. Your father's holding Mansfield. Those beady little rat eyes glare at me like I'm a monster. And your dad? He stands there and shakes his head in disapproval. I can't bear it."

Mansfield's ghost was here, too? Why was Shadow ignoring the ghost rat? In the back of the house, the toilet flushed. Claudia squeezed my arm, digging her nails into my skin. She brought her nose close to mine. The smell of her lavender perfume filled my nostrils. I glanced behind me.

"If I tell him to go," I said, "will you stay away from my hearing on Monday?"

"Yes, yes."

I wasn't sure if I believed her, but it was worth a try.

"Go on, Dad."

"He shook his head," Claudia whispered. "Try something else."

Like my Dad would listen to me. He must have brought Mansfield here to make a point. If he felt a moral standard had been breached, Dad would stick around until he was sure it wouldn't happen again.

"Dad was always good at accepting my apologies. Maybe if you confess, he'll disappear."

"All I did was curl up Mansfield's body," she said in a hushed voice to a spot beyond my head. "Tucked him into a ball with his head under his back leg, like he was sleeping. I placed him in a corner of Austen's cage and pushed shavings around like he burrowed himself into a little nest."

This wasn't an apology. This sounded like rationalization. I could almost feel Dad's disgust.

"I was trying to spare the woman," Claudia pressed on, "Mrs. Bellweather assumed Mansfield died peacefully in his sleep. Isn't that how we all want our pets to leave this world?"

Shame on her. My stomach knotted as I visualized the old woman discovering her pet's body stiff and lifeless.

"Uh, Claudia, that's not an apology."

She frowned then pasted on a fake sad face.

"What I did was wrong. I'm sorry."

Claudia glanced toward the hallway then stood and bent over me. Her floral smell, a sweet, innocent scent, was all a sham. I don't know what she intended to do, put a butter knife to my throat and force my Dad to leave? Fortunately Mark rounded the corner, and Dr. Griffin straightened as if someone had jammed a stick up her butt.

She lunged past me into the kitchen. He took a look at my face and raised his eyebrows. I imagined what he saw: a deer-in-the-headlights expression, pale cheeks, and ashen complexion.

I reached behind my chair groping the space behind me. A warm pocket of air would mean Dad hadn't left. No temperature change. Perhaps he was satisfied with the apology and decided to return Mansfield to rat heaven. More likely, he stepped out of reach.

The sudden appearance of my dad's ghost disturbed me. So many weird things had happened in the last two days. Dad sabotaged Kyle's attempt to befriend me. I became a star football player's tutor. But the rat's death was the most troubling of all. When Mansfield died in my hands, something shifted. I didn't know who I was anymore. It would be so nice if something made sense.

"Sarah," Mark said, picking up his fork. "Tell me more about yourself."

Thank goodness he dropped the topic of my father's cancer. But what else was there to say?

"Um," I said. "I can play piano."

Claudia slunk into the dining room, placing a second pitcher of ice water on the table, even though our glasses didn't need refilling. A lame excuse for having fled.

She glanced behind me, jerked backward, then straightened in her chair. It seemed Dad still lurked nearby, after all. I imagined he was trying to instill his Relationship Rule #10 on Claudia: Never pretend to be something that you're not.

I smiled at Dr. Pullman as I launched into a summary of how I worked the whole summer, how I studied for the SATs on the weekends, and how I walked Shadow daily. Dr. Pullman nodded, all the while staring across the table at Dr. Griffin. If I said I cheated on my last exam, it probably wouldn't have registered.

A waft of warm air passed by. Claudia shivered then jumped to her feet and started collecting plates.

"I'll do the dishes," she said and hurried away.

Good. The sound of running water would mask my conversation with Dr. Pullman. Claudia might try to influence Dr. Pullman's decision to come to the hearing.

"So what do you think about Monday?" I said.

"I have to admit I am pretty uncomfortable with the idea of a young girl living alone," Mark stared at his hands as he spoke. "But I also think children should not be forced to live with people they aren't related to if there is a reasonable alternative."

The ambience of the room seemed to change. Dr. Pullman realigned his unused spoon next to his plate then took a sip of water. The man did not take this decision lightly.

I was afraid to breathe. My body fell still as I waited to hear his final answer.

"You seem like a very responsible young lady, Sarah. I'm really sorry your dad died and left you in this situation." Dr. Pullman took a long sip of wine then finally looked me in the eye. "But he did. And the question is, can I support your desire to live on your own? So let me first ask, is there any reason to suspect that you wouldn't be safer at your guardian's house?"

The clank of glasses emanated from the kitchen. How would Claudia answer the question if she were to answer truthfully? Would she say that I should stay next door since she would never bother me with others around? But I had another enemy in my guardian's house. So far Margaret had only done minor things like ruining my homework and gifts, but what would she do if my stay weren't temporary? I hadn't really contemplated this scenario. I had focused my energy on getting the courts to grant my request. But what if they didn't?

"Margaret," I blurted. "My guardian's granddaughter hates me. She's ruined my homework a few times. She wants me gone. I don't know what she'll do if I don't move out soon."

Dr. Pullman looked alarmed. "Have you told your social worker?"

"I can't. If she moves me to a different home, how can I keep Shadow? Besides, I was doing just fine on my own before social services discovered my living situation."

I was really glad Claudia didn't hear the last part. I wasn't doing all that great. But the ghost was out of my house, and Claudia was mostly out of my life. Things were fine now. Dr. Pullman whistled through his teeth.

"Wow. I hadn't thought about poor Shadow. Well, you've certainly laid out a strong case for yourself."

Shadow, my sweet dog, chose that very moment to lay her head on Dr. Pullman's knee. Mark shook his head.

"Oh, good grief. If I agree to do this, you have to promise to behave like your father was still in the house— no parties, no boyfriends over, honoring curfew. Do we have a deal?"

"Yes, yes and yes."

In the next room the water had been turned off, and the clatter of dishes had stopped. Claudia appeared and picked up the unused silverware. Dr. Pullman looked up at her and smiled.

"Did I hear you talking about boyfriends?" she asked. "Sarah's seeing Kyle, did she tell you?"

"Kyle?" Dr. Pullman frowned. "Kyle Bowman?"

Great. Just when things looked like were going my way, Dr. Griffin had to ruin it. And the worst part of it was, it wasn't true. Kyle and I weren't even friends at this point.

"Actually," I said, "Kyle and I had a misunderstanding and he doesn't want anything to do with me anymore."

Dr. Pullman's gray eyes studied me for a long moment. I met his gaze. I had nothing to hide.

"I mean it about no boyfriends over," he said in a stern tone. "If I agree to do this then you should expect me to pop by your house to check on you without any notice."

No problem there. Since I had no friends, the only thing he might catch me doing was studying or playing with Shadow.

"That's fine. You'd be welcome to visit anytime."

"Good," he said to me. "I can appear on your behalf on Monday."

"Thank you sooo much." Relief flowed from my shoulders to my knees.

"It's a shame you can't come, Claudia," Dr. Pullman added.

"Well…" Claudia began.

Noooo. This couldn't be happening. I reached out knocking my water glass over. Claudia jumped to her feet, bolted into the kitchen, and returned with a wad of paper towels. I righted the glass, but most of it had already spilled. While she mopped up the water spreading across the table, her gaze kept darting over my shoulder. Her lips were drawn tight and her movements were as twitchy as a rat's nose.

"Let me help," I said.

"No, I've got it."

Liquid had leaked through the crack where a leaf was inserted and dripped onto the floor. Claudia disappeared under the table. If I didn't do something quickly, when she finished, she would offer to come on Monday.

"Claudia's amazing," I said. "Did she tell you she brought Mrs. Bellweather's rats to my house?"

A loud smack reverberated from the underside of the tabletop, making the table shake. Dr. Griffin rolled back onto her heels and rubbed the crown of her head.

"Are you alright?" Dr. Pullman said.

"I'm fine," she said, but she left the wet paper towels on the floor and eased herself into her chair. She smiled at Mark who stood and massaged her shoulders.

"You're sure you're okay?" He parted her hair. "No lump,"

"I'm fine," she repeated. "Really."

Dr. Pullman nodded and returned to his seat.

"Anyway," I continued. I gave Claudia a meaningful look. Her chin dropped a tad which I took to mean we had better come to an agreement fast. "Mansfield, the older rat, was having a hard time ... adjusting to having a cage-mate. Well, Claudia, she took him into a ... whole new realm."

A warm swath of air covered my wrist. Dad squeezed hard to show his displeasure at my glossed-over version of the events. I flicked my arm to dislodge his grasp. He held firm for a moment then pinned my wrist so it lay on the table right next to my plate.

"Really?" Mark said.

"Oh, yes. When she returned the two rats to Mrs. Bellweather, they were sharing a cage without fighting."

Claudia chewed on her lower lip as she glanced over my shoulder. I was glad I couldn't see Dad's expression. He must be furious with me.

Mark's eyes were lidded with love. He leaned across the table and took Claudia's hands between his palms. It dawned on me that I had made Claudia even more appealing to the man. One of my SAT vocabulary questions came to mind. Only one word fit the way Mark appeared at that moment: besotted. Claudia inclined toward him with a similar look on her face, only she kept shooting furtive glances beyond my head.

The warm claws of the ghost rat poked into my shoulder. I flinched. In moments, Mansfield had travelled down my pinned arm and headed toward my plate. Now I understood my dad's punishment for my bad behavior. Oh, gross. How would I possibly be able to finish my dinner after a rat had crossed it—even if it was a ghost? How could my father do this to me? The prickly sensations reached my wrist and traveled to the back of my hand. Please, not my food. Keep it off my plate. Why didn't Dad do something?

"Get him off already."

Oh crap. I spoke the words aloud.

Mark's hands released Claudia's as if he had touched a hot burner. Claudia's face flamed scarlet. The words and their alternate meanings hit me. Mark's chair scraped the hardwood floor as he pushed away from the table. He was a proper man and he had taken my outburst as a crude remark.

"Really, Sarah," Claudia said with a huff.

The warm paws and spiky toenails disappeared from my hand. Dad, at least, had taken my words for their proper meaning. But why was it whenever my father appeared I blurted things out loud? Was he trying to sabotage my chances to move back into my house? Didn't he realize how miserable I was living with Margaret? He had said I was in danger. Was he now afraid something would happen to me if I lived on my own? Or did he like Mr. O'Shawnessy so much that he thought I was better off there? Well too bad. Shadow didn't deserve to stay alone every night, and I didn't deserve Margaret.

I couldn't let Dr. Pullman retract his offer to help me. I scrambled for a way to repair the damage. Would one of Dad's relationship rules help? Telling the truth was out of the question, but Rule #9: "Treat others the way you want to be treated" applied here. If someone insulted me, I would want an apology.

"I'm sorry," I said, folding my arms across my chest. "What I said. I didn't mean what you think."

Claudia's cheeks remained rosy pink as though she had contracted a fever. She picked up the spare water pitcher, grabbed the soaked paper towels from the floor, and escaped into the kitchen.

Mark lifted his palms as if I held him at gunpoint and he wanted to surrender. His quick grin was probably meant to put me at ease. Yet my face warmed all over again. I tucked an errant strand of dark brown hair behind my ear and studied the tapered ends of my sweater. I wanted to disappear under the table.

"I was a teenager once," Mark said. "Let's leave it at that, shall we?"

Hope swelled in my chest. Did this mean he would still be my witness?

Dr. Griffin hurried in, collected my half-eaten dinner, and put a giant ice cream sundae in front of me. She had even put whipped cream and a cherry on top. She picked up Dr. Pullman's empty plate.

"Whipped cream?" she asked.

He nodded.

"Dig in," he said. "No need to wait."

After Dr. Griffin left, I picked up my spoon and pushed the cherry aside. He still hadn't said he would support my petition.

"You did say eight o'clock, Monday morning, right?" he said.

I sat up straight. I suppressed the urge hug him. He didn't even try to encourage Dr. Griffin to come along this time.

"Yes, thank you," I whispered.

"Now eat up," he said. "I couldn't possibly tell the judge you're a normal teen if you don't eat ice cream, now could I?"

I plucked the cherry from my dessert and popped it in my mouth then jabbed my spoon into the dessert and proceeded to demonstrate how much I loved sundaes.

CHAPTER FIFTEEN

*"Then you should say what you mean," the
March Hare went on.*

I escaped early from Claudia's house, swung by the store, and bought a new potted mum. I dropped Shadow next door and arrived at Mr. O'Shawnessy's by 9:00 p.m. I didn't expect Margaret to be home since she usually hung out with Paul until her 11:00 p.m. curfew on Saturday night. But when I walked in the front door, there she was lounging on the couch with ear buds in while my guardian watched one of his favorite BBC shows.

"Sarah," Mr. O'Shawnessy exclaimed. "Come sit. Have some warm cow's juice."

Drinking a mug of heated milk before bed was his habit. No matter how many times I said no thank you, Mr. O'Shawnessy continued to offer the vile brew. Margaret occasionally obliged his request, but not this evening. She shot me a look that told me to get lost.

"No milk for me, thanks."

Even if I had wanted a warm drink and to plop down on the couch next to him, I would have declined. This was the opportunity I had been waiting for. I hadn't dared to call Paul until Margaret wasn't with him. Now that I knew her whereabouts, it was safe to call him—as long as I did it out of earshot. I disappeared into my bedroom long enough to pick up the dying mums then reappeared in the living room.

"I'm going to toss out this old plant, and I remembered that I forgot to give Shadow her biscuit," I said to Mr. O'Shawnessy. "I'll be right back."

I swung by my car and picked up the new mums. The moment I stepped inside my house Shadow greeted me with her "roo roo roo" glad-to-see-you bark.

I set the old and new flowers on the table, kissed Shadow on the top of her head, and gave her a biscuit. I peered out the kitchen window. Margaret's car was still there, so I dialed Paul's number.

"Yo," Paul's familiar voice answered on the first ring.

"Paul, it's Sarah."

"Sarah." I heard the smile in his tone.

"I only have a few minutes. Did you tell your mom about the tutoring on Monday?"

Silence, which meant he hadn't. One of Mr. O'Shawnessy's sayings came to mind: This guy was as sharp as a beach ball.

"Paul?"

"It's cool," he said "I'll make it right "

I had zero confidence in this promise, but I let it go. Just as I had struggled with how to broach the subject of the hearing with Dr. Pullman, I couldn't find the words with Paul. Moments ticked by.

"I will, I will," Paul said.

I felt bad that he interpreted my hesitation as disbelief. I pulled out the box of dog treats. Shadow barked. Her tail came to life like a grandmother wagging her finger at a disobedient child.

"Hey, was that Shadow? Are you at home? Can I come over?"

I didn't need to see Paul's face to know what the guy was thinking. He figured out I was at home alone without parental supervision.

"Yes, yes, and absolutely not," I said. "I got in trouble because my guardian saw you hug me yesterday. I can't have anyone over. It's one of his rules."

And then I saw my angle. It wasn't honest, but desperation drove me forward. I would do anything, say anything so Paul would show up as a witness.

"Paul," I said with sugar in my voice. "You can't come over. But tomorrow though, we can get together for tutoring, just the two of us." I paused to let that settle in.

"You want to get started on a Sunday?" Paul gushed. "I don't study over the weekend, but if that's the price I have to pay, I'll make an exception."

I didn't much like taking time from my studies, but I wasn't about to stop the ruse now. I reached into the box.

Shadow danced at my feet. I flipped the milk bone into the air, smiling as my smart pup snagged it before it hit the floor. I took a deep breath as if I were about to dive into a pool and swim a race.

"I need a small favor," I said still using my flirty voice. "I want you to come to the courthouse on Monday morning at eight and testify about me. I'm trying to establish that I'm capable of taking care of myself, so I can live on my own. So I need you to tell the judge that I am getting along well with others at school and that I'm a responsible person."

"Uh ... but you don't have any friends. I can't lie to a judge."

I squatted down next to Shadow and pulled her close. Paul's words stung. Even someone as dense as this guy had noticed how unpopular I was. It wasn't like I hadn't tried. Margaret had managed to sabotage every effort I made to connect with my classmates.

"And won't they put me under oath? I can't prejudice myself."

I assumed he meant perjure. I had to give him credit. Paul was a moral person. Still, I wasn't about to give up that easily.

"Aren't you my friend?" I meant to use a sugary tone, but my voice cracked with emotion.

Paul didn't respond. I had been foolish to think he would fall over himself to help me.

"Never mind. I shouldn't have asked."

"Wait," he said. "I can say you're responsible. I can tell them how you volunteered to tutor me. That would help, wouldn't it? That wouldn't be a lie."

"Really? You'll be a witness? You'll miss school."

"Yeah," he said. "I have P.E first period. My mom won't care if I skip it."

His tone conveyed his sincerity. It was hard to believe that yesterday in art class this same guy had stuck his feet out in the aisle and forced me to step over them. Of all people, why did the one person who was nice to me have to be Margaret's boyfriend?

"Are you sure you can get a note from your mom?"

"Yeah. She'll be so happy when I tell her that you're tutoring me in biology that she'll probably insist that I help you."

"Thank you soooo much," I gushed for the second time this evening. "You have no idea how much this means to me."

I wondered if the judge at the hearing would ask about the tutoring. If Paul were to be asked if he had found my teaching helpful.

"This will work out great for both of us," I said. "You said you had a test on Tuesday and it might be better if you had more time to prepare."

"Yeah? I'd like to see you. Only ... I'm supposed to go Halloween costume shopping with Margaret."

Again? I thought that's what they were doing at the mall today. I had to give Paul credit; he was a trooper.

It would not be good to disrupt Margaret's plans. But I bet we could fit in an early morning session over coffee. The green-eyed monster I lived with wouldn't be up until at least eleven.

"How about nine in the morning at your house?" I said. "Or if that's too early for your family, we could meet at a coffee place."

"Nine?" A groan skated through the phone lines. "That's like sunrise. Even my mom sleeps in on Sunday mornings. Can we say ten at Starbucks? I'm gonna need some strong coffee."

Ten might be too close to Margaret's uprising from her throne. I didn't want to risk it. Besides, I suspected he needed a lot of help.

"Nine-fifteen. Not the Starbucks downtown on North Main, the one near you on Railroad Avenue."

"That's so early," he sighed. "But, okay, I'll be there."

I hit the off button. My victory didn't feel right. I should have come clean and told him I wasn't interested in him that way. I should have told Paul to call Margaret immediately and tell her of our plans. But I feared he might change his mind about attending the hearing. I thought about Relationship Rule #6: Never make a promise you don't intend to keep. I imagined Dad watching me at this very moment, shaking his head in disappointment.

The slightly tangy smell of the mums caught my attention. I planned to unearth the hood ornament from the soil in the old mums and transfer it amidst the roots of the new plant, but suddenly even this small task overwhelmed me. I wanted to walk next door and go straight to bed. I tossed Shadow another biscuit. By completing that task at least I hadn't lied to Mr. O'Shawnessy. At least I showed a trace of honorable behavior today.

* * *

The door to Starbucks had a strand of bells tied on the inside handle so it sounded like reindeer arriving every time someone entered. The place was packed. Several people stood in line in front of me.

A quick survey of the tables revealed I had arrived before Paul. Not surprising since I arrived a full ten minutes early to scope out the place and make sure no fellow high-schoolers were there. If I had recognized anyone, I would have intercepted Paul and found a different venue.

This Starbucks apparently didn't attract the teen crowd—either that or it was too early. Amidst the bustle of patrons, only one empty table remained in the small space. I arranged my sweater on the back of one chair then returned to the line. A large bulletin board was positioned next to the reindeer door. Business cards littered the corkboard. A notice about an upcoming concert in the park caught my eye as did an ad for a roommate. Dad had made sure I had a comfortable cushion of money, so I didn't need to rent out a room in my house, but I had two extra bedrooms and company might be nice. I looked closer and noticed Penny owned two cats. Shadow would not appreciate a feline invasion. So much for that idea.

At the counter, I ordered myself a tall Caramel Macchiato and Paul a grandé Bold Pick of the Day. After my order was prepared, I took a seat toward the rear of the crowded room. My spot provided a clear view of the front door. I savored a sip of my drink before pulling the biology textbook out of my backpack. I had just flipped open the book when I heard Paul's voice.

"Yuuu-nit," Paul said. "Dude, this is way skip."

Unit? Dude? Skip? There was something oddly familiar about those words, but I couldn't quite place it.

"What?" I stammered.

He swaggered over to the table, turned the chair backwards, and straddled it as if it was a horse. He placed a one-inch, white binder on the table.

I expected him to wander in disheveled, but his hair was slicked back, and he wore a collared shirt. Muscles bulged from the short sleeves. Buff and... What was I thinking? This was Margaret's boyfriend.

"You know," he said. "Unit. Get it?"

"Uh...no."

I leaned forward to check out the notebook, and I got a whiff of cologne. This was not good. He dressed up like this were a date. But shouldn't I have expected as much? Hadn't I led him on to get him to testify on my behalf?

"Really?" His brow furrowed. "I was sure you'd have read *The Feed*."

That's right. The jargon came from M.T. Anderson's sci-fi book about kids that had commercials running in their heads all the time.

"Yeah, I read it," I said.

"I knew it," Paul puffed his chest out like a gorilla about to drum his pectorals.

Was Paul in a remedial English class where the students were reading that book instead of Shakespeare?

"It's sooo ... brag," he said. "Like it's so totally cool the way those robot kids can like, you know, know everything and chat in their heads."

"Yeah," I said. "Anyway, shall we get started?"

Paul rested his elbows on the seatback. I was surprised and pleased that he remembered his notebook. It even looked organized with colorful tabs. I wouldn't have expected him to be neat.

"Sorry," he said. "It was meg-null that I was late."

Meg-null? Oh, well. He seemed so pleased with himself, I decided to ignore his newfound vocabulary. One of two things would happen. Either the popular crowd would start talking like him or shame him into stopping.

"Well. Have some coffee and then we'll review your last test to see what you got wrong."

I reached for the binder.

"Whoa," he said, pulling the notebook out of reach. "Can't have you looking at that. That's top secret."

For a moment, I thought he still channeled M.T. Anderson. Then I realized it was more likely that his furrowed brow and fidgeting was caused by his embarrassment over his score.

"If you want my help, I have to see the material."

"What? Dude, that's not biology, it's the playbook."

Playbook? I couldn't recall that term used in *The Feed*.

He cocked his head and looked askance. A sly grin spread across his face. He glanced around at the dozen men and women who occupied nearby tables. No one paid either of us any attention.

"Well, I guess I could show you one page," he whispered. "But you can't tell Coach, okay?"

Ah. Now I understood. Locker room strategy. Game winning formulas. He flipped open the cover and showed me a two-dimensional drawing of a football field. The players spread across the field were depicted by a series of Xs and Os. Arrows indicated which direction they should run after the hike. The quarterback would roll to the right. At the top of the page, the play was labeled "Pro 34 Right Power." A series of hand signals were drawn at the bottom of the page. The binder held at least a hundred sheets.

"Wow. Do you know all these plays by name?"

"Yep. And the hand signals." Paul sat up straight in his chair. He formed a fist, shook it twice to the left, and bonked his forehead with the flat of his hand. "That's a Pro Right X-Crash 32 Sweep."

I nodded. If this guy could memorize a notebook full of football jargon, he was capable of learning the basics of biology.

"Hey," he said. "Are you going to the game next Friday?"

Tess and I had gone to a few football games at my old school last fall before Dad got so sick. At first, I enjoyed the hot dogs more than the action on the field. But I soon got caught up in the excitement when our team scored. The idea of attending a game at this school filled me with dread. I would be mortified sitting in the stands alone. I didn't have a single friend. Worse, no one would want me there.

"Can't," I said.

"Oh," Paul's lips puckered into a pout. "I'd like you to see me play."

Perhaps he needed to be reminded his girlfriend would be there rooting for him. As would a whole slew of cheerleaders, no doubt.

"Margaret, will be there."

"Uh," his eyes seemed to have found something interesting on the floor, "doubt that."

Alarm bells jangled in my brain. Margaret never missed his games. Oh crap. Had he told her about the tutoring? Had she freaked out and broken up with him?

"What happened?"

"After I talked to you last night, I called her up. It's over."

Normal English at last. But he didn't seem sad about the breakup. Had he dumped her because I flirted with him last night? If so, Margaret would blame me. A knot formed in my stomach.

"What exactly did you tell her?"

"The truth. I told her I didn't want to go Halloween shopping." Paul's green eyes held mine. "Look, I know you aren't into me. I'm not stupid. I know you only said you'd tutor me today so I'll go to your hearing. I'm disappointed you felt you had to lie to get my help."

It was my turn to study the floor. I had been a jerk.

"My mom says you should always say what you mean," Paul continued. "You weren't honest with me. I thought you were better than that."

I imagined my father might have said the same thing. Margaret had a way of bringing out the worst out in me. But I couldn't blame my behavior on her.

"You're right. I thought I was better than that, too. I'm sorry. I understand if you don't want to speak on my behalf at court on Monday."

"No, I'm coming. I can see you've had a hard time—largely because of Margaret. She's hot and everything, but I don't know. I'm tired of her games. You should hear the stuff she says about people. It's mean. Don't worry. I didn't say anything about you when I broke it off. I only told her I needed to work on getting my grades up. But she went crazy and told me that if I didn't go shopping with her today, we were through." Paul shrugged. "So, it's over."

I nodded. He had a lot more substance than I had given him credit for. The slump in his shoulders and the droop of his head revealed his sense of loss.

"I'm sorry," I said. "I'm sure it's hard to break up, even if it feels like the right thing to do."

Paul stood, flipped his chair around, and settled down long enough to take a sip of coffee. He pushed his playbook aside.

"Let's do this," he said.

"Good idea. What chapter are you on, and what concepts has Mrs. Confetti been focusing on?"

Paul's brow furrowed. He shifted in his seat and bit his lower lip. He didn't know what they were studying? The third lesson dealt mostly with atoms and molecules. Or had they progressed to Chapter 4?

"Cell biology?" I asked.

"Yeah. Yeah, that's it. We're learning the differences between plant and animal cells and how they work."

"Great," I said. "Let's start with the differences. Can you tell me which type of cell contains chlorophyll?"

"Easy," Paul grinned. "Plant."

His enthusiasm was infectious. If he wanted to learn, I would help him. Maybe these tutoring sessions weren't going to be a burden after all.

"Excellent," I said. "And what is the purpose of chlorophyll?"

"It's like gasoline, right? Makes fuel or something?"

I took a sip of caffeine. This was going to be a long morning. I moved on trying to explain the process of mitosis, a type of cell division. Paul reclined in his chair, shaking his head. I lost him at interphase, which was

the easiest step—a resting stage between cell divisions..
How would I explain in a way he could understand, the
complicated processes of telophase when two nuclei are
formed? My cheeks puffed up with air at the enormity of
the task at hand. I let my breath escape in one long stream.
Paul leaned forward, reached across the table, and placed
his hand over mine.

"Don't give up on me, okay?"

The doorbells jingled. The air shifted. The whole
place seemed to go quiet, even though it still buzzed with
conversation. At the front door stood a boy with a nest of
wild red hair and skinny arms. His jaw clenched. Kyle.

The drop dead gorgeous guy of my dreams cinched
his lips together and shook his head. Unruly locks tumbled
over his brow. My heart constricted as he backed out of the
coffee house. I tried to tell myself that his reaction was a
good sign. He wouldn't have been angry if he didn't have
feelings for me. But when the door closed and the bells fell
silent, I was left with a sense of finality.

The empty place where Kyle had stood moments before
left a void in my heart. I squinted as if to conjure his return.
A faded flyer on the bulletin board by the door caught my
attention. How had I missed the smiling face of the toddler
ghost boy on the notice when I first walked in? I rose to my
feet, navigating around tables to get closer.

Below his picture in capital letters were the words
'MISSING -REWARD.' Whatever information had once
been written underneath the ragged edges of yellowed

paper had been ripped away. No name, no date last seen, no person to contact with information or how to collect the reward, nothing.

CHAPTER SIXTEEN

Alice: "I believe I can guess that."

The picture of the little ghost boy on the yellowed flyer showed him in a baby swing at a playground. He gripped his toes and smiled up at the camera. Behind me, a barista announced Dora's tall caffé latte was ready.

A loud snap crackled and warm air encased my wrist then tugged, trying to draw me away from the bulletin board. Two days ago, Dad had warned me not to pursue the identity of this child, but how could I not? What if this was Faye's son? Or someone else's? Somewhere his parents might hold on to the hope that their child still lived. Perhaps, they spent every spare moment trying to locate their boy. But he was dead. Shouldn't I tell them so they could move on with their lives?

I jerked my arm from Dad's grasp, not caring if Paul watched from our table across the room. I retrieved my iPhone from my pocket. Before Dad could stop me, I took a photo of the little boy. I heard a snap, crackle, and a pop that suggested my father left angry.

Paul approached. He leaned against the wall, towering over me. His brow wrinkled with concern. A tingling sensation flitted through my veins at the sight of the smooth, taut skin of his biceps.

"What are you doing?" he said.

"Who is he?" I said, pointing at the flyer.

Paul shook his head. "I was in fifth grade when it happened. No one talks about it anymore. Why?"

I couldn't tell him that I had seen the boy's ghost. Once again, I would have to lie ... or maybe not. I remembered my cover story.

"I'm doing my senior project on missing children," I said.

"Well, you'd best leave this kid out of it."

"Why?"

"I'll tell you, but you have to promise not to include it in your project."

I was not making any such deal, but maybe I could leave the family alone, yet still give the cops any information I uncovered.

"I have to know who not to speak to about my project, right?"

Paul sighed. He inclined his head until his cheek brushed against mine. My breath caught, and I was suddenly confused. Paul wasn't my type; Kyle was. So why did part of me want to move away, but the other part want to turn my face toward his and wrap my arms around him?

"That's Kyle's little brother," Paul whispered in my ear. "I don't want to talk about it."

Kyle? I took a step back, my heart thudding in my chest. Kyle's brother? Was that why the little ghost boy had been in my art class? Did the toddler follow his older sibling around like most little brothers? Was Faye the mother? An aunt? Now more than ever I needed to find out what happened. If I could uncover the truth, perhaps I could help Kyle and his family.

I had a thousand more questions: What was the toddler's name? When did he disappear? Were the police still looking for him? But I couldn't ask Paul or he would know that I had no intention of leaving it alone.

"Let's get back to biology," Paul said.

I wasn't going to get answers from him, so we might as well.

"Okay," I said.

As we settled across from each other, Paul leaned his elbow on the playbook. Before Kyle had walked in, I struggled with how to teach Paul about mitosis. The sight of the football notebook gave me a flash of inspiration. I fumbled in my backpack and extracted my artist sketchpad.

"Awesome," Paul said. "We're taking a break, right? You're going to draw me like you said in art class."

"Nope. I am going to teach you about mitosis in football language."

"Huh?"

I flipped open the pad. At the top of the page, I sketched a locker room with a coach standing next to a blackboard, while a group of football players sat watching. Above this, I wrote "interphase." Below this, I dropped to the center of the remaining white space on the page and drew a small circle. Starting with prophase, the first stage of cell division, at the twelve o'clock position, I progressed clockwise, penciling in the remaining phases of mitosis: metaphase, anaphase and telophase. I then drew a football scenario next to each of these phases.

"Okay," I said, turning the pad so he could see. "Let's start with interphase. This is when the cell is not dividing, like the athletes studying a playbook. See. During interphase, the cell's chromosomes are decondensed, and the cells can synthesize products. The chromosomes are called chromatin. So this is like practice. You are spending time with your teammates, and you might discuss strategies, but you are not actually executing them. Does that make sense?"

Paul puckered his lips, then slowly nodded his head. "Interphase is like off-field activities. The team is together, but separate, and is called chromatin. Got it."

"That's right," I said. "Excellent."

"Then, it's game time. The first quarter in mitosis is called prophase." Next to the word, I drew a group of players in a pre-play huddle. "Prophase is when the chromosomes start to coil. See these two strands at the center? Each of these is called a chromatid. Are you with me?"

Paul nodded. "Interphase, practice, prophase, huddle," he mumbled.

He didn't speak with confidence, but at least his eyes hadn't glazed over. He hunched over the table studying the drawing. I soldiered on.

"So each of these strands or chromatids are attached at the centromere and the nuclear envelope disappears. See," I said, pointing to another drawing in the book next to the depiction of huddled jerseys, where teammates lined up in two straight lines. I skipped the nucleolus disappearing. "And the last thing that happens in prophase is the spindle forms. Consider the spindle like the football. The spindle guides the separation of sister chromatids into the two daughter cells. Kinda like two teams are formed around the football so you can have a scrimmage."

Now, Paul nodded vigorously. "Interphase is playbook; prophase is team bonding and scrimmage. Then," he craned his neck, "me-ta-phase."

"Great!" I said.

"Hah!" He pointed at my picture of two lines of colorful jerseys scrunched together on opposite sides. "I can guess that one. The offensive front line."

I grinned. As I had hoped, his passion for football had tackled his preconceived notion that he wasn't capable of learning difficult material. I talked him through anaphase, when the chromosomes move away from one another, before describing the activities of telophase in football lingo.

"Wow," Paul said. "I'm going to have to memorize the terms, but this makes total sense to me. You should become a teacher."

My face warmed under his praise. Once again, he reached across the table and clutched my hand. I eased my fingers from his grasp with a twinge of reluctance, noting the tingle of heat lingering on my skin.

"Thanks." I said, ripping the sheet from my sketchbook and keeping my gaze downcast. "But I think we've covered enough today. I'll try to come up with some football analogies for meiosis for our session tomorrow afternoon."

Tomorrow after school. If things went as planned, I would be free of Margaret. I had to convince the judge, which shouldn't be hard with Dr. Pullman and Paul by my side.

"Did your mom give you a note for skipping first period tomorrow?" I asked. "Do you know how to get to the courthouse?"

"Yep. Don't worry. I'll be there."

* * *

The closer my Civic got to home, the more I dreaded going inside Mr. O'Shawnessy's house. It was after eleven a.m. Margaret would be awake. Had anyone let her know I held Paul's hand at Starbucks? Walnut Acres was a small town.

It seemed everyone knew everyone else's business. My best hope was that Margaret wouldn't hear of the event until Monday morning at school. Now, more than ever, I needed my court hearing to go well.

Margaret's car wasn't anywhere in sight when I pulled into my driveway next door. Good. I would check in on Mr. O'Shawnessy and toss tonight's dinner ingredients into his slow cooker. That way I could disappear to my house for the day and limit my contact with Margaret.

I only needed to suffer through one Sunday. Most of my belongings were still in boxes, so I could move next door with limited packing. By Monday afternoon, Margaret would be out of my life. Well, except for school. But I didn't share any of her classes, so I would only have to watch my back at lunch.

The front door was locked confirming Margaret was gone. She never left the house unsecured. I rummaged for the key and unbolted the latch.

Mr. O'Shawnessy was asleep in the recliner in the front room. I tiptoed into the kitchen, assembling the ingredients as quietly as a calm summer night in the mountains. The task complete, I proceeded to my room to get my laptop and SAT prep book to take next door.

Before opening my bedroom door, the smell of coffee hit. I carefully pushed open my door. That was odd. I noted open dresser drawers, a Starbucks cup on top of my computer—I never kept liquids near my laptop. The green logo left no doubt. Margaret had learned I had been at Starbucks with Paul this morning.

I refused to believe Kyle was the one who had told Margaret, but he must have mentioned it to someone because Margaret had sought revenge.

I walked on leaden legs to my Apple and lifted the lid. The keyboard had been flooded with brown liquid. Like a robot, I moved to my dresser. Coffee had saturated or splattered every piece of clothing. Hours of laundry lay ahead.

My gaze registered the skewed closet door. I wasn't sure I could face the closet, but my hand shoved the door open despite my fear. The fabric of my favorite dress resembled a grass hula skirt. Thank goodness I bought new clothes for my hearing. At least they're still safe. Tiny piles of shredded paper cluttered the hardwood floor. A square piece had been placed in front of the mess like a name card at a formal dinner place setting. The paper held the pages of the problem set I worked so hard on Friday evening. Another message. She was angry that I hadn't let her copy my math homework. Did she jot down my answers to the problems before destroying my work?

My shoes had been shoved into the corner and, from the aroma, I suspected they too had been doused with coffee. I fingered the tattered remains of my dress. When I noticed the full-length mirror on the back of the closet door, I recoiled. Margaret had penned a message in bright red lipstick: "This is just the beginning. YOU WILL PAY."

My knees gave out. I stumbled backward landing on the edge of my bed. I reached out and flung the empty Starbucks cup across the room. I slammed the lid on my ruined computer. I hadn't I backed up my hard drive since school let out last June. My laptop had held the final version of a twenty-page English essay that was due tomorrow. At least I had printed a draft and it was safe next door on my dining room table, but it would still take time to retype the paper. Worse, during the summer I had kept notes on all the SAT vocabulary words I missed on practice tests. How was I supposed to recreate those months of work before my test next week? Of all the ways to hurt me, Margaret had sabotaged something I cared deeply about. School. My future.

I wished I could rouse Mr. O'Shawnessy from his nap and show him what his precious granddaughter had done. But I would never hurt that sweet, old man. And Margaret knew it.

I wanted to storm down the hall to her room and throw all her clothes into a tub of bleach. I wanted to hack into her Facebook page and post pictures of my room to show her friends what she did. But how could I without a functional computer? I couldn't retaliate anyway. Margaret would tell my guardian, and my behavior would be discussed during the hearing. Not only would I be denied emancipation, but Mr. O'Shawnessy could rescind his offer to be my guardian. I could lose more than my independence; I might lose Shadow.

Margaret's reign was foolproof for now. I tried to console myself that bad karma usually comes full circle, but in my heart I didn't believe it. Margaret always seemed to get what she wanted. Margaret always won.

Margaret. Even her name caused heat to bubble through my veins. Evil Queen suited her better. A bitterness like sour gummies entered my mouth. The sensation was so sharp it made my teeth ache. Until that moment, I hadn't realized hate had a taste.

I longed to pull her hair until she apologized. I wanted to scratch her cheek with my fingernails, to mark her for life, so every time she looked in the mirror there would be a reminder not to mess with me. But more than cause her physical pain, I wanted to expose her true nature to the world.

I pounded my fists into my pillow until frustration left my body, and I could face cleaning up the evidence of Margaret's treachery. My soiled clothes were shoved into the laundry basket. I looked up the nearest Apple store on my iPhone. Dad had left me financially sound, so I could buy a new computer. Maybe an Apple genius at the store could salvage some of my files from my computer, but those appointments sometimes took days to schedule. I could redo my essay and math work this evening. Most of the damage was fixable. Not the dress though, which had been a gift from my father. Even if I could find the same style, it would not be the item Dad bought me before he died. She knew how special that sundress was to me. I bit down hard on my lip.

At dinner, I would be forced sit across the table from Margaret and pretend nothing had happened while Margaret displayed her venomous smile. The red words scrawled on the mirror drew my attention. *This is just the beginning.* She wasn't done.

My new computer would be stored next door. Where was Evil Queen Margaret at this moment? Was she planning her next move with her little worker bees in tow? One more day of hell. If I didn't get emancipation, this wouldn't end well—for either of us.

CHAPTER SEVENTEEN

"Get to your places!" shouted the Queen in a voice of thunder...

On Monday morning, the sun radiated an intense light that outlined the edges of every object it touched. The cooler air announced the fall season would soon morph into winter. I wouldn't have cared if it were pouring rain. Today was the day of my hearing. Today, I would gain my independence. Today, I would return to my house and Shadow. Best of all, I would be rid of Margaret except at school.

A shiny new computer, all my redone homework, and most of my freshly laundered clothes were stored next door. The only thing I hadn't accomplished was repotting the new mums with the hood ornament, but I could do that this afternoon.

The chili I made for dinner had been delicious, and I had been spared having to share the meal with Margaret. She ate at a friend's house and had come home late. I hadn't seen her since she trashed my room because she was in bed when I left to feed Shadow this morning. When I collected Mr. O'Shawnessy to drive him to the courthouse, the Evil Queen was primping in the bathroom.

As I turned into the public parking lot, and my day in court had finally arrived, my nerves threatened to overwhelm me. The judicial building was a two-story monolith that blotted out the sun. I pulled into a slot to the right of my social worker's brown Jetta. Mrs. Wright sat in her car scribbling notes on a yellow legal pad. I didn't like the frantic way her hand moved across the page. She leapt out of her car and rushed to my car window before I killed the engine. The way she descended on me suggested something had gone wrong.

"Sarah," she said. "Judge Heart's assistant needs to know your character witnesses' full names right away. Lord knows why."

She hadn't even said hello. Why was it so urgent to have their names when we would be stepping into the courthouse in a few moments? We could introduce them to the judge then. But whatever.

"Dr. Mark Pullman and Paul Marks," I said.

A twinge of pride laced my voice. I had done the impossible. I had located two people to speak on my behalf on short notice. The judge would have to be impressed with a star high school football player and a respected veterinarian.

I stepped out of my Civic, looking around for my witnesses, while Mrs. Wright dialed a number and spoke into the phone. Dr. Pullman stood at the far end of the lot. I waved him over.

"One of them is already here," I said.

"Great, great," she said.

I pulled Mr. O'Shawnessy's collapsible walker from the trunk, opened the passenger door, and helped my guardian to his feet. Mrs. Wright nodded a greeting then rested her hand on my arm.

"We have another problem," she said. "This judge, well, I know this isn't professional, but she's a piece of work. The court clerk called me at 7:00 a.m. saying you needed death certificates for both of your parents. I already had your father's in your file so I brought that, but she wants to see your mother's as well."

My mother's death certificate? But that wasn't possible. Would this mean my chance to be rid of Margaret was doomed? My temper flared.

"Are you kidding me?" I screeched. "I don't have one. She died the day I was born." My voice escalated and hit a high note I didn't known I could reach. "Dad didn't keep any documents on her. And honestly, I don't think I can get one anyway."

"Now there, lass," Mr. O'Shawnessy said, patting my arm. "No sense getting your feathers ruffled. Ye know no matter what the courts decide, ye can stay on with me. Truth be told, I'll miss ye terribly."

I smiled at him, but I couldn't bear the thought of even spending one more night near Margaret. If it weren't for Shadow and the Evil Queen, I wouldn't have cared whether I moved out. I had grown quite fond of my guardian. But I would never feel safe with Margaret just down the hall, and I missed sleeping next to my dog. Last night, I wedged my desk chair under my bedroom doorknob. I had to escape today. I just had to.

"Well I don't have my mother's death certificate," I said again. "And I probably won't have one a week or a month or maybe even a year from now. Why did the judge have to decide she needed this on the day of the hearing?"

"I don't know," Mrs. Wright said with a twinge of exasperation. "Like I said, Judge Heart is a stickler. Anyway, we'll explain the situation and maybe she'll let it go. Regardless, we better get inside. Your emancipation hearing was the first on the docket. We don't want to upset the woman."

Dr. Pullman approached. He wore a suit and tie. I smiled and could have hugged him for dressing up. Surely, Judge Heart would be impressed. I searched the lot for Paul. We still had fifteen minutes, but I had asked him to arrive early. Where was he?

As if conjured by my thoughts, Paul's beat up truck swerved into the lot. He pulled into the empty slot on the other side of my Civic. When he emerged from the cab, I grinned at his collared white shirt and black dress pants. Not too formal, but classy enough to impress the court. How could I lose with these two witnesses and Mr. O'Shawnessy at my side?

I introduced everyone and the four of us headed inside. The courthouse had a stone entry with large Greek columns that seemed too extravagant for the expected amount of criminal activity in this sleepy town. Paul rushed forward to push open the heavy wooden door for Mrs. Wright.

The courthouse was a cacophony of sound. A child crying, a woman swearing, the echo of stilettos in a narrow corridor. Mrs. Wright led us down a hallway and into a room. Only a conference table surrounded by eight chairs occupied the room. Where was the intimidating judge's bench and witness chair? The setting seemed too informal given the effect of this decision on my life.

Mrs. Wright took the chair to the right of the head of the table. I settled in next to her as Dr. Pullman helped my guardian take the seat on the other side of me. I was sandwiched between my two greatest advocates. She directed Dr. Pullman and Paul to sit across from us. It was 7:55 a.m. and we were all present and accounted for. Being on time should work in my favor. Yet, I had a bad feeling. What if she insisted I provide my mother's death certificate?

The door opened and the Honorable Judge Alice W. Heart entered. The woman had the pinched face of someone who never smiled. Her mousy brown hair had been pulled back into an austere bun. There was absolutely nothing warm or fuzzy about her.

Her pencil-thin arms poked out of her billowing, black robe suggesting there wasn't an ounce of fat on her skinny frame. She was probably one of those Type A exercise fanatics. No doubt she was not one to bend the rules. Her world would be black and white. It wouldn't surprise me if she didn't know the color gray existed. While I applauded her efforts to keep murderers behind bars, I did not want this by-the-book woman deciding my fate.

She breezed by the backs of our chairs, bumping into Mrs. Wright's with a motion that appeared to be deliberate. If she had a heart, it was probably as cold as a dragon's or rather a dragoness's.

The door opened again. A petite woman wearing large, thick glasses and carrying a small typing machine, positioned herself at the end of the table, directly across from the judge. Lucky her. She could sit as far away from the Dragoness as the room allowed.

The judge glanced at her watch. She nodded at the court reporter whose fingers poised to type.

"Let the record show this hearing began precisely at eight a.m. and we are here to discuss the emancipation of Ms. Sarah Whitman under Family Code Section 7120, Case Number 12-5736. The Honorable Alice W. Heart will preside over the hearing. In attendance are Ms. Sarah Whitman, Mrs. Wright, her social worker, Mr. Patrick O'Shawnessy, her temporary guardian, and two character witnesses, Mr. Paul Marks and Dr. Mark Pullman. Mrs. Wright you may now speak on behalf of your ward."

Her ward? The Dragoness made me sound like a prisoner or a juvenile delinquent. No wonder Mrs. Wright had called her a piece of work.

"Thank you, Your Honor." Mrs. Wright said in a tone that offered anything but respect.

Tension sliced the air leaving no doubt these two had a history, and their past encounters hadn't ended well. I didn't care about their issues with each other. All I cared about was that the ruling be decided in my favor.

"If it please the court," Mrs. Wright continued in a clipped tone that suggested she didn't care about the judge's desires. "I'd like Mr. Patrick O'Shawnessy, who has been acting as Sarah's guardian since last spring, to speak. Then I'll have Sarah introduce her two character witnesses. After that, Sarah has a few things to say before you make your decision."

A few words to say? What was Mrs. Wright doing? We hadn't talked about my speaking on my own behalf. She had told me not to worry, just answer any questions the judge posed, and tell the truth.

Mrs. Wright proceeded to give a brief summary of how I came to be an orphan, glossing over the incident that led to my hospitalization last spring and the discovery of my status as a minor living alone, before providing a nice description of her own impressions. She then asked Mr. O'Shawnessy to describe how I handled my responsibilities under his guidance. He had nothing but good things to say.

Dragoness nodded; her face expressionless. Then, the judge cleared her throat.

"Mr. O'Shawnessy, is it your testimony that you believe Sarah is capable of handling her own affairs?"

"Aye. She's a bonnie smart lass."

I flashed him a grateful smile.

"Okay, Sarah," the judge said. "Why don't you introduce your character witnesses?"

"Yes, Your Honor." I sat straight in my chair and inclined my head in Dr. Pullman's direction. "This is Dr. Mark Pullman. He is a veterinarian at the emergency animal clinic. He treated my dog last spring."

"Yes." He turned his head to address the judge. "Sarah is a very responsible young woman. When her dog had an accident last spring, she immediately brought her in for treatment. She even paid her bill on time."

"Thank you, Dr. Pullman, but have you had any opportunity to meet with Sarah recently?"

"Yes, I had dinner with Sarah and my colleague, Dr. Griffin, who is also an acquaintance of Sarah's, this last Saturday evening."

I cringed. I wish he hadn't mentioned her. Dr. Griffin was not well-liked and most people suspected her of foul play in the death of her prom date and parents. Would Dr. Griffin's reputation sully his testimony? Even if the judge didn't react to her, the dinner itself hadn't gone well. Would the judge ask for details? Would Dr. Pullman mention my outburst?

"I have to say," Dr. Pullman added, "Sarah conducts herself well. Polite to a fault and she has excellent table manners. She even offered to do the dishes."

I grinned at him. He had come through for me.

"Thank you, Dr. Pullman," the judge said. "That will be all. You are welcome to leave now, if you need to get back to your job."

Dr. Pullman made no move to leave. He winked at me and leaned back in his chair. I liked his show of support by sticking around.

"And, who else have you brought Sarah?" the judge asked.

"This is Paul Marks," I said, nodding in his direction. "He is a fellow student at Walnut Acres High and the football team's quarterback."

"Well, Mr. Marks," the Dragoness said. "What do you have to say?

To my surprise, Paul pulled out a 3 by 5 inch index card as though he were about to give a speech. His blond hair fell over his forehead. His green eyes connected with mine as he cleared his throat.

"Yes, ma'am." A bead of sweat rolled down his temple. His voice wavered, but he soldiered on. "I came here today to say that Sarah is my tutor for biology. That she is an amazing artist and that she is super smart. That is what I want to say."

"Thank you, young man," the judge said. "Would you say Sarah has adjusted well to the school?"

I held my breath. Paul wouldn't lie, but the judge hadn't asked if I were popular or had made friends. Would he realize there was more than one way to interpret her question?

"Yes, ma'am. Mrs. Durgette, the art teacher, is very impressed with Sarah's work. Sarah did this amazing still life last week where she made a pear into her dog's head and now it's hanging on the classroom bulletin board."

The judge nodded.

"Thank you, Mr. Marks. Now, you said Sarah is your biology tutor. Has she helped your grade improve?"

Great. Paul hadn't had a test yet. He couldn't say yes.

"Um, well, not yet, ma'am. Sarah just started teaching me this weekend. But if you'd like, I can explain mitosis to you."

I cringed again. What if Paul started spouting off about how pre-game practice equals interphase and prophase is equivalent to the huddle? To my relief, the Dragoness shook her head and told him that wouldn't be necessary.

Then she dismissed Paul, not giving him the opportunity to stay. He gave me a thumbs-up as he left the room. He had done his best for me. I owed him big time.

The judge faced me. I was supposed to speak next. I had been too worried about how the judge would react to Dr. Pullman's and Paul's testimonials to plan a speech.

"Now, Mrs. Whitman," she said. "What say you?"

"Your Honor," I said, studying my fingers. "Um ... let me first say that I appreciate the court's interest in my welfare."

I shifted in my seat. Everyone's attention rested on me. This was my moment to shine and my mind was blank. I tried to think of what my father would do in this situation. Probably he would find a relationship rule to follow. I sorted through them in my mind and landed on Relationship Rule #10: Never pretend to be something that you're not. Who was I though? And if I couldn't answer that question, did I have any right to ask the court to treat me like an adult? But, of course, I knew who I was. I was my father's daughter. I sat up straight in my chair and lifted my gaze to the judge.

"You see, Judge," I said. "I have had to grow up fast. Last year, my dad had cancer and he was so sick that I had to do everything. I cooked, I cleaned, I paid the bills. I drove him to doctor's appointments, and yes, I even cleaned his bedpan. My Dad knows ... knew me better than anyone, and he felt I was ready to live on my own."

The judge studied me; her face unreadable. Mrs. Wright nodded encouragement. Dr. Pullman nodded at me. Mr. O'Shawnessy smiled. Buoyed by their support, I pressed on.

"Except for today, I haven't missed any school. I get good grades and, as you have heard from Paul, I am tutoring a fellow student. I studied all summer for my SATs. I plan to go to college. I've taken on the responsibility of a rescued dog, and as you heard from Dr. Pullman, when she had a health issue, I took her to the vet. I know I can take care of myself and I hope you will grant me emancipation. It was my father's dying wish. He loved me more than anything, and he would never have put me in a situation he felt I wasn't capable of handling. He even crafted a list of rules to live by to help me be a good person."

Whoops. Had I gone too far mentioning the rules? Would she ask what they were?

The judge tented her fingers and pursed her lips. She flipped open her case file. I could see financial statements mixed in with some loose yellow legal pages. I had forgotten to say anything about how Dad had arranged for the bank to pay the mortgage and other expenses. He also provided a generous allowance.

"Well, Miss Whitman, you have certainly stated your case for emancipation. It appears you're set up to handle your finances in a responsible manner, so as long as the rest of your paperwork is in order, I see no reason to deny your request."

I suppressed an urge to let out a whoop. I smiled at the judge. I could go home. I could sleep cuddled next to Shadow tonight. And no more Margaret.

"Mrs. Wright, I believe I asked you for death certificates for Sarah's parents," the judge added.

Oh no. I held my breath. Mrs. Wright pulled a copy of my father's death certificate from her file and slid the paper over to Judge Heart. The judge sneered at my social worker, before her gaze dropped to the form in front of her.

"As for the mother's death certificate," Mrs. Wright said, "I'm afraid I wasn't able to locate one on such short notice. But even if I had more time, what you've asked for will be difficult. You see, she died when Sarah was born, and her father didn't speak of her mother. She doesn't know her mom's maiden name and Sarah's birth certificate seems to have an error. It only lists her mother's first and married last names. Sarah does not have a copy of her parents' marriage license. You'll have to accept Sarah's word on this issue."

Judge Heart stiffened the moment the words were out of my social worker's mouth. Mrs. Wright should never have phrased it like a command.

"I'll have to?" Judge Heart frowned. "Mrs. Wright, I will not tolerate your insolence. I don't have to accept any such thing."

"Your Honor," Mrs. Wright said. "I've seen dozens of cases where it wasn't possible to provide information on both parents. Some mothers don't even know who the fathers are."

Crap. Why was Mrs. Wright being so argumentative? My social worker turned to face me and shifted her eyes toward the ceiling. At least she did that out of view of the judge.

My social worker took a deep breath and turned to face the judge.

"I'm sorry, Your Honor," Mrs. Wright said. "Of course, you will make up your own mind. I hope you won't punish Sarah because I spoke out of turn."

"I must act in the best interests of the child, even if that means more work for you," the judge said then glowered. "It just so happens my schedule has unexpectedly had an opening for next Monday. I think a week should be sufficient for you to come up with a death certificate. For all I know, this girl is a runaway or was kidnapped, and her mother is frantically looking for her. We will reconvene next Monday."

I opened my mouth to protest, but Mrs. Wright clutched my arm and squeezed hard. She leaned close and whispered in my ear to hold my tongue. She was right. It was only a week. If I spoke out, I might be denied emancipation at the next hearing.

The judge gathered her papers, shoved them in the folder, turned to Dr. Pullman, wished him a good day, and strode out of the room. She didn't glance in my direction. The court reporter stood and scrambled after the Dragoness.

"I'm sorry, Sarah," Mrs. Wright said. "That woman brings out the worst in me. I believe she meant to punish me, not you. I have another hearing down the hall, and I have to run. I'll call you later."

She gathered up her briefcase, pulled her cell phone from her pocket, punched a few buttons, and rushed out the door. I slumped back in my chair. How could things have gone so wrong so fast? I had brought the witnesses. I had done everything right.

How would I survive another week living in the same house as Margaret? Dr. Pullman stood. I should thank him for coming, but the words stuck in my throat. I gnawed on my pinky.

"I've got to get going," Dr. Pullman said when he reached the door. "I can see how disappointed you are, Sarah, but things usually work out for the best."

I nodded, though I couldn't see how spending even one more second near Margaret would benefit either of us. How would I find a death certificate for my mother when I didn't know her full name?

"No worries, lassie," Mr. O'Shawnessy said. "Ye know I'll be pleased to still see yer smilin' face after school today. Now, ye best take me home so ye can get back to yer studies."

Again I nodded. I rose to my feet. I retrieved my guardian's walker from the corner of the room and helped him to his feet. The walls closed in on me as we navigated the hallway and exited into the parking lot. The air I took into my lungs made my head spin. I would have to sleep not one, not two, but seven more nights under the same roof as Margaret. When I emerged from the courthouse, the huge building cast a dark shadow over me.

CHAPTER EIGHTEEN

"The question is," said Alice, "whether you can make words mean so many different things." [2]

Morning classes proved uneventful. I hadn't seen Margaret in the halls. Her worker bees kept inside their hives. This was a very good thing since my disappointment in the court delay had festered into anger, but instead of directing it at the judge, I had focused my resentment at Mr. O'Shawnessy's Queen Bee granddaughter.

The more I stewed over my ruined computer, homework, and clothing, the more I wanted revenge. Instead of paying attention to my teachers, I fantasized about what punishment I would like to inflict on the self-crowned Margaret. Destroying her beauty had been the theme. My ideas for retaliation started small—plucking her eyebrows until only shiny skin remained, dying her hair pink with green stripes, drawing a Hitler moustache

---

2   Lewis Carroll quote from the 1871 novel *Through the Looking Glass*.

in indelible ink. Each time I remembered the hours I spent redoing my homework yesterday, each time I thought about how she ruined my chances of making even one friend at school, my thoughts of retribution poured from the dark places of my heart. These were things I would never do, but I enjoyed imagining them—bleaching her hair white, taking her clothes out of her gym locker so she would have to wear her workout uniform the rest of the school day, shaving her head in the middle of the night. But each fantasy ended in guilt. These options would devastate dear Mr. O'Shawnessy and disappoint my father.

I still didn't trust myself not to deliver an open-handed slap across her smug face. So I slunk through the less traveled corridors between periods.

Somehow I made it to lunch avoiding the She-Devil. The break posed a bigger problem since Paul and Margaret shared my lunch period. Paul might try to sit with me to find out about the hearing. The last thing I needed was for Margaret to see Paul talking to me. She would come storming over, and I wasn't sure I could rein in my impulse to hit her. So I went straight home at the bell, even though my pass didn't release me from school for another fifteen minutes.

The further I distanced myself from Walnut Acres High, the more anxious I became. I wasn't sure of the source of my worry. I didn't think it was over leaving school early. Or even Margaret. No. It had something to do with home.

The bad feeling morphed into panic the moment my Civic turned into my driveway. It wasn't that anything looked unusual, but the very air filling my lungs felt wrong. I had the awful premonition that I forgot something important. Had I left Shadow water? Had I forgotten to unhook her leash after her walk this morning because I was in a rush to get to the hearing? Maybe her lead had become wrapped around a tree, and she strangled herself.

Blood ricocheted through my veins. I thrust the gearshift into park and ran to the front door, calling Shadow's name. My fingers shook as I tried to insert the key into the lock.

A sharp bark came from the other side of the door. Normally, I would tell her to be quiet, but now I welcomed this behavior. She was alive. Yet, my heart still thudded in my ears. Something felt wrong.

Using two hands, I slid the key in, twisted the knob, and shoved open the door. And there she was. No leash dangling from her collar. She wasn't panting. My dog was her usual, happy self—yipping and wagging her tail. I threw my arms around her muscular neck. I had been so sure something was amiss. Now, I felt foolish.

"Good girl," I said. I shook my head at how I overreacted. "Let's get you a treat."

As I walked into the dining room on my way to the kitchen, the two potted mums—one shriveled and dried, the other vibrant and glowing with yellow flowers— caught my eye. Thanks to Margaret I hadn't hid the hood ornament in the soil under my new mums and taken them next door as planned. How stupid of me. Dr. Griffin had a key and knew exactly where I would be this morning. I had foolishly left the silver eagle unprotected.

I didn't need to lift the root system of the dead plant to confirm the silver eagle was gone. Soil puddled around the base of the dying plant. Dr. Griffin hadn't even tried to cover her deed.

I walked over anyway, hoping I was wrong. I picked up the dried mums by the base of the plant and stared at the remaining dirt in the pot. No silver object. Without the hood ornament, I didn't have leverage over Dr. Griffin. I sank into one of the dining room chairs. I wasn't safe here anymore and neither was Shadow.

"I'm sorry," I said to my dog.

She crawled up onto my lap, panting in my face. I hugged her against my chest. Why hadn't I changed the locks immediately? I had been an idiot to think that whacko vet would stay away. For the second time today, the desire to take revenge threatened to overrule my better judgement. I wanted to storm over to Mrs. Bellweather's house right now and tell her the truth about her dead pet rat. But there was no proof of Dr. Griffin's deception. Even if Paul confirmed what happened, why would Mrs. Bellweather take the word of two teens over a licensed veterinarian?

Instead, I went to my new computer and Googled locksmiths in Walnut Acres. I found a local company and called. I needed to schedule the appointment around 4:30 to keep my tutoring session with Paul.

"J&J Locksmith," a gruff male voice announced.

"Yes," I said. "I need to have the locks at my house re-keyed at 4:30 today."

"Today? I usually book out a day or two. But you're in luck. My 3:15 cancelled. How many locks are we talking about?"

I did a mental calculation. The front door, one to the garage, and one side door that connected to the outside. The sliders didn't have keys.

"Three."

"Yep, shouldn't take long. I can fit you in at 3:15."

But 3:15 wouldn't work. I had to plan around Paul's football practice schedule, and he and I were meeting for tutoring at 3. After all he had done, I couldn't back out on our deal. He had a big test tomorrow.

"Can't you move your last appointment of the day to 3:15 and come here at 4:30?"

"No, miss. Do you want the appointment or not?"

Shadow nudged my hand with her nose. Without the hood ornament, I had no way to keep Dr. Griffin away from her. What if she came back while I was tutoring Paul and stole Shadow? I couldn't take the risk. I would offer to tutor Paul at 4:30. It could work out.

"I'll take it," I said then rattled off my address.

I sat to eat my lunch. Shadow placed her head on my knee. I patted her head but did not want to encourage begging behavior so I resisted slipping her any food.

"Sorry, girl."

She was getting a raw deal. Even after I had my locks changed, I would have to secure Shadow's doggie door and keep her inside the house whenever I was gone. My poor dog would have to pay the price for my negligence. I wolfed down my sandwich then took Shadow's leash from the peg on the door and attached it to her collar. I locked the door behind me, even though it hadn't helped secure my home earlier today.

* * *

The first thing I noticed when my Civic turned into the high school parking lot was that the front lawn was empty of students, which meant the five minute warning bell had already sounded. The second thing I noticed was Principal Huntsman. He stood next to my designated parking spot. Walnut Acres had strict parking rules, and I had been lucky that seniors got first dibs on assigned spaces.

I took my foot off the accelerator and slowed to a crawl.

I didn't want to get in trouble for driving too fast on top of a lecture about the terms of my off-campus pass. Someone—probably Margaret—must have tattled about my early exit at lunchtime. Still, this small infraction didn't seem so extreme that it would warrant him intercepting me before I returned to the classroom. What else had I done?

The car maneuvered around the man. Shadow yipped and wagged her tail. To her the tall man represented a human who might pet her. I cut the engine, my heart pounding. At six-foot-five, Huntsman towered over even the tallest student. He was fit and chipper, and only his polar-bear-white hair suggested he was on the cusp of retirement. Principal Huntsman always wore a suit and tie, even on the warmest days. He ruled the school with an iron fist, but he would give a kid a break in certain situations. Yet, he still frightened me because the man was so physically imposing.

I opened my car door, removed my backpack from the passenger seat, and told Shadow to stay. Then I turned to face the man. He smiled. Maybe this would turn out okay. I would apologize and promise I wouldn't leave early again and that would be the end of it.

"Sarah," Principal Huntsman extended one hand. "May I have your backpack please?"

My backpack? My brain riffled through the contents trying to figure out what he wanted with it. I handed over the canvas bag. He unzipped the main compartment and plunged his hand into the very bottom as though he knew exactly what he was looking for. Margaret must be behind this. An image of my unzipped backpack sitting on my bed formed. But when I pulled stuff from my backpack during my morning classes, nothing appeared disturbed.

The moment Principal Huntsman's hand emerged clutching the baggie with Shadow's pills, I understood. A leaden ball settled in my stomach as my pulse leapt into overdrive. Because of an increase in prescription drug abuse by teens, Walnut Acres High had instituted a zero tolerance rule. No student was allowed to carry medicine of any kind onto the high school grounds. All prescriptions were to be administered by the school nurse, provided the student had a doctor's note. The punishment for failure to comply was a minimum twenty-day suspension. Judge Heart would never agree to my emancipation if the principal suspended me.

Principal Huntsman waved the baggie under my nose. His face turned an awful shade of magenta. I shrunk back, leaning on my Civic for support.

"Don't you realize the school could lose its federal grant money if even one student is found using unauthorized drugs on campus? That's why we spent valuable district money on a hotline number to report illegal activities. Fortunately, a student left an anonymous tip to report your transgression. Now, we can deal with the issue without police involvement."

"But ... but those are my dog's pills," I said.

Shadow pressed her nose against the rear window as if to confirm my statement. Mr. Huntsman only glanced at her before shaking his head. The principal must have heard lots of lies in his tenure. I thought about Dad's Relationship Rule #5: Always be honest, but I couldn't exactly explain that the medicine was a precaution against seizures after I used Shadow as a medium to see ghosts.

The final bell rang. Great. Now, I would be late for class again. Mrs. Durgette was already annoyed with me. I hurried to explain.

"Sometimes Shadow gets diarrhea from car travel," I said, "so I wanted to have a few pills handy. I was afraid I would forget to bring them, so last Friday, I put in enough pills for the week."

"Your dog's, huh? Same one that eats homework?" Principal Huntsman scoffed. "What's the name of the medicine?"

"Metronidazole," I said without hesitation.

Principal Huntsman raised an eyebrow. The speed and sincerity with which I responded seemed to have given him pause. He pulled out an iPhone and tapped a few buttons.

"Spell it," he demanded.

I enunciated each letter then added that the drug was used in pets for inflammation of the bowel, and if he wanted, I could bring him to my house right now and show him the vial of pills. Ten remained in the bottle and they would look exactly like the ones in the baggie.

To my relief, Principal Huntsman nodded. "I believe you, Sarah. I'm going to take these pills to the school nurse. You can pick them up after class. But from now on, you will have to administer medicine to your dog either before class or drop them with the nurse. Do you understand?"

"Yes, sir. Thank you."

He pulled out a piece of paper and a pen from the breast pocket of his jacket, scribbled a hall pass, and handed it to me. He pocketed the baggie and strolled in the direction of the front office without another word.

As I made my way back to class, I stewed over the Black-Haired Demon. She went too far this time. I vowed to retaliate—something that would put a stop to her wreaking havoc on my life—but something that wouldn't also hurt my guardian. I had no idea what to do, but I would think of something.

* * *

It felt like *Groundhog Day* walking in late to Mrs. Durgette's class. Once again, I waited in the back while she droned on about her expectations for behavior in class. When she described the importance of respecting other people's work, she walked to the rear of the room and stood beside me. The lecture was because of me, and all but two of my classmates glared in my direction. Not Paul, who only glanced over his shoulder once and winked at me, and not Kyle, who kept facing forward with his shoulders hunched toward his ears.

"Well, Ms. Whitman," Mrs. Durgette concluded. "Why are you late once again?"

I handed her Principal Huntsman's note. I hoped she wouldn't read it aloud. Shadow leaned against me as if to express her solidarity.

Mrs. Durgette raised one eyebrow. "Very well. Please take your seat."

My proximity to Kyle would only make him hate me more. There was nothing to be done though. I couldn't exactly ask for a different seat with Mrs. Durgette's patience with me already stretched. Kyle turned his face away as I took my place. I got out my sketchpad and pencils.

"Let's talk about light and shadow before we get started."

Oh joy. Another lecture. Shadow sat beside me and I stroked her head. My fingers itched to place my fingers between her eyes. But I didn't have Shadow's pills anymore. What if she had a seizure?

When my index finger hesitated on Shadow's forehead. In a brief flash I saw the little ghost boy curled on the floor and sobbing behind Mrs. Durgette. Before I could change my mind, I fused my middle finger with my first in the space between Shadow's eyes to get a better look.

The ghost boy wore the same clothes. His crying was more intense than last time. Today he had a stuffed toy clutched in both of his hands. The object was orange with four green legs. The child sensed me. He looked up and threw the object at me—an orange jack-o'-lantern with green arms and legs and a green stem centered on the top of its head. The stuffed toy's eyes were black triangles, the nose a black circle. The smiley black mouth had a single orange tooth. The toddler pointed at it and screamed. I suspected he wanted me to get the toy and return it to him. He wanted the impossible.

"Ms. Whitman," Mrs. Durgette's voice startled me, and I jerked my hand away. "We're waiting for an answer."

What had she said? Should I ask her to repeat her question or simply state that I didn't know? From the expression on my teacher's face, admitting I hadn't heard her instructions seemed like a bad idea.

"I don't know," I mumbled.

"Certainly, you must have some idea."

I glanced over my shoulder at Paul. He mouthed something. I made a face of confusion. He lifted his finger and scratched his head, clearly point to the ceiling. Mrs. Durgette mentioned something about light and shadow. Could Paul be referring to the fluorescent lighting? Same word, different meaning when the two opposites were used in the context of art.

"Light?"

"Yes. Light was one of the essential elements missing in art before the Renaissance. And that's why three-dimensional art wasn't around back then."

"And, Mr. Marks," Mrs. Durgette said, "What was the other missing element?"

Now it was Paul's turn to be mortified. He caught my eye, and I smiled. I thrust my chin at Shadow. His brow furrowed and then he smiled.

"Shadow," Paul said.

"Exactly," Mrs. Durgette said. "Well done, Paul."

Paul? Was she downgrading Paul's status as a troublemaker? Good for him.

I patted my dog's head. Shadow panted heavily. A cold sliver of fear pierced my heart. Had my brief use of her to see the ghost boy harmed her? The pills I intended to have close at hand were now three corridors away. But she shouldn't need them. I had only viewed the child through Shadow for less than a minute. There must be another reason for Shadow's distress.

The temperature was warmer than usual in the classroom. Maybe she was just hot. I wished I had brought her a water dish.

"Ms. Whitman," Mrs. Durgette said. "Can you pose Shadow for us now?"

I rose from my seat. Did my dog hear the ghost boy screaming? Would Shadow balk at getting closer to him? My answer came soon enough. Shadow stood, but then planted her feet. She was not going anywhere. I didn't blame my pooch. The toddler could break glass with his high-pitched shrieking.

"I think she needs water," I said, hoping that after a moment, the boy would pipe down, and Shadow would do as I asked.

Shadow's tongue lolled out of the side of her mouth. I never should have put my fingers between her eyes. It had been risky and foolish.

"She does seem too warm," Mrs. Durgette agreed. She walked to the back of the room and filled a water container.

While Shadow lapped water, I stroked her head until my breathing slowed. But when I tried to lead her to sit in front of the fireplace prop, again she refused to budge. I needed my father to come and move the child. I closed my eyes and mumbled "Dad, please help."

I sensed Kyle stiffen. Had he heard me? I hazarded a glance.

"Unbelievable," he whispered under his breath.

Before I responded, I heard the familiar snap and crackle of air announcing my father's arrival. I waited a moment giving my dad time to calm the ghost toddler then I told Shadow to come. This time she complied. Dad must have quieted the boy. Shadow trotted up and took her position in front of the backdrop. Now there was nothing more to do but draw.

CHAPTER NINETEEN

Alice: "Would you tell me please, which way I ought to go from here?"

We only had a few minutes left before art class was over. Kyle hadn't so much as looked at me the entire class. We were supposed to be quiet while drawing, but most people would hazard a whisper now and then. Whenever I glanced at him, waves of negative emotion— either dislike or disgust—radiated from him. What would he do if he knew the ghost of his baby brother was sitting in this room? Would he want to tell him how much he missed him? Maybe the child cried so much because he wished his brother would pay attention to him.

And how did my father fit in? Dad used to love to watch me draw and paint. Had he stumbled across the child when he visited me in art class? And why didn't he want me to try to find out more about this little ghost boy?

Paul had warned me to leave it alone, too. Did Paul know about the events surrounding the boy's death? Why else was he so adamant that I shouldn't be asking questions? What if a child killer lurked in Walnut Acres?

"Two minutes," Mrs. Durgette announced, drawing me back to the present. "Pack up your supplies and clean your area."

The classroom erupted in activity. I called Shadow to my side

"Good, girl," I crooned.

I scratched her hind end. Her nose lifted into the air in appreciation, making me laugh. I scooped up pencils, flipped my sketchpad closed, and shoved them into my backpack. My fellow students complimented each other's work or discussed after-school plans. No one said a word to me.

I studied Kyle's drawing as he wrestled with his pencil box, trying to open it. The thickness in the grout around the brick fireplace had been evened out so I no longer saw the word "liar." His outline of Shadow's body was well proportioned except for the ears, which were bigger than they should be.

"Nice job," I said to Kyle.

He frowned. A lock of curly red hair tumbled down his forehead as he flipped his sketchpad closed. He was so gorgeous. If only he would give me a chance to explain. But not now. I needed to hurry home to meet the locksmith.

"Can we talk later?" I said. "Maybe this evening?"

I thought I saw his resolve flicker. But before he answered, Paul clapped one of his massive hands on my shoulder.

"Ready for our date?" he said.

Kyle flung his backpack over his shoulder, snatched his artwork from the easel, and walked out of the room without a word. I could have killed Paul at that moment.

"What is wrong with you?" I snapped, unable to contain my anger from both his interruption and the way he touched me.

"What?" Paul said, releasing his grip and stepping back. "What did I do?"

His smile faded. His eyes pleaded like a shelter dog's. I felt bad about my outburst after his supportive testimony this morning at my hearing.

"Never mind," I said. "But I can't do the tutoring session now. I have to go home. I'm having the locks changed. Can we meet at 4:30 instead?"

"You promised." Paul's chin dropped to his chest. "And I can't later. Didn't you hear the morning announcement about Friday night's game being moved to tomorrow? Coach has extended our practice. He just sent out a text. It starts after sixth period and we have to plan on sticking around until ten tonight. Now is the only spare time I have today."

What did he want me to do? I couldn't risk Dr. Griffin barging into my house whenever she wanted, so cancelling the locksmith wasn't an option. I promised Mr.

O'Shawnessy no boys in the house. My guardian would be angry if I betrayed his trust—maybe mad enough to decide I wasn't ready to live on my own when Monday's rescheduled hearing rolled around.

Still, Dad's Relationship Rule #6 was to never make a promise you don't intend to keep. I had made a deal. Paul kept his part of the bargain. I couldn't renege on my end of the deal.

"You're right," I said. "We'll have to meet at my house. We can study at the dining table while the locksmith works. Try not to let my guardian see you come in the house though. You drive yourself over so you can leave in case the work isn't done, and you need to leave for practice."

"But my mom's expecting us. She was so excited to meet you."

I wonder what he said about me. I really should thank her for letting Paul out of school this morning to testify at my hearing.

"How about if I drive by your house and introduce myself while you're at practice?"

Paul chewed on his lower lip then smiled.

"I have a better idea. Tutor me at your house now then come to the game tomorrow night and sit with my mom and dad. Then you can watch me do something I'm good at."

I imagined the bleachers at Walnut Acres High would be like my old school: parents in one section, students in another. I would be the only young person sitting in the parent section, but I also wouldn't be anywhere near Margaret. Paul had helped me. If this was what he wanted, then so be it.

"Great idea," I said. "So I'll meet you at my house in a few minutes. I've got to swing by the nurse's office first."

* * *

I was surprised to see a woman waiting on my porch. I assumed the locksmith would be a man. She tapped her foot with impatience as I fumbled with my front door lock. My dog was sensitive to the moods of people. When she bristled and growled at the agitated woman, I put her back in the car.

The business card in my hand held the locksmith's name: Mary Warzueski. The dark-haired woman was in such a hurry to start work that she hadn't even introduced herself. She was younger than I thought at first glance— probably in her mid-fifties. There wasn't anything pleasant about her. She didn't seem to know how to smile. Her pale arms resembled the spindles I drew to demonstrate the prophase stage of mitosis. Her demeanor was as cold as the metal keys she made.

You would think Ms. Warzueski was about to miss her Academy Award announcement the way she fidgeted. After I showed her the locks that needed to be changed, she started re-keying the back garage door lock.

I heard the deep rumble of Paul's truck coming down the street. He parked on the street, so with a little luck, Mr. O'Shawnessy would see the locksmith's truck in the driveway next to my car and assume Paul was an employee.

Paul rapped on the screen door and walked inside without waiting for me to push open the door. He held his arms wide as if welcoming a hug. I suppressed an impulse to step into his embrace because, in truth, the thought of snuggling next to him sent a rush of hormones through my body. I had felt safe nestled against his chest on my porch only a few short days ago. His silky blond hair seemed to hold an invitation to run my fingers through those golden strands. I shook off the feeling and stiffened my spine.

"Let's start," I said, pointing at a dining room chair. "We don't have much time."

I took the seat across the table from where I indicated Paul should sit. I had tossed the wilted plant, but the new pot of yellow mums that I hadn't bothered to return to my bedroom next door provided a cheery centerpiece. Late afternoon light made the whole room glow yellow.

A mischievous smile spread across his face. His mother must have had her hands full when he was a young boy. Paul slid into the seat to my right, moving the chair close so that the hair on my arms brushed against him. Heat radiated from him, and it seemed as if the whole room had been engulfed in flame. My thoughts constricted like sand trying to trickle down an hourglass. I leaned away to get my backpack and focused on my breathing until my head cleared enough to begin the lesson.

I reviewed each of the stages of mitosis, asking questions here and there. He impressed me with his retention of the terms. Football analogies had made the difference. Next I tackled meiosis.

When I reached into my backpack and pulled out my football analogy sketches, the information on missing children and the photo of the little boy I had printed last night spilled onto the floor. Paul picked the pages up and put them on the table without a second glance. I didn't want to draw his attention to the photo, which sat askew on the pile, so I let it be. He would be upset with me if he noticed the content. Paul studied each of my drawings. Because of the extra work from Margaret's destruction, I hadn't been able to put much thought or time into them.

"I think you need to explain these," he sighed.

"Of course. So, meiosis, is a special process of cell division," I began, "that is necessary for sexual reproduction in eukaryotes."

"Sex?" Paul grinned, shifting his weight to close the gap between us. "This is going to be gooooood."

My face flushed into what must have been a brick red. My tongue seemed to have swollen into a nonfunctional ball. I hoped Paul didn't see how he affected me. I must conduct myself as his tutor, not his girlfriend.

"Pay attention." I said, but a smile formed despite myself. "This is very similar to mitosis, but there are two important differences. The first has to do with the shuffling of genes in the chromosomes."

I located the sketch of an injured athlete leaving the field and a benched player taking his place and put it on the top of the pile.

"So in meiosis, the chromosomes recombine into a different genetic combination in each gamete. Mitosis is the process to replace dead or damaged cells. So in mitosis division occurs once resulting in two separate pairs of each parental chromosome in each cell."

Paul nodded. "And the other difference?"

I liked that he asked. I liked that he hadn't made any sexual jokes. The guy did want to learn.

"Good question." I showed him the sketch of twin football players in red jerseys, each with the same number (double zero), and standing next to four players in green uniforms with different numbers (10, 11, 12, and 13). "So the outcome of meiosis is four genetically-unique, haploid cells, whereas two genetically identical diploid cells are produced from mitosis."

I blushed once more as Paul's expression gleamed with admiration. "Wow. I totally get this. Do you know how many times I tried to read the text last night?"

"You read your biology text on a Sunday night?" I blurted.

It was his turn to blush. "It's your fault. You've changed my whole perspective on school. I always thought it was a waste of time ... but now ..."

"But now, what?"

"Well, I dunno, I guess it seems possible that I can learn this stuff. I've always been able to skate through classes because the school placed me with teachers who were avid football fans. They looked the other way when I didn't turn in homework and were lenient on test scores. I thought they believed I was too stupid to learn, so who was I to question their judgment? But now, well, you've shown me a whole new side of myself."

His words moistened my eyes and I looked away. It felt good to be appreciated. Paul, this great big oaf, had a whole new outlook on learning because of me. The idea that I could make a difference stirred inside me. This awakening sense of accomplishment filled me with confidence. Dad had said that power was a weighty thing and that, above all else, it can be abused. That's why he emphasized Relationship Rule #1: A successful relationship needs to have balance. Balance of power, balance of respect, and balance of compassion.

I turned to face Paul. "That's one of the nicest things anyone . . . has . . . ever . . . said to me."

As I spoke his lips inched closer to mine. I didn't want to pull away, and at the same time, I did all at once. His nearness intoxicated me. It would feel so good to have his arms cradling me to his chest.

"All finished with the garage," Ms. Warzueski said as she entered the room.

I stood up so fast the chair tipped over backward. Paul's face blanched. I imagined my cheeks were about as red as the rose in Salvador Dali's painting *Rose Meditative*. I righted my seat.

The locksmith smirked. "Yah, I'll just work on the front door now then I can get out of you two lovebirds' way."

A red knot of anger swelled in my chest. I hired her to fix my locks, not judge me. I was about to respond with a "you just do that." But then the woman gasped and put her hand over her mouth. Her eyebrows arched toward her forehead and she took a step backward. Paul turned to see what the woman was looking at and frowned.

"Oh, no, Sarah," he said, moving my drawings to cover the photo of the ghost boy. "I'm so sorry, Mrs. Warzueski."

"It's okay, Paul," the woman said in a tight voice then scowled at me.

What was going on? I looked at Paul, hoping he would explain. He took me by the arm and escorted me out back.

"Didn't I tell you to leave it alone?" he said in a hushed whisper. "Mrs. Warzueski is Kyle's mother, and the missing boy is her son. I bet she struggles every day to forget what happened, and here you are reminding her again."

"What? That's Kyle's mom? But his last name is Bowman."

But the moment I said it, I knew I wasn't using my head. Divorce, remarriage, maintain a maiden name—any number of reasons would explain the differing last names.

"Kyle's real dad died in a car accident when he was three. She remarried when Kyle was in the first grade. He's had a tough life. Now do you understand why you should leave it alone?"

I nodded. I felt awful. No wonder this woman was so unhappy. She knew her child was missing, but she probably still clung to the idea that her boy might be alive. Both Paul and my dad told me to drop it. I should have listened.

"You're right," I said. "I'm sorry. I ... I didn't know."

But now the damage was done. Poor Kyle. Not only had my stupidity put him in a bad mood, but now he would come home to an upset mother. I hung my head. I made things worse for everyone I came in contact with. My lower lip trembled and I felt tears pooling behind my eyes.

"Hey," Paul patted my shoulder. "Don't cry. Let's go back inside, okay?"

We settled into the same seats at the table. Paul pushed an errant strand of hair out of my face then he leaned close and gave my hand a squeeze. He was such a nice guy—too good for me.

"Now, where were we?" he asked.

His hand still covered mine. My heart sputtered as I remembered how he had been about to kiss me. I glanced at Mrs. Warzueski's stiff movements. It seemed wrong to be flirting after what happened. I pulled my hand out from under Paul's to retrieve one of my drawings.

"Haploid cells," I said. "Let's review. With meiosis, we start with a diploid cell. The chromosomes duplicate how many times?"

"Once," Paul said with confidence.

"Great! And how many successive divisions to create the four haploid cells?"

When Paul hesitated, I showed him the scoreboard I had drawn that showed the game was in the second quarter, and the score was four to zero. It was a stretch to relate this to football, but he got the analogy right away.

"Two," he grinned.

By the time we reviewed the material, Mrs. Warzueski had finished changing the locks on my doors. After I wrote out a check, she thrust a new key into my hand, and then she was out the door. As soon as the woman backed down the drive, Paul told me he needed to leave for practice. I followed him outside, intent on retrieving Shadow. Paul paused at the end of the driveway.

"Can I call you later if I have questions? About the lesson I mean."

"Of course."

I wanted him to have questions. Lots of questions. The truck's engine roared to life and then he was gone.

I fingered the key in my hand. I had a burning question of my own. Was it right to stop trying to find out what happened to Kyle's stepbrother knowing that Ms. Warzueski lived every day wondering what had become of her son?

Shadow yipped and scratched at the car door. Instead of looking toward me though, her gaze was fixed on something on the ground in the ornamental rocks by my front porch. She obsessed over squirrels, but I didn't see any bushy-tailed creatures in the yard. Maybe she was just being a silly pup.

"Stay." I opened the car door and reached for her leash.

Shadow rocketed by me to the landscaped area that captivated her. I scrambled after her, but the trailing lead eluded my grasp. She stopped short, barking at one of the larger dark-colored rocks. As I caught up to my girl, I grabbed her collar. Coiled and well camouflaged in the shadow of the rock was a large reddish snake.

I drew back, pulling Shadow with me. A quick glance at the tail confirmed it was not a rattlesnake. But what if it was another poisonous species?

I guided Shadow into the house then whipped out my laptop and Googled "snake photos." I riffled through the pictures until I found a match. It was a corn snake—a docile species that was not inclined to bite.

Dad had always emphasized the importance of respecting and appreciating things that were different. He told me spiders and snakes played an important role in the ecosystem. I decided to relocate it because I didn't want it slipping inside my house. I went to the closet and pulled out a pillowcase.

Catching the snake proved easy. It coiled around my arm, flicking its tongue in and out. It was so calm that I wondered if it might be someone's escaped pet. I guided the reptile into the pillowcase where it settled in as if this activity were an everyday occurrence.

A car rumbled down the street. Crap. Margaret was home—the witch who destroyed my computer and my favorite dress, who called the school to report I brought pills to the high school. If I let her get away with it, what would stop her from doing something worse? The pillowcase in my hand bulged then grew thin again. I tied a knot in the cloth and texted Tess—the one person who had befriended me when dad was ill and still kept in touch. The one person who would approve of my plan.

* * *

I lay awake on my bed, nestled under the covers, ears trained for the scream I expected. What was taking so long? The red numbers on my alarm clock indicated it was 12:02. Margaret must have crawled into bed by now.

My phone buzzed. Tess' text read: *Did she find it?*

I typed the letter *N*.

K. Going to sleep. Text me in a.m.

K.

Could the corn snake I placed at the foot of her bed under the covers while she brushed her teeth tonight have slithered away undetected? It was petty of me, and it wouldn't make up for my ruined computer and clothes but scaring her gave me a satisfying sense of power.

For the first time today, I wasn't angry that my petition for emancipation wasn't granted. If I had moved back into my house next door I wouldn't have been able to seek revenge on Margaret. If only she would discover my little present.

What had gone wrong? I was sure turning on her electric blanket on a low setting would keep the animal in a heat-induced stupor. Perhaps the reptile sensed Margaret's serpentine nature and fled to the closet. It couldn't leave the room. Before I released the creature, I made sure it wouldn't be able to slide into Mr. O'Shawnessy's bed and frighten the old man. The weather stripping at the base of Margaret's door would prevent its escape.

Fatigue threatened to pull me into sleep. What was taking so long? Had the snake crawled into her UGG boots? If so, she wouldn't get her surprise until the morning.

My mind drifted as time lagged. Thoughts of Paul sent tingles through my body. I had been disappointed when he hadn't called tonight. Practice had probably run late. I looked forward to watching him play football tomorrow. Stealing Paul from her wasn't part of my revenge. I really liked him, and she didn't deserve him. I envisioned running onto the field and throwing my arms around him after he made the game-winning points. I imagined Margaret fuming on the sidelines as the cheer squad dripped with envy. Paul was handsome. He was popular. He was the quarterback. He could pick any girl, and he had chosen me.

I hugged my pillow, wishing it were him. I had misjudged him, labeled him as a dumb jock. But he was kind and sweet and a true friend. He came to my rescue when I needed help.

I hoped Paul would invite me out for a post-game pizza tomorrow. I hoped he would drive me home and try to kiss me goodnight. And I would let him.

How quickly my feelings had changed. Hadn't I dreamed of having Kyle do the very same thing a few short nights ago? I still needed to make things right with Kyle though. He probably still thought of me as a liar and a jerk who considered him a loser.

Poor Kyle. His little brother was dead, and he didn't even know that for sure. I had to find a way to reveal the boy's fate. My thoughts fell quiet the way they always did before I lapsed into sleep. The screech came then, jarring me into a sitting position.

"Help!" Margaret screamed, "Help!"

My smile spread from ear to ear. I forced it to disappear, put on my most innocent face and jumped into action, bursting into the hall.

"What's wrong?" I yelled over Margaret's cries for help.

"Get it out of here," Margaret cried. "Please, Sarah."

I charged into her room. She cowered in the far corner. The bed covers lay in a crumpled mess at the foot. The snake lifted its head from the tangled sheets. As I drew closer, its tongue flicked in and out.

"What's the matter?" Mr. O'Shawnessy poked his head into the hall.

"There's a corn snake in Margaret's room," I said. "It's harmless. Go back to bed. I'll take care of it."

"Aye, that's a good lass," Mr. O'Shawnessy mumbled.

His medicine must have made him groggy, because he retreated into his room and shut the door without another word. I lifted the calm snake by the tail. The creature that terrorized my nemesis and I headed for the front door. Margaret shrieked and shrank back.

Hah! Mr. O'Shawnessy would never suspect I masterminded his granddaughter's traumatic experience. In fact, I was the hero. I was glad she was frightened, but more than that I was pleased she had needed my help. Maybe the more I forced her into situations like this, the less she might feel compelled to hurt me. Dad's Relationship Rule #1 said you needed to have a balance of power. But that implied both parties were fair-minded. Margaret would never relinquish her advantage without a struggle. At least for today, I tipped the scales a little in my favor.

I stepped outside and clutched the neck of my pajamas tight against the brisk night air while my eyes adjusted to the dark. The moonlit night provided enough light to walk across the yard and release the snake in the brush where I hoped it would slither away.

Movement caught my eye at the end of my driveway. I froze, squinting in the darkness. My hand clutching the snake released the reptile as realization hit. At the bottom of the sloped driveway stood a tall, lean figure dressed in black. A jack-o'-lantern mask covered the person's entire head—an effective disguise since I couldn't see a thing behind the teardrop eye holes, triangle nose, or multi-toothed smile.

Moments before I shivered in the cool autumn air, now I felt nothing. The figure resembled a giant version of the pumpkin toy the little ghost boy had thrown in the classroom. Could the person who stood less than fifty feet away be his killer? Could this person have known I had taken an interest in the missing child?

In the dim light, I couldn't tell whether the slender form was male or female. Other than Paul and my father, the only person who knew I was looking into the case was Mrs. Warzueski. If Kyle's mom had murdered her own son then she would have no problem doing the same to me.

The dark figure raised its left hand and pointed its index finger at me. My mind screamed for me to run, but it was as if the asphalt driveway encased my feet. The jack-o'-lantern head swiveled from side to side then the figure took a step toward me. I could see an object in the person's right hand, but I couldn't make out what it was. Why wouldn't my feet move?

The familiar crackle of air alerted me to my father's presence. Warm hands clutched both of my upper arms and shoved me backwards. His actions broke the spell. I turned and fled to my guardian's house, slamming the door and locking it behind me.

CHAPTER TWENTY

In another moment down went Alice after it, never once considering how in the world she was to get out again.

I leaned against the front door inside Mr. O'Shawnessy's house, half-expecting the jack-o'-lantern killer to try to push the door open. I imagined the doorknob turning like in a creepy slasher movie.

Who could it be? Mrs. Warzueski might have told any number of people I was curious about her missing son. With a second chance to study the person's body type, maybe I could determine who had lurked under the mask.

I crept into the living room then inched the curtain back, afraid the jack-o'-lantern face might be peering inside as I looked out. My fear of a peeping pumpkin was unfounded. No one stood in my driveway.

What would have happened if I hadn't gone outside? Would the killer have gone inside my house? Would they have taken Shadow? Did they intend to kidnap me?

It could have been Dr. Griffin. She was crazy enough. But the body shape hadn't been right. Or at least I didn't think so. He or she had been tall and thin, but I had been so frightened that now I couldn't estimate their height. It could have been Mrs. Warzueski. What did Kyle's dad look like? Faye was too stocky. Or was she?

"What are you doing?"

I whirled around and slammed my knee on the coffee table. The pain jolted me. I hopped a couple steps away from the window. Somewhere in the chaos, I recognized Margaret's voice, which kept me from screaming and waking Mr. O'Shawnessy. I held my hand over my heart as if this might stop its wild pulsating. Air filled my lungs when I finally caught my breath.

"I . . . I was making sure the snake wasn't heading back this way," I lied, rubbing my throbbing knee.

"You didn't kill it?"

"No," I said. "Of course not. Corn snakes are harmless."

"It's still out there? What if it comes back in the house? Get rid of it!"

"I'm not killing it. And anyway, it's gone."

"Let me see." Margaret stepped around me and jerked the curtain aside. "Where did you dispose of it?"

I toyed with the idea of telling her I dropped it outside her window, but I had enough excitement for one night.

"On the grass in front of my house," I said, edging close behind her so I could see.

I now had a clear view of the street and my front lawn, as well as the driveway. The figure in the pumpkin costume had disappeared.

Where had he or she gone? If it was Mrs. Warzueski under the orange head, she had access to my house if she kept a key when she re-did my locks. She had only given me one. Didn't they usually come in pairs? But Shadow would be barking. She never made a fuss until someone got near the house, so she must be okay. Pumpkin Head must have left thinking I would call the police. But I couldn't involve the authorities for the same reason I hadn't called them when Dr. Griffin broke into my house—to do so would jeopardize my emancipation.

"Is that it?" Margaret said pointing at a fallen tree branch under the ash tree in my yard.

Where had the snake gone after I dropped it on the driveway? I had a vague sense the reptile headed toward the rock where I found it, but I wasn't sure. I doubted I could see it now, even if it was slithering straight toward the window where Margaret and I stood.

"No. I've been meaning to pick up that dead branch. I don't see the snake. It's definitely gone," I said.

"Are you sure?"

"Absolutely."

"Oh, by the way, that weird veterinarian friend of yours stopped by tonight when you ran to the store for milk. She said to tell you to let the past stay in the past, whatever the hell that means. She said if you did that, things would go

well on Monday. Her eyes looked kind of …wild. She's sus.
You should stay away from her."

Sus? Wow. If clueless Margaret thought Dr. Griffin
wasn't to be trusted then Claudia must have been acting
cray-cray."

I nodded. But I still puzzled over the message. What
past had Dr. Griffin referred to? The rat's faked death
and lying to Mrs. Bellweather? Or the hood ornament
that linked her to the death of her high school boyfriend?
Perhaps she meant my interest in the ghost boy's death. If
so she probably discovered from Mrs. Warzueski that I was
looking into the case.

"What did that crazy woman mean anyway?" Margaret
placed her hands on her hips.

When she asked a question, she expected an immediate
answer. But I couldn't say what I didn't understand myself.

"I have no idea," I said.

"You're sure the snake's gone?" Margaret said.

"Yep."

"Okay, then. I'm going to sleep."

She turned and headed down the hall. No "thank you,"
no "I can't believe how brave you were." Not from the likes
of her.

My prank hadn't accomplished anything. The sweet
taste of revenge had been fleeting, and I woke poor Mr.
O'Shawnessy. It had been a waste of time.

I took one more peek. An empty street. During one of our
many cross-country moves, Dad had mused about roads.

He said car accidents happened because of them, traffic jams clogged them, but the asphalt remained unchanged, despite the frustration and heartache that had transpired on it. My dad was a wise man. He had told me to steer clear of the little boy, but I hadn't taken the time to consider the consequences. I had jumped in, and now I didn't see any other path than to wait for the splash because I wouldn't feel safe until the murder had been solved and the killer put behind bars. With a last name for the missing child, an internet search might provide enough information to clear up the murder.

I wished I had my laptop, but I now kept it locked in my own home to keep it away from Margaret. No way was I going back outside to get it tonight. My sleuthing must wait.

* * *

As I walked to my first class, a flurry of texts from Tess arrived, filled with praise over my snake prank. Her support left me feeling somewhat justified in my actions, even if it hadn't turned out the way I planned. Morning classes passed with surprising ease. Eliza, one of the wannabe-popular students, had said hello to me in the hall. At lunch, Paul cornered me by my locker, grinning, laughing, and playfully punching me on the shoulder.

"Guess who passed his biology test with a B?" he said.

"You." I said with a smile.

He nodded. "Come sit with me?"

How tempting was that? With Paul Marks at my side, others might be more accepting of me. But I didn't even want to think what Margaret's reaction would be.

"Can't. I'm leaving school to get Shadow."

When I collected my dog at home to take her to art class, I didn't see anything suspicious—no moved furniture, no open doors that I had left shut this morning With the sun shining and chasing away the crisp fall air, the pumpkin-head killer's visit felt like a distant nightmare.

I managed to make it to class on time, and Kyle half-smiled at me as I sat next to him. Mrs. Durgette announced five minutes into class that the rest of the period was to be used to work on our projects.

"Sarah, please position Shadow in front of the backdrop."

I rose from my seat, guiding my dog to sit before the cardboard fireplace setting. She swung her rear around so she faced the class.

"Sit," I said to Shadow.

She wagged her tail but made no move to comply. I repeated the command and added a hand signal by lifting my hand in a scooping motion. Her head dipped as if looking at an object next to her. Her ears tipped forward, and the taut muscles supporting her lean frame twitched, but she remained standing. My girl lived to please me. What was going on?

When I applied pressure to her rear, lukewarm air surrounded my arm. The temperature was all wrong to be my father whose ethereal presence tended to be at least ten degrees warmer. Only one other spirit occupied this classroom. The little ghost boy. That was why my dog refused to sit.

"It's okay, girl."

I squatted and guided her rump to the ground. A circle of tepid warmth encompassed my neck as the toddler wrapped his pudgy arms around me, so I could easily pick him up. I had no choice but to place my arm under his bottom, lift the child, and take him with me to my seat. My fellow students probably wondered why I had my elbow jutting out at a weird angle like a folded bird's wing.

I returned to my easel with as much dignity as I could muster. Once settled, a new problem arose. The child had latched onto to my right side so my only choice was to draw with my left hand. I pretended to be contemplating my painting as I pondered my next move. Weighted, warm air, the size of the child's head, pressed into my chest. I suspected the toddler had fallen asleep. If I woke him by shifting his body to my other side, he might cry and upset Shadow again.

Around me the other students improved their sketches. I couldn't sit here idle the whole class period, but I was at a loss as to how to proceed. Mrs. Durgette had started her tour of the room at the back of the classroom and had almost reached me. She paused at Kyle's easel to compliment his work, before stepping behind me.

"Sarah," Mrs. Durgette said. "Just because you brought in your dog does not exclude you from completing the assignment."

"Sorry," I stammered. "I'm trying to figure out what to do next."

"Well, get on with it."

I gripped a charcoal stick with my left hand and began shading a section of Shadow's tail. Satisfied, Mrs. Durgette moved on to another student. Black marks appeared outside the outline. At this rate, my picture would be ruined.

After ten minutes, I stood with my crooked arm fused to my side and released Shadow from her pose. I stooped to Shadow's level so that my arm was hidden behind her and out of the view of others in the classroom. After a short break, Shadow was once again in position. My elbow jutted out at a strange angle again as I returned to my seat. My limb tingled from being stagnant in one position. Amazing how heavy air feels when it's occupied by a spirit.

"Sarah," Mrs. Durgette exclaimed. "What's wrong with your arm?"

My classmates chortled. I longed to keep walking straight through the doorway and never returning. But that wasn't possible. Not with my emancipation at stake. My initial thought was to claim an injury while playing tennis yesterday, but she might have noticed that I had been fine when I first came into to the classroom. Or she might send me to the school nurse forcing me to take the child along.

"Nothing," I said. "It fell asleep is all."

Flexing my fingers a few times, I slunk back to my chair. I busied myself sorting through pencils. How long did toddlers nap anyway? Would he wake before I needed to give Shadow another break? I decided to stretch the time for Shadow's sit-stay to twenty minutes, even though this was a lot to ask of her.

My sweet pooch whined after fifteen minutes and stood. I didn't blame her. I called her to my side so she wouldn't head for the door. I leaned over to kiss her head.

"Good girl," I whispered.

"Okay, class. The dog needs a break. Color in your sketches while we give Shadow five," Mrs. Durgette announced.

My drawing now looked like the scribbles of a child the age of the one I held in my arms. And for my sacrifice my arm felt as stiff as a frozen side of beef. I wasn't any closer to finding answers as to the boy's killer either.

After I confirmed that Mrs. Durgette wasn't watching, I placed my fingers between Shadow's eyes. The sleeping child had a sweet round face with his mother's cheekbones. His red hair must come from his mother's side. Wait. The label on his shirt might have his first name on it, but to lift his collar, I needed to shift his weight onto my chest. My numb arm demanded relief, and I decided to risk it. The moment I moved, he startled awake, and the waterworks erupted. Tear-filled blue eyes stared at me in accusation. Shadow whimpered but didn't pull away.

The child's curled fist rose, and I thought he might punch me, but instead he threw a crumpled piece of paper that had been hidden in his hand at my face. I recoiled and sensed Kyle lean away from me.

"Fly," I said to Kyle by way of explanation.

Kyle's only response was to resume his work to add detail to the fireplace mantle. At least Mrs. Durgette was distracted as she explained the importance of proper perspective to Harvey and didn't notice my body contortions.

My body twisted to counter the boy's moves as the toddler struggled to get off my lap. I wiggled my tingling fingers while trying to hold on. A few students tittered, but I held tight, hoping to get a look at his shirt tag before he escaped. When Kyle scooted his chair further from me, I let the boy go. He landed on his bum, but to my relief he stopped crying. He used my leg to pull himself to his feet then pointed at the paper that had landed on my chest.

I smoothed the tattered remains in my palm against my head so that Kyle would think I fixed my hair then examined the paper. It appeared to be an emergency card like the one I wore on preschool field trips, but the mangled paper was almost unreadable. At one end, I could just detect the seven digits of a phone number.

The little boy reached for the paper with his chubby hand. I committed the sequence to memory and handed the rumpled card to the child. I was rewarded with a smile before he toddled away. My gaze swept the room, but my father had not made an appearance.

"Sarah," Mrs. Durgette said, "do you think Shadow has rested long enough?"

"Yes," I said, dropping my hand from my dog's head.

This time I held my arm at a natural angle as I moved to the front of room. Then, after I situated Shadow, I focused on fixing my Shadow drawing.

After the bell rang, I rushed to the nurse's office and, once in the car, I gave Shadow a pill as a precaution against a seizure from using her to see the ghost boy. She gobbled it down with a piece of string cheese and rewarded me with a lick on my nose. Her ears tipped forward like they did when she was on alert.

As I drove home, I repeated the phone number on the boy's paper. The moment I walked in the front door of my house, I extracted my cell from my backpack and dialed the number, but I hesitated before I hit "call."

Caller ID on the other end might reveal my name. Even if the person didn't have that phone feature, and I disconnected without saying anything, if they hit redial and I didn't answer, they would get my voicemail and know who had called. What if this number belonged to the killer? This phone call might prove deadly.

Should I buy a burner phone? Dial the number from a phone booth? I didn't have time to drive around looking for either of these things with a physics exam to study for and the football game tonight. Then I remembered the school directory. I unearthed my copy from under a pile of junk mail. I flipped it open to Bowman. The numbers on the ghost boy's paper didn't match Kyle's cell phone, his mother's, or father's contact phone numbers. I found my receipt from the locksmith's company. The numbers didn't match Kyle's mother's business number either.

Was it possible that the boy found a scrap of paper somewhere, and it had nothing to do with his death? Before I could change my mind, I hit the call button. The phone rang twice before a man came on the line.

"Hello?"

The voice sounded familiar, but I couldn't place it.

"I'm sorry," I said. "I think I misdialed. Who is this please?"

"Sarah? Is that you?"

Holy Mother. The killer knew me. But who was this? Should I hang up? I had been a fool to make this call.

"Sarah, you're scaring me. Are you home alone? Should I come by?"

This man knew where I lived? Who the hell was this? Is this the person who was hiding behind the jack-o'-lantern mask?

"No," I blurted. "I just misdialed. I'm sorry to have bothered you."

"No bother. Claudia and I enjoyed dinner the other night."

Dr. Pullman. Of course, that's where I had heard that voice. Relief flooded through me. But this didn't make any sense. Why would the child have his number? I swallowed hard. I needed to pull myself together.

"Yeah, me too. Dr. Griffin, I mean Claudia, is such a good cook. Anyway, I need to get ahold of my classmate. I'm studying for my physics exam and have a question on velocity and acceleration. It was nice chatting with you though."

"You, too. And don't ever hesitate to call . . . especially if you are in trouble."

My finger shook as I hit the off button. Did Dr. Pullman make it a habit of befriending children then kill them? Had he started with toddler boys and graduated to teen girls?

CHAPTER TWENTY~ONE

Alice felt so desperate that she was ready to ask help of any one...

An unwritten rule requires parents to sit on the forty-yard line to the southernmost goal line of the high school stadium near the scoreboard, while high school students claim the other seats which are closest to mid-field and the goal line near the snack shack. Paul had shown me a photo of his parents and had explained they would be wearing orange. This last bit wasn't helpful since most of the Walnut Acres High fans had adorned themselves in various shades of that home-team color. I scanned the bleachers for Mr. and Mrs. Marks in the adult section. Paul assured me that he had described me to them in detail, and they would watch for me. I had waited until the last moment to arrive to avoid leaving Shadow alone for longer than necessary.

The stadium burst at the seams with people. Northridge, our biggest rival, remained unbeaten. Winning this game would put Walnut Acres High in first place in the league. Our team had asked for our support and the Walnut Acres community had rallied. The air crackled with anticipation.

With my attention on the seats above, I didn't watch where I was going. I walked straight into someone. My gaze took in his wavy red hair, slender arms, and tapered swimmer's waist. Of all the people to crash into, it had to be Kyle. He turned with brows narrowed.

"Kyle." Impatient fans rushed by, pressing our bodies together. "I'm sorry. You must think I'm stalking you."

"Sarah," his expression softened.

The high school band launched into the *Jaws* movie theme. The music was beyond loud. He leaned toward my ear and shouted.

"I'm glad I ran into you. Want to sit together? I've been thinking it over. I really want to hear what you have to say."

His timing couldn't have been worse. But how could I refuse when I have asked him so many times to let me explain? And what would I say to him now that I had fallen for Paul? Or had I? Maybe if Kyle were ready to forgive and forget, I might not want to be with Paul. Was my fantasizing last night because of real feelings for Paul, or because I was convinced Kyle didn't want anything to do with me? I didn't know what to think.

The crowd rose to their feet. A deafening roar erupted from the stands. Our football players rocketed through a poster displaying the word "Winners." Paul led his team, fist pumping the air, to the delight of the crowd. The very sight of him took my breath. His gaze seemed to search the stands. Was he looking for me?

I turned to where his attention was directed. Two parents in the middle section of the bleachers jumped up and down with such enthusiasm that I feared the stadium might collapse. I squinted. Was that them? The small space to the side of the woman could be a saved seat for me.

The home team fans sat as the opposing team made their grand entrance, creating a commotion in the seats across the field. I heard my name from the seats above. Those enthusiastic people had been Paul's parents. Mrs. Marks waved her arm and pointed to the tight space next to her. I couldn't just turn and walk away with Kyle. I had been spotted.

"I'm sorry, Kyle," I said. "I want to talk, I really do, but I can't now."

"After the game?"

I should have said yes without hesitation. It was the right thing to do, even if it was to meet with him briefly to apologize and explain the "loser" note I scrawled. But what if we won, and Paul wanted me to go out for pizza to celebrate with his teammates? Not only could I share his success with him, but this could also be a chance to finally make friends at this school.

"Sarah," Mrs. Mark's voice caught my attention.

I turned to wave at Paul's Mom. When I looked back, Kyle had already moved on, picking his way through the throng toward the teen section of the stands.

No time to worry about Kyle now. The band played a few opening notes of the national anthem. I wanted to be in place to show my respect. I took the stairs two at a time so I could settle in.

"Sorry," I said, pressing my way through a wall of parents.

Paul's mom rose to her feet. I didn't really know what to expect, but I never anticipated a welcoming hug. She was about my height and, well, solid. Not fat, just big-boned with a little bit of pudge, probably from the cookies she made. Paul's father was completely lost in the pregame enthusiasm. He shook my hand and that was that.

"Sarah," Mrs. Marks said once I sat. "I wanted to thank you for agreeing to tutor Paul. Did you hear what he got on his biology test?"

I had, of course. He scored 80 out of 100.

"Yes," I said. "He worked hard."

"Well, it's more than that," Mrs. Marks gushed. "You've given him confidence. I saw your mitosis drawings. You found a way to teach him. I always knew he was smart, but he didn't see it. Thanks to you, he has a whole new perspective on his ability to take tests."

"I really didn't do that much," I said, feeling my cheeks redden.

"Don't be modest," Mr. Marks said.

He must have been a linebacker in his day. The man was fit, but solid. Paul had inherited the man's blond hair and green eyes.

"He would have never done it when he was seeing that awful Margaret," Mrs. Marks whispered. "She called him constantly, distracting my boy from his studies. And the drama. Good grief, doesn't she know that nobody loves a drama queen?"

Her words made me smile. This was Dad's Relationship Rule #3: Nobody loves a drama queen. Even if they say they do. My father would have liked this woman.

"You are a breath of fresh air." Paul's mom patted my leg then turned her attention to the game. "Oh look, we've won the toss."

On the field, a red-haired woman stepped into centerfield carrying a microphone. I squinted. Was that Faye from dog class? What was she doing here? The announcer's voice boomed, welcoming the spectators from the home and opposing teams.

"Tonight, we have a special treat," the man continued. "Our very own Honorable Judge Faye Shoeman will sing the national anthem."

I faced the flag. As I listened to my agility classmate belt out the high notes, I struggled to process this information. Faye was a judge. Is that why Matthew had said the woman got a lot of slack? Was it possible that she wasn't related to the ghost boy?

After it ended and the crowd quieted, the players assembled for introductions. As quarterback, Paul's name was first. The crowd exploded in applause. Mrs. Marks went into another frenzy. Paul scanned the stands until he spotted me. His face shone as he waved. I wondered if Margaret was there. Had she seen who Paul had acknowledged? I cheered along with the crowd to blend in.

The athletes now assembled for the kickoff. Was Paul relating the formation to the prophase stage of mitosis as he called numbers for the snap or was his mind only on football? In moments, he had the ball, dodged a potential sack, and rolled clear to throw a thirty-yard pass. First down. The crowd roared approval. Three plays later, Walnut Acres had six points on the scoreboard. The kick was good and we were ahead seven to zero.

People stomped their feet, making the bleachers shudder earthquake-style while they chanted. "Paul Marks, Paul Marks." How could Paul not love this adoration? How could I not love him? Paul was a hero.

"So," Mrs. Marks said, "Paul said your hearing didn't go your way. You must be disappointed, but I have to admit I was a bit relieved. You are much too young to be living alone. I mean, Walnut Acres is a safe place to live, but things happen, even here."

Did she mean Kyle's little brother? Could she know of a connection to Dr. Pullman? She might know if Mrs. Warzueski was ever a suspect. If I asked, would she tell Paul that we discussed the boy's disappearance? He would be annoyed since he wanted me to stop investigating.

On the field, Northridge had failed to get a first down, and Paul headed to the scrimmage line. If I broached the subject at halftime under the guise of my senior project, I could mention the boy's disappearance. For now though, I turned my attention to Paul.

We got a turnover, Northridge kicked a field goal, then Paul ran the ball over the goal line for a second touchdown. We had a solid lead at halftime: 14 to 3. But the game was far from settled. Northridge was known for their comebacks.

"Can I buy you a hot chocolate?" Mrs. Marks yelled over the cheerleader's halftime cheer.

A warm drink sounded good. Fall was definitely in the air. I shivered in the chill, but more importantly, the snack shack was at the entrance and far enough away from the intercom system that I might be able to hear her above the din.

"Yes, thank you," I said. "I'll come with you."

As we took our place in line, I tried to find a natural transition to the missing ghost boy. My senior project was a good place to start. Several folks wearing orange or black, even someone in Northridge-red, congratulated Mrs. Marks on Paul's performance. A few teens chatted or fussed with their cell phones. After no one seemed to pay any attention to us anymore, I opened my mouth to tell Mrs. Marks about my senior project. Someone touched my shoulder.

"Hello, Sarah," Dr. Pullman said, "I was wondering if I'd run into you tonight."

"Dr. Pullman," I blurted. "What are you doing here?"

I felt small standing next to him. He had to be at least six feet from head to toe. He was dressed in black, all he needed was a jack-o'-lantern mask to complete his outfit. But had the figure at the bottom of my driveway been this tall? It had been dark and Pumpkin Man had been far away, not to mention how frightened I had been. Then again, almost everyone was dressed in orange or black tonight. Still this didn't seem like a coincidence. I searched for Dr. Griffin, but if she was here, he must have left her in the stands.

"I used to be the kicker for this team back in the day," he laughed. "I still come to the big games."

His manner was easy. He was so likeable. I couldn't picture him killing a toddler.

"Dear?" Mrs. Marks said.

I had been so jarred by Dr. Pullman's appearance that I had forgotten to introduce Mrs. Marks.

"Oh, I'm so sorry," I said to her. "Mrs. Marks, this is Dr. Pullman. He's a veterinarian and also spoke on my behalf at my emancipation hearing."

Mrs. Marks offered her hand. "Nice to meet you."

Was that an expression of surprise that crossed his face? Did he think I came alone? Had he tracked me down to invite me to sit with him?

Dr. Pullman shook her hand. "Marks? As in the quarterback's mom? He's amazing."

The line moved, and Mrs. Marks stepped to the window.

"Whipped cream, Sarah?" Mrs. Marks asked.

"Yes, please."

"Three hot chocolates with whipped cream," she said, stepping close to the window.

"Is Dr. Griffin here?" I asked.

"Uh, no," he said.

The man suddenly seemed anxious to get away. He backed up, glancing between Mrs. Marks and me as though trying to decide how or why the woman would treat me to a warm beverage.

"Well, I better get back in line," he said. "Nice to see you."

Then he turned and disappeared into the concession stand line. Mrs. Marks handed me my hot chocolate and we headed back to our seats. I was disappointed that I had missed my opportunity to gather information on the ghost boy's disappearance.

She hadn't reacted to Dr. Pullman with recognition. Paul had said his mother always provided food whenever there was a community emergency. She must have followed the events of the little Warzueski boy's case. If Dr. Pullman had ever been a suspect, she would have known, but she hadn't even flinched when he offered his hand. The only connection between the toddler and the man was a phone number. Old numbers were reissued when people changed their contact information. Maybe Dr. Pullman was the nice guy he appeared to be.

Back in our seats, I glanced around the stands. I couldn't find Dr. Pullman in the crowd. The cheerleaders finished their routine for the halftime entertainment, and the band blasted the prelude to Survivor's "The Eye of the Tiger." Then padded football players exploded onto the field. And there was Paul leading the charge. This time he didn't look into the stands.

Forty-five minutes later, Paul led his team to victory. The fans went wild. I was swept onto the field with everyone else. In the crush of humanity, I lost Paul's parents. Up ahead, Paul's teammates and fellow students thumped him on the back. He was smiling, and laughing, and not looking at anyone except the people around him.

Margaret created a furrow through the crowd like a plow horse. When she reached Paul, she flung her arms around his neck and kissed him full on the lips. I wanted to slap her. I wanted to put a snake in her pants. Who the hell did she think she was? When Paul leaned into her, I turned my back. An ache slid into my heart. I wanted to go home. I wanted to pull Shadow into my lap and match the rhythm of her breathing with mine.

As I left, I noticed Dr. Pullman waving at me to come toward him. The urgency in his expression sent alarm bells jangling. His interest in me, his presence here, creeped me out. At least a dozen people separated us so I pretended I didn't see him.

Now, I was scared and upset. I had parked far away due to my late arrival. Would Dr. Pullman follow me then force me into his vehicle? In this chaos, what would prevent the man from snatching me right under everyone's noses? I searched for Paul's parents, but the crowd had swallowed them.

I didn't want to walk to my car along darkened streets, but I didn't have anyone I could ask to drive me home, except maybe Paul. He would help me, even if he and Margaret had reconciled. But the coach herded Paul and his teammates toward the locker room. In this throng of people, I had no way to intercept him.

For the second time tonight, I felt a hand on my shoulder. I almost screamed, convinced it was Dr. Pullman. But when I whipped around and saw the mop of red hair, I relaxed. I was so glad to see Kyle. I smiled wide.

I took his wrist and said. "Let's get out of here and go someplace where we can talk."

CHAPTER TWENTY-TWO

"I'll be judge, I'll be jury."

Kyle's two-door, silver Ford Escort shone in the glare of the stadium lights. He followed me to the passenger side to open my door like a gentleman. We agreed that he would give me a ride to my car a few blocks away. From there we would caravan to Pinky's Pizza to talk. I expected Kyle's considerate behavior to meet with my father's approval, but the buzz and crackle of my father's arrival suggested otherwise. What was his problem? I crossed my hands over my chest, so Dad couldn't grab an arm and try to pull me away.

"That was an exciting game, wasn't it?" I said.

Dejected-looking people dressed in red passed by, heading to their vehicles. Most of the fans in orange and black were probably still on the field celebrating. No sign of Dr. Pullman, but there was enough of a crowd for him to blend with the masses in his dark clothing.

"Yeah," Kyle said, stepping aside to give me room to enter the car. "I wasn't sure the team would pull off a win when Northridge scored and tied the game in the third quarter, but Paul came through with a quarterback sneak."

Dad tried to block my entry into the car. I elbowed my way inside. Kyle walked behind the vehicle then paused at the driver's side. His fingers flew over his phone keypad. I imagined he texted his parents to tell them of his plans, reminding me that I should call Mr. O'Shawnessy. I reached into my pocket. Crap. I had left my phone in my Civic.

Dad's Relationship Rule #11 was to never forsake safety. Keep a cell phone on you, meet dates in public places and never, ever, get high or drunk on a date. Double crap. I should be driving myself and I should have brought my phone.

Yet, a short car ride with someone I knew seemed better than walking back to my car alone with Dr. Pullman stalking me. Besides, a five-minute drive separated me from my Civic. After that I would be surrounded by other people at Pinky's and have my phone.

"I'm three blocks over on Main Street in front of Wells Fargo," I said as Kyle settled into the driver's seat and started the car.

We exited the lot then Kyle turned right at the first stoplight. But at the stop sign, he turned left in the opposite direction I expected.

"Don't forget my car," I said.

"It's going to be a real pain to find parking at Pinky's," he said. "Don't worry, I'll take you back to your car afterward."

I studied his face. He seemed relaxed. What he suggested did make sense. Still, I wanted my phone. I could ask to borrow his to call Mr. O'Shawnessy. But if I did, Kyle would know I didn't have one. I decided to wait until we got to Pinky's. If Margaret was there, I could ask her to tell Mr. O'Shawnessy that we were both at the pizza place. But what if Paul came too? I couldn't bear to watch Margaret drape herself on him like a necklace. And what would Paul think of me arriving with Kyle?

The silence in the car felt awkward. If I apologized, maybe I wouldn't feel so weird.

"So," I said, "what I wanted to tell you is that I didn't plan to write "loser" on that paper. I was actually trying to say loose rat, but Mrs. Durgette came and I was rushing. You see I had to go straight home after school. I know it sounds crazy, but I had to get home to catch my neighbor's escaped pet. I am so sorry. I messed up and made things worse."

I looked for Kyle's reaction as he made a right turn onto California Avenue. Pinky's was a few blocks up. His expression hadn't changed. I wondered if he'd heard me. As he accelerated, Kyle kept glancing in the rearview mirror.

"Not again," he said between clenched teeth. "I texted her, I told her where I was going and who I was with, and still my mom pulls this."

Huh? I turned in my seat. A silver Lexus was less than a car length behind. I recognized the vehicle without having to look at the driver. Dr. Pullman had followed us. I slouched in my seat then felt silly. The man must know I was inside since he had tailed us. But what did Kyle's mom have to do with any of this?

"Pulls what?" I said.

Kyle's whole body tensed. His fists gripped the steering wheel as if we were hydroplaning and about to crash.

"This is your fault," he said through clenched teeth. "Do you realize what you've done?"

I was lost. What had I done? I leaned against my door, putting as much distance between us as I could.

The car swerved into Pinky's lot, jerking me so hard I had to brace against the dashboard to keep from slamming my shoulder back into the car door. As Kyle had predicted, there wasn't a parking spot to be had. A line of red-clad teens funneled into the front door. Northridge fans had swarmed the place.

Crap. A car in front of us had its emergency lights on. The driver must have hopped out for a moment. We were trapped.

I considered bolting from the vehicle, but with my car parked about six blocks away, that seemed foolish. Kyle's gaze remained fixed on his rearview mirror. I turned around, but Dr. Pullman had not entered the lot. Had he stopped up the street? Was I safer staying with Kyle? He had told the truth about Pinky's.

"I'm sorry, Kyle. I don't seem to be able to do anything right around you. Can you tell me what I did? Maybe I can fix it."

He honked his horn. A boy chatting near the entrance to Pinky's came jogging back to his car, waving an apology. I looked behind us again, but the silver Lexus wasn't in sight.

"It's too late, Sarah. When my mom saw that picture of my stepbrother on your table, she went off the deep end again. It had taken over five years, but Mom had finally started letting me go out by myself. Now, thanks to you, she's got my uncle tailing my every move again."

"Dr. Pullman is your uncle?"

Kyle nodded. Since Kyle's last name was Bowman that would mean that Mrs. Warzueski was Dr. Pullman's sister. I scratched my head. Here I thought the man was stalking me, when he had come to the football game because of Kyle. This explained why Dr. Pullman's phone number had been on the little boy's paper. Putting a card in a toddler's pocket with Mom and Dad's information along with an emergency contact was common practice. Hadn't Dr. Pullman been surprised when Dr. Griffin said Kyle was my boyfriend? He would have been interested in who his nephew was seeing.

Kyle slammed the palm of his hand on the wheel. "Err. I wish Tobin had never been born."

"Oh, Kyle. You don't mean that." I touched his arm. "I'm so sorry. Missing children is the topic for my senior project. That's why I had a copy of your brother's photo. If

I had known your mother was the locksmith, I would have hidden it. Is there anything I can do? Anything at all?"

The warm air of my father's hand covered my mouth. My father was in the back seat spying on us. Good grief. What did my dad think I meant by "anything at all?" Kyle wouldn't take advantage of me that way. What was the use of the relationship rules if Dad didn't trust me?

Kyle's shoulders slumped. He exhaled a long sigh then pushed red curls from his forehead.

"No, the damage is done." Kyle shook his head. "I'm sorry I yelled at you. It's just so frustrating that my mom's so overprotective."

I pasted a smug look on my face and turned toward the back seat to make a point with my father. Kyle's car lurched forward as the vehicle in front of him moved, providing enough space for him to swerve around.

"There's no parking, so we might as well go get your car and go home," he sighed. "But I'm glad you told me about the loser thing. I should have let you explain sooner, but it's all good now. Hey, are you going trick or treating tomorrow?"

He transformed when his mood changed. His dimples deepened as he smiled at me. I didn't want to spoil the mood by telling him that I had fallen for Paul when I had already caused him so much trouble. Besides, for all I knew, Paul was with Margaret, or a cheerleader, or maybe the whole pom-pom waving squad right now. He could have any girl, so why would he bother with me?

Except Paul did like me. I felt it. Why risk changing that by accepting Kyle's offer? Anyway, neighbors tended to frown upon older kids trick or treating for free candy.

"I think I'm a little old," I said with an embarrassed laugh.

Thank goodness we were almost back to where I parked. I glanced over my shoulder. Dr. Pullman had the decency to hang back a few car lengths, but he was still there. Poor Kyle.

"Take a right here. That's it. The white Civic."

Kyle maneuvered his car next to mine and turned in his seat to face me. His awkwardness charmed me. Did he plan to ask again? My answer wouldn't change, and I felt bad that I didn't feel the same about him anymore.

"You should come. The Shell Ridge neighborhood caters to teens, and the homeowners don't mind. It's a tradition for seniors at Walnut Acres High to trick or treat as a group."

The warm air of my father's hand covered my mouth once again, but I twisted in my seat and leaned forward to extricate myself from his ghostly protest. I wanted to decline, but guilt descended. Hadn't I just asked if there was anything at all I could do to help him? Going trick or treating might lift his spirits. And this was a group event, not a date. I would tell Paul of my plans and suggest the three of us hang out together.

"Sounds fun," I said. "I'll meet you there. What time?"

"Eight o'clock."

He waited for me to get inside my car before driving off. I pulled my phone from the console. I had three texts from Paul asking me to call. The last text said, *@ Extreme Pizza, please come.*

"Yes," I said aloud, bobbing up and down with enthusiasm, then felt foolish, afraid someone witnessed my outburst.

No one lingered nearby. Only a few cars had passed since Kyle left. If Dr. Pullman's had been one of them, I had missed it while checking my messages.

My phone also showed two missed calls from Paul. I hit call back. Paul's phone rang and rang. I imagined restaurant racket masked the ringtone. I would drive over and surprise him then phone Mr. O'Shawnessy and describe my plans.

Extreme Pizza was a mile or so away near Paul's home. I should have anticipated the same parking problem as Pinky's, but I had been so excited about Paul's invite and hadn't thought through what to do when I got there.

People clustered around the entrance. The front door had been propped open. The loud music vibrated in my chest. I craned my neck to see inside as I coasted by in my car. The place was packed.

I exited the lot, scanning the street for a place to park. Not a space to be had. I drove around the block. No luck. The next block over was in a residential neighborhood without streetlights. Justified or not, I had been frightened enough for one night. Walking alone on a dark street in an unfamiliar neighborhood was a bad idea.

I circled back. Still nothing. Frustration set in. It was 9:30. My driving curfew was ten. It would take fifteen minutes to drive home. Disappointed, I double-parked in the Extreme Pizza lot and dialed Paul's number. Maybe he would come outside and at least I could congratulate him in person. No answer again.

"Paul, it's Sarah," I said to his voicemail. "I'm so sorry. I've been trying to find a parking spot but it's impossible, so I'm heading home. Great job tonight. I am so proud of you. Call me later."

As I pointed my Civic toward home, I tried not to think of the cheerleaders surrounding Paul or the way Margaret had flung herself on him. Maybe he was too busy kissing her to bother responding to my voicemail. No, Paul was over her. What I needed to focus on now was my immediate problem. I needed a Halloween costume for tomorrow night.

The mall might hold a few remnants. Dad had taken me to the Superstore on Halloween when I was twelve. We lived in Kansas City and the only costumes left in my size were for tall kids: Barney or Hello Kitty. I had been angry with Dad for waiting so long, now here I was in the same situation.

I had a set of white sheets to make a ghost costume. Once the idea formed, it seemed perfect. The outfit would be a tribute to Kyle's stepbrother, Tobin.

* * *

By 10:30, I finished my costume. I examined the bottom edge of the sheet, jagged in traditional ghost fashion. It was perfect. But I still hadn't heard from Paul and all I could think about was Margaret kissing him on the field. Were they back together?

Margaret had come in fifteen minutes ago, pushing the limits of her curfew, as usual. She didn't look my way. What did that mean? If they were together, Paul must be home by now. I had to find out. I picked up my phone and dialed his number. It rang five times, and I almost gave up when he answered.

"What do you want, Sarah?"

His voice was crisp, the words staccato. I was taken aback. I had tried my best to come to the celebration. I never expected him to be this upset, unless ... he really was back with the Evil Queen and was deflecting his guilt as anger. I kept my voice low in case Margaret pressed her ear to my door.

"I ... I want to congratulate you," I whispered. "What's wrong?"

"Don't give me the innocent 'I don't know what you mean' act. Margaret said she saw you leave the game with Kyle."

Margaret—always behind the drama in my life. At least, this time she had told the truth. But had she used it to reel Paul back into her web?

"Oh," I said. "She's right. I did. But it's not what you think."

"Really? One of the best days of my life, and I wanted you by my side, but you go running off with your...your boyfriend."

"He's not my boyfriend. He never was." I had hurt Paul's feelings, and I wanted to apologize. "I tried to reach you. But there were so many people."

"Really? You're not interested in Kyle?"

Disbelief laced his tone. Why did my best intentions always result in a mess? Relationship Rule #5 came to mind: Always be honest. And it was true. I wasn't interested in Kyle. Not anymore.

"Nope. Are you kidding? I wanted to be with you. Except everyone else wanted to stand by your side too."

"There were a lot of people, weren't there?"

I could hear the smile in his voice. But the thought of all those people surrounding him reminded me of what I witnessed.

"Yeah, including Margaret. Did you like her kiss? Is that why you didn't respond to my texts?"

I closed my eyes and held my breath. I tipped my head back and waited.

"What? No. Absolutely not," he said.

All the tension melted away.

"Okay," I said.

"I'm glad we got that settled," he said.

"Me too," I said. "You're amazing. I'm sorry I missed out on the celebration. I really did try to come to pizza."

"So ... Coach gave us the night off tomorrow night. Let's go trick or treating now that I'm free to make myself into Tarzan or a vampire or ... or a eukaryote."

I laughed then bit my lower lip. How could I explain that I had already made plans with Kyle?

"Actually, I just finished my costume and there's no one I would rather go with more than you."

"Yeah? Then this is the best day of my life."

I shifted from foot to foot. It wasn't right to burst his bubble. He was so happy. He deserved to have this one perfect day.

"There's just one thing. I ... I ... Oh, Paul, this is going to sound so wrong."

"What is it? You can tell me. If we can't talk then we don't really have anything."

I gnawed a fingernail. The thing I loved most about him was his moral center.

I thought how I had judged him as a dumb jock. But since our tutoring session, and after he abandoned his M.T. Anderson jargon, he had been speaking intelligently. We were good together, but my actions tonight might cause him to walk away.

"I want you to come with us," I said at last. "Me and Kyle. I already agreed to go with him."

Everything went still. I waited for him to speak. The end of the line held only dead silence.

I looked at the phone and saw we had been disconnected. If I were in his shoes, I probably would have hung up too. I hit redial, but Paul didn't pick up. Maybe this was his way of saying we didn't have anything.

I sighed. I needed to give Shadow her evening bone and lock her doggie door so she couldn't go outside to bark at raccoons or cats and annoy the neighbors. The image of the jack-o'-lantern killer formed. I no longer felt comfortable making the short jaunt over to my own house in the dark, but I had no choice.

I pulled the flashlight from my dresser drawer and poked my head into the hall. No light filtered under the bedroom doors inside the house. Margaret and Mr. O'Shawnessy must have gone to sleep already. I tiptoed to the front room window in the dark and pulled the curtain aside. No figure stood at the base of my driveway or on my front porch. What if the killer lay in wait inside my house? I told myself not to be ridiculous. Shadow would be barking.

I dashed across to my front porch, stepped inside, locked the door behind me, and flipped on the light. Shadow jumped up, her hind end wiggling so fast I couldn't keep track of the metronome of her tail. I flung my arms around her, scratching behind her ears until she calmed. At the back door, I slid the lock on the doggie door.

"Okay, girl. Now, let's get you a bone."

The photo of the ghost boy caught my eye as I passed through the dining room. Tobin's smiling face tugged at my heart. Who could kill an innocent child?

I selected a dog bone from the box and tossed it in the air. Shadow caught it before it hit the ground then trotted off to enjoy her treat.

In the dining room, I studied Tobin's innocent face. I told myself to leave it alone. My meddling had already caused enough damage, but curiosity took hold. I would just do a quick computer search.

I Googled "Tobin Warzueski."

I clicked on the first hit. It was an old article featured in an e-zine magazine called *Crime-Lit.*

Most people think of Halloween as an evening of candy collection. The goblins and ghouls are imaginary fiends that can't hurt you. No one ever expects one of those costumed figures to run off with your child, but that's what happened to the Warzueski family in a small community in the town of Walnut Acres. Ten-year-old Kyle and his baby stepbrother Tobin left their home at 7:30 p.m. At 9:30 p.m., a strange man ran up behind them and snatched the toddler. To this day, no one knows what happened to Tobin.

Wow. Poor Kyle. It hadn't occurred to me that Kyle might have been the last one to see his brother.

The rest of the piece focused on how to keep your child safe on Halloween night and the importance of having an adult escort. I exited back to the search results and clicked on the next entry. It was an article from the local newspaper *Diablo Centennial* on November 1, the day after the abduction. The kidnapping made front-page news, complete with photos. The first picture showed a close-up of Mrs. Warzueski's stricken face. She clutched her eldest son to her chest. Only Kyle's cluster of red curls were visible. The rest of him was masked by his mom's embrace. The photo next to it showed the same picture of Tobin used for the flyer. The third was a map, showing the location of the incident. The kidnapping had occurred less than a block from the high school. The last photo showed a policeman poking through construction debris with a German Shepherd. The cop had a pot belly and a giant handlebar moustache. The caption read, "Detective Mathers investigates the site of the new high school wing with his cadaver dog for signs of the missing boy."

The high school. Why hadn't it occurred to me before? Dr. Griffin had said that ghosts were often location-bound, unable to wander far from where they were killed. No wonder the little boy hung around in my art classroom. The police dog must have missed his scent, because I was convinced the boy's remains were buried under the foundation.

CHAPTER TWENTY-THREE

From verses read by the White Rabbit: "A secret, kept from all the rest,"

After a final hug and belly rub for Shadow, I sprinted across my driveway back to my guardian's house. No jack-o'-lantern figure lurked in the shadows. I was too tired to floss my teeth, so I collapsed onto the bed. But my brain wouldn't switch off.

I needed a convincing story as to how I might know that Tobin's remains were under my art classroom. Short of a confession by the killer, what would compel the authorities to destroy school property by digging for a body?

I must have dozed off at some point, but it seemed like I had only drifted off for a moment, when my phone jarred me awake. Even in my sleepy state, the ring tone, Bob Marley's "Redemption Song," meant Mrs. Wright was calling. The song's theme of independence had been the perfect fit since freedom was what Mrs. Wright meant to me.

I hit the answer button.

"Hello, Mrs. Wright," I said, ending with a yawn.

"Good morning, Sarah," my social worker said in a resigned voice. "I'm sorry to call so early but I wanted to catch you before school. I'm having a tough time locating your mother's death certificate. I must have wrong information. I have the date of your mother's death as your birthday, the location as Akron, Ohio, and her name as Marianne Whitman, no middle or maiden name."

I rubbed the sleep from my eyes and yawned again. Dad had said my mother had died birthing me and I was born in Akron.

"Sounds right to me," I said.

"I've already tried variations in the spelling of the first name and searched nearby counties. I changed the date since you were born just after midnight and it was possible your mother passed on shortly before you were delivered. There were no matches. I need something more."

Something more? My father had been a closed book on the subject of my mother. I had been through his papers and there was nothing. Not his marriage certificate, not even a wedding photo.

"I can't help you. My father refused to talk about her."

"The name on the certificate should be the name she used at her death. I'm grasping at straws here, Sarah. What about your aunt in Arizona? Would she know anything?"

"No. As I've said before, my aunt isn't well in the head. Dad said he and my mom eloped."

"There has to be something in your medical records."

"I doubt it. We moved a lot because of Dad's job. I haven't really been sick much. I only went into the ER for bronchitis once and clinics for shots. When I tried out for tennis two years ago, I had a physical at the school, but my dad wrote in the health history."

"All right," she said with a sigh.

I didn't like the sound of defeat in her voice. What was wrong with the judge? Even if my mother were alive, she wasn't likely to ride into town on a white horse after seventeen years and suddenly decide to raise me.

"What happens if we can't get the death certificate by Monday...or ever?" I asked.

"Any other judge would look the other way. With Judge Heart, who knows? We might get lucky, and she'll be in the mood to clear out cases. I'll bring the documentation to show how thoroughly I searched for the death certificate."

"Isn't there something else you can do?" I said. "Can't you request a different judge?"

"I'd have to have cause and, even if granted, your case would be placed on the bottom of the pile. You could be looking at a six-month delay."

Six more months of Margaret? Really? Pull the trigger now. I groaned aloud.

"Hang in there, Sarah. You're like a poster child for a mature teen girl. I've got a good feeling about this."

"Thanks, Mrs. Wright. I appreciate your confidence."

I hadn't put the phone away before it broadcast the lyrics to Green Day's *"Warning."* Dr. Griffin. Should I answer it? Was she calling to gloat about having her hood ornament back and celebrate that I had nothing over her anymore? Except I did. In a small way. I knew the truth of Mansfield-the-rat's cause of death.

"Hello," I said.

"Sarah, Sarah, Sarah." Dr. Griffin tsked into the phone as if it pained her to voice her disappointment. "Why didn't you leave it alone like I asked? Didn't that snotty girl tell you? Do you think you live in a rabbit hole and nothing you do affects what happens above ground? Well, I've got news for you. Your nosey nose has messed up my dinner plans tonight."

"I have no idea what you are talking about," I said.

But all of a sudden something clicked, and I suspected I did. If Kyle had told his mother of his trick or treating plans, she probably told him Dr. Pullman would have to chaperone us.

"Lose the Miss Innocent act," she spat. "Fix this, Sarah. Stay home and pass out candy with Kyle so Mark won't be forced to babysit a couple of teenagers. If you don't, I'll be at the courthouse on Monday, and I'll have a lot to say to the judge. Someone needs to remind that decision-maker about the dangers that can befall a young girl living alone."

Annoyance clouded my thoughts. I took a lungful of air and closed my eyes. It wasn't her place to tell me who I could go out with and when.

"I'll take your opinion under advisement," I said then disconnected.

Poor Kyle having to be shadowed like a little kid. Would it be so awful to stay home and pass out candy with Kyle as Dr. Griffin suggested? Wouldn't that be better than having Dr. Pullman tailing us through the streets in front of our classmates? Besides, we wouldn't run into Paul. I stared at the red numerals on the clock: 7:45 a.m.

Great. I had overslept. Now there was no time to review the material for my physics exam. I rolled out of bed trying to get my head around key facts that would probably be on the test. Light exhibits properties of waves, but sometimes it can act as a particle. A wave is defined by four properties: reflection, refraction, diffraction, and . . . My mind went blank. The last component started with an "I." What was it? Oh, yes. Something I had been doing too much of: interference.

* * *

I didn't have any morning classes with Kyle. No way to contact him about changing our plans from trick or treating to passing out candy. My plan was to intercept him at lunch before he joined the other seniors. I hovered in the hallway to observe the senior lunch hang out.

Paul had been one of the early arrivals to the walnut tree. He didn't look like a guy who led his team to the championships. His shoulders drooped, and his deadpan face appeared as if it had forgotten how to smile. Margaret batted her green eyes at him, but he kept looking toward the spot of grass where I usually ate by myself.

I wanted to make up with Paul, but at the same time, I didn't want any guy dictating who I hung out with. One of the rules I had forgotten came to mind: Relationship Rule #7: Run like the wind from possessive guys. Did that apply to Paul? Hadn't I told Dr. Griffin that Kyle was my boyfriend in front of Paul when he helped lift the couch, even though it was a lie? If Paul said he had made plans to trick or treat with Margaret, how would I feel? But I couldn't ditch Kyle who had been through so much. Besides, Relationship Rule #6 was never make a promise that you don't intend to keep.

A cluster of students congregated at a bank of lockers further down the hallway. Kyle's red curls glowed like a beacon. It was impossible not to spot him in a crowd.

"Hey," I said, weaving through a group of freshmen to reach him.

The familiar snap, crackle, pop announcing my father's appearance didn't faze me today. From the direction of the sound and the waft of warm air immediately before me, I knew he had materialized to block my path to Kyle. What was his problem? What did Dad know about relationships anyway? He never dated. For all I knew, he had knocked up my mother, never married her then was so filled with remorse when she died that he idolized her. Or maybe she never loved him, and that knowledge was too painful, so he destroyed the reminders of her. I wish he had saved something, like a special dress wrapped in plastic that retained her apple scent. I wish he had thought about what I might want. I hugged my lunch to my chest and side-stepped my father.

"Sarah," Kyle grinned, holding up his paper sack. "I brought my lunch today since I know you have to get Shadow and don't have time for the cafeteria line. Want to eat at the picnic tables with me?"

I nodded, relieved that I wouldn't have to sit out front with Kyle within Paul's view. A few seniors ate at the tables, but mostly juniors gathered there. We seated ourselves at the table closest to the office. It was always the last to fill up, since the principal had a view of this one from his desk. After a moment, a breeze carried a waft of warm air from my right. Dad must have taken the spot next to me.

"Ready for tonight?" Kyle asked, pulling a sandwich from his bag.

I was hoping to ease into this conversation, but maybe it was just as well to tackle the issue head-on. Like medicine, it was better to get it over with quickly.

"Uh ... I wanted to talk to you about that," I said, pulling an apple from my lunch. "I was thinking it would be fun to pass out candy together at your house instead."

Kyle wrinkled his nose as if he caught a whiff of rotting fish. "Err ... our Halloween celebration involves turning out the lights and going to bed early. We haven't answered the door since Tobin ..."

How insensitive of me. I hadn't thought how Kyle's mom would feel having costumed children on her doorstep—every little kid would be a reminder of what she had lost. Even Kyle must have a lot of emotions to sort through every time October rolled around.

"Oh," I said. "I didn't realize."

"I used to get so angry," he said.

Kyle bit into his sandwich like a lioness taking down its prey. It appeared his resentment still ran deep. I would probably be bitter too if I had been imprisoned in my home while my friends were out raking in the candy. My father scooted closer, trying to push me off the seat, but I anchored my feet against the table legs and held my ground.

I considered suggesting that he come to my house to pass out candy instead, but that probably wouldn't work. Not only would Mr. O'Shawnessy object, but Dr. Pullman might follow Kyle there and park out front. I was out of ideas.

Kyle looked at me askance. I took a bite of fruit and straightened my posture so that it didn't look like I was resisting falling to the ground, which was the challenge I faced.

"Well, it will be fun going one last time," I said hoping to brighten his mood.

"Yeah. And it will be even better if you come."

What a moron I was. Of course, he would go without me. I approached this problem all wrong. I should convince Dr. Pullman to keep his date with Dr. Griffin. Why should

Kyle have to miss out on his last chance to celebrate Halloween? Why should I change my plans because of an overprotective mother? Kyle was almost an adult and we would be hanging out with a big group. No one would kidnap her teenage son.

"You're right. We're seniors. It will be our last chance to dress up and knock on doors. Where should I meet you? And what sort of evil monster should I look for?"

Kyle laughed. I loved those dimples.

"I was going to go as a rhino," he said. "But I changed my mind and now my costume is top secret."

Before Paul had charmed me, I longed to sit with this boy and eat lunch. Now, here I sat across from him, and all I felt was confused.

"I can pick you up," he said.

"Thanks, but my guardian is strict. He thinks I'm too young to be alone with boys. I'll meet you there."

"Okay, if that's how it has to be. Let's say the corner of Fremont and Azalea; it's a block away from the main gathering spot."

"How will I know it's you if I don't know what costume you're wearing?"

"What are you dressing up as?" he said.

"Well, I had to improvise. I made a ghost outfit from a sheet last night. It's pretty lame, so you won't have a problem finding me. I'll be there at eight sharp."

"Now, fess up. What's your costume?"

He chuckled. "You'll have to wait and see."

He looked like a little kid with that mischievous grin. This evening meant a lot to him. That he picked me to share it with him made me feel special.

Dad nudged me harder and harder. I slid out from the bench before Dad succeeded in unseating me with a stronger shove. I had just enough time to get Shadow and return on time if I left now anyway.

* * *

Back at school I realized I forgot to bring Shadow's medicine. I had been preoccupied with thoughts of Kyle and Paul. I dreaded walking into art class and seeing Paul. One look at his disappointed face and I would want to bail on Kyle tonight, but it wouldn't be fair to ruin Kyle's last Halloween when he had lost so much.

The first thing I noticed as I entered the classroom was Paul's empty seat. He looked healthy at lunch so there was only one reason I could think of as to why he wouldn't be here. Could I have hurt him that much so that he would rather cut class than face me?

Mrs. Durgette set us straight to work the moment the bell rang, so I didn't have a chance to observe the ghost boy. Ten minutes into class, Shadow stood. Mrs. Durgette announced a break, and I called my dog to my side, crooning over how good she was.

Kyle elbowed me and lifted a sheet of drawing paper to show me the ghost he sketched. The shoes poking out from beneath the jagged ends of the sheet were my Converses. I had been so caught up in my drawing that I hadn't noticed that he had been working on a drawing other than our current assignment. I nodded. He would know how to find me tonight all right.

Mrs. Durgette launched into a lecture on shading techniques. Basic stuff that gave my mind an opportunity to wander. I scanned the room looking for where Tobin had stashed his pumpkin toy. He hadn't had it yesterday. What if he kept his treasures near where his bones lay? If I knew where that was, I could advise the police where to dig.

If I had brought Shadow's pills, a quick peek might provide information as to the whereabouts of the remains. I told myself a few minutes wouldn't matter. I had been careful to use her for only short periods, and Shadow hadn't had any ill effects. She had only gone into seizure when I had used her ability for fifteen minutes straight.

I slipped my fingers between Shadow's eyes. My father stood less than a foot away, towering over me, with his hands on his hips and an expression that would make a mosquito run for cover. He wasn't just angry, he fumed. I gasped and withdrew my fingers. Everyone looked up.

"What's wrong?" Kyle whispered.

"Ms. Whitman," Mrs. Durgette bellowed. "Is there something you'd like to share with the class?"

"No, Ma'am," I said, scrambling for an explanation for my exclamation. "Shadow's nose was cold and it surprised me. I apologize."

"Well, if your dog is distracting you then it's a good thing that this is her last day in class. Everyone has almost finished this assignment, so let's get back to it. Let's put her and her cold nose up front, shall we?"

What? Shadow was supposed to come to class for the next two days. Now I only had today to figure out where Tobin might be under the classroom floor. Whether my father liked it or not, and even though I didn't have Shadow's medication close at hand, I needed to use her to find the body which might help solve the crime.

At the next break, I didn't hesitate. My fingers flew into position. This time I was prepared for my father's wrath. He stood in exactly the same spot, and it occurred to me that maybe he blocked my view of the burial spot. My hunch was confirmed when I tried to crane my neck, and his body shifted. I scanned the rest of the room, but neither Tobin nor his toy was anywhere in sight. Had my father hidden him? Was he asleep behind Mrs. Durgette's desk?

Shadow's brief respite was called to a close, and I had to pose her again. As I positioned her, I drew an imaginary line from my father to the corner of the room. The drywall was discolored near the baseboard. What if the bones were in the wall, not under the foundation? I slipped my fingers in place, pretending to adjust the angle of Shadow's head. Tobin lay curled in the corner, asleep. He clutched the stuffed pumpkin and sucked on his thumb.

"Ms. Whitman," Mrs. Durgette said. "Is there a problem?"

I dropped my hand from Shadow's head. Cyndi twittered along with a few others. Even Kyle gave me an odd look. How long had I been staring at that corner? I shook my head.

"Sorry, I thought I saw a spider."

Shadow sneezed twice and blew her sit-stay. She bolted to Tobin's corner of the room. I called her back and settled her, but she rose to her feet, shook her head, and went back to sniff the toddler.

I grew alarmed. Sneezing and head shaking had preceded a seizure the last time I overused Shadow as my ghost-viewing medium. If only I could run to the nurse and get her medicine, but I had left the metronidazole at home. I should have never risked putting my fingers between her eyes.

The classroom had grown so quiet that I could hear the clock tick. Shadow's mouth opened into a lazy pant. She seemed fine now and didn't resist when I guided her rump into a sit with gentle pressure. Only ten minutes remained until class ended then a short drive home. She would get her pill and be just fine.

I gave Shadow a hand signal to stay then I took my place behind the easel. Kyle frowned as I selected a pencil. My face must reveal my anxiety. It seemed like hours, not minutes until the bell rang. I tried to stay focused on my drawing, but my attention kept traveling to the corner where Tobin lay sleeping. Each time my gaze went there, Kyle shifted in his seat.

Shadow wasn't her chipper self when we left the classroom. Her shortened tail stood still at half-mast. Even the tips of her ears drooped. I hurried my dog into the back seat of my Civic and cursed the line of cars blocking my exit from the parking lot. If only Margaret hadn't called the hotline, Shadow's medicine would be in my backpack. If only I had remembered to bring her pills. If only I had listened to my father and Paul and left the mystery surrounding Tobin's death alone.

CHAPTER TWENTY~FOUR

... said the Gryphon in an impatient tone: "explanations take such a dreadful time."

"Hang in there, sweet girl," I said, pushing the car to the maximum allowable speed limit. Shadow sneezed twice and shook her head over and over. Oh, what had I done?

I rushed inside my house, leaving my dog in the car. I grabbed one of her pills and a piece of cheese, then rushed back. Shadow gobbled the mozzarella with the tablet hidden in the center, then her mouth fell open into a lazy pant. The pill would take a while to work. I considered carrying her into the house, but in the end, I let her walk.

She collapsed onto her dog bed, and I curled around her body on the floor next to her. She whined and licked my face.

Should I call a vet? If I did, how could I explain? Last spring when I rushed her to the emergency clinic, Dr. Pullman had never questioned my explanation that Shadow had skidded into a wall and hit her head. But what would he think if I said Shadow had another brain injury? Would he be suspicious?

I stroked Shadow's sleek red fur until she dozed. A knock, knock, knock on my door jolted her from sleep. I cursed the intrusion as she scrambled to the entrance, barking and growling.

When I peered through the peephole, Dr. Griffin's turquoise eye blinked back like she was trying to see inside my house through the portal. She must have seen or heard me, because she stepped away about a body length from the door. She opened her lemon yellow purse. Her hand dipped inside, then reappeared clutching the hood ornament.

"I know you're in there, Sarah," she said, waving the shiny eagle. Then she resumed her position at the peephole. "Open the door."

Wielding an object that she had used to murder her boyfriend provided even more incentive to keep a locked door between us. This woman was crazy if she thought I was opening the door now. Shadow's bark morphed into an excited yip. I stroked her back to calm her.

"What do you want?" I said.

"I need to talk to you," she hissed. "Mark says that Kyle is still going trick or treating tonight."

"I tried my best. He's going with or without me. I don't see why you can't convince Dr. Pullman to stay with you if it's so important—that man adores you. Explain how embarrassing a chaperone would be for Kyle. He'll listen to you."

Dr. Griffin puckered her lips and she shook her head.

"Do yourself a favor and stay home tonight, Sarah. If you do, I won't disrupt your emancipation hearing on Monday. If you don't, well, you can't say I didn't warn you."

Witch. It wasn't my fault Dr. Pullman had agreed to his sister's request that he shadow Kyle. It wasn't my fault that Kyle's mother was overprotective. I wasn't giving in to Dr. Griffin's blackmail.

"Get off my property," I yelled. "And stay away from my hearing. If you don't, Mrs. Bellweather will get an earful ... and ... and so will Dr. Pullman."

Dr. Griffin smirked. "And who do you think these people will believe? You and another teen or me, an adult and a respected veterinarian?"

I didn't know about the respected part, but she was right. I had nothing on her without the ornament, which made her a threat, not only to me. Would she hurt Dr. Pullman if he didn't do as she wished?

"Last chance, Sarah."

I said nothing.

After a moment, I peeked through the peephole to see Dr. Griffin retreating. Shadow whined and scratched at the door. If I opened it, she might chase after Dr. Griffin and bite her on the butt.

"Sorry," I said to her.

Shadow sneezed then launched into a barking fit and lunged at the door as if her arch nemesis, a squirrel, teased her from the other side. I tried to catch her, but she danced out of reach. Her eyes bulged, and white rimmed the edges. Then she backed away, canted to one side, and collapsed.

"Shadow," I yelled, dropping to my knees.

Oh, no. Oh, please. I put my hand on her ribcage. A faint heartbeat fluttered under my fingertips. Her breath came in violent shudders. I didn't know what to do, but the woman outside would. I couldn't stand by and let Shadow die. I flung open the door. Dr. Griffin had only made it to the end of the drive.

"Wait," I shouted. "Help. Something's wrong with Shadow."

Dr. Griffin sprinted to the front door. Shadow's paws paddled the air, and her eyes had glazed over. Her breath came in unsteady hiccups.

"You've used her." She spat the words with such vehemence that my breath caught. "You selfish girl."

I deserved that. My throat constricted, but I forced myself to hold in the tears. I could indulge my feelings later. I took a deep breath.

"I gave her a metronidazole pill about ten minutes ago."

"The medicine should have kicked in by now," Dr. Griffin said.

Dr. Griffin should know. Her border collie had died when she had used her to communicate with the spirit world one time too many. Now, I might have done the same. She had warned me not to use Shadow to see ghosts, but I hadn't listened.

My dog trusted me. She had sat still during art class while I put my fingers between her eyes and watched Tobin. Now I had done it too often and for too long, and she could die.

"We've got to get her to Dr. Pullman," Dr. Griffin said.

When the veterinarian hefted her and rushed out the door, I didn't try to stop her. If Shadow stopped breathing, the vet would know what to do. I snatched my keys and backpack and followed, locking the door behind me.

"My car," I shouted. "I'll drive."

I burned rubber as I swerved onto the street. Please, please, I prayed. I'll kiss Margaret's boots, I'll do her chores. I'll make nice with her the rest of my life. I'll do anything, just don't let Shadow die. Not like this, not because of me. I could never forgive myself.

Dr. Griffin cradled my dog in her arms in the passenger seat. Shadow's labored breathing made my own chest seize When white froth appeared around Shadow's muzzle, tears travelled in rivulets down my cheekbones. Not now I told myself. Dr. Griffin had her phone next to her ear.

"Mark, it's Claudia. Are you at the clinic? Good. Please wait for us. Sarah and I are bringing Shadow in. I don't have time to explain. Five minutes. Set up a crash cart, okay?"

A crash cart? Like her heart might stop? No, no, no. This couldn't be happening. I floored the accelerator. Dr. Griffin's nails dug into my arm.

"Slow down," she snapped. "You'll kill us all."

I eased up on the accelerator. She was right. Several youngsters in costume accompanied by their mothers walked along the sidewalk. I didn't want any more tragedies on my conscience.

"Now tell me what happened. How long were your fingers between her eyes?"

How much should I confess? If I took the time to explain the full story, would she use it against me? I had to at least reveal what I did today.

"I used Shadow twice. No more than a few minutes each time. About an hour ago and again about a half hour ago."

"Weren't you supposed to be in school?" Dr. Griffin said, stroking Shadow's back. "Never mind. I remember now. Shadow was part of your art class project."

Shadow groaned then her quivering body stilled. For one awful moment, I thought she was gone, but then her breath settled into a regular rhythm.

"I think we are through the worst of it." Dr. Griffin let out a long sigh. "My dog survived a similar episode. If Shadow survives, you can't do this anymore. Do you hear me, Sarah? You could kill her."

"I won't. I'm done. I promise."

As I guided the Civic onto the freeway on-ramp, Dr. Griffin bent down and kissed the top of Shadow's head. She cared for my dog. I had to give her that much.

"Were you talking to your father?" she asked.

Did it matter who I had been conversing with? Should I tell her about Tobin? What if I didn't, and Shadow died because I withheld this information?

"I wanted to find out where the remains of Dr. Pullman's nephew are," I said.

"Tobin?" She looked at Shadow and then back at me. "You've seen his ghost?"

I nodded. I guided the car off the freeway, thankful how close the clinic was to my house. I willed my dog to hang on.

"Yes, I've seen Tobin. I had good intentions. Shadow has pointed out where his body is buried. I thought I might be able to give the family closure. I never intended to hurt Shadow."

The women stiffened. Her face took on the pale shade of a moon as I turned into the clinic parking lot. Dr. Griffin's hand trembled on the door handle. Did she know about the events surrounding Tobin's disappearance?

"Stop so I can get out," Dr. Griffin demanded.

"Okay, just a sec."

I drove close to the entrance. Dr. Griffin jumped from the car and ran inside with Shadow. I found a parking space and took the keys from the ignition.

What would she say happened to Shadow when Dr. Pullman asked? I had no idea how to explain. Dad's list didn't cover what to do when none of his relationship rules fit a situation.

As I reached for my backpack in the backseat, I noticed Dr. Griffin had left her purse on the floor of my car. The hood ornament. If I had the object, I could keep her away from my hearing. I could blackmail her into staying away from Shadow. It felt wrong to steal it back this way since she had helped me. But how could I not?

I sifted through her purse until I located the silver eagle. I couldn't keep it with me though. Across the parking lot, four planter boxes with geraniums lined one wall. But I had hidden the eagle in a potted plant before. Next to flowers were three garden gnomes adorned with dog faces: a pug, a basset and a collie. I double checked that no clinic window looked onto the lot then lifted the basset. It was hollow underneath. I stashed the ornament inside, then carrying both my backpack and Dr. Griffin's purse, I entered the clinic.

The smell of disinfectant and bleach burned my nose. No one staffed the reception desk. I hit the bell on the counter. When no one came, I collapsed into a plastic chair, putting the backpack and purse on the seat next to me. A few moments later, a young vet assistant appeared. She had frizzy red hair and wore a kelly-green smock and scrub pants. I recognized her. Leah had been here last spring when I had brought in Shadow.

"How is she, Leah?" I said, rising from my seat.

"Fine, fine. Dr. Pullman put her on an IV and gave her a mild sedative. We'll need to run tests, of course. But the doctor says her blood pressure is slowing, and her heart rate is strong, so the prognosis is good."

"May I see her?"

"Not yet. Dr. Pullman's working up the labs and Dr. Griffin is assisting. He asked me to let you know there's nothing to worry about and to get you started on paperwork."

"Okay, whatever you need."

She handed me a clipboard then disappeared through the interior door again. Leah had written my name and Shadow's name at the top and had checked the box as a returning patient. I stared at the first question: Has your address changed? It had. I lived next door now. But would I be home Monday? And did it matter? I still received my mail at my house. I checked the "no" box.

Next I confirmed my credit card information was up-to-date. The last question was difficult: Is there anything else we should know about your pet? I couldn't exactly write in that she sees ghosts. I couldn't say she had collapsed after I used her to see a missing child, so I could prove where the child was buried. I could tell them though, that I had given her a metronidazole pill, so I scribbled in the information. I wondered what reason Dr. Griffin had given Dr. Pullman for Shadow's seizure. Maybe she hadn't said anything.

Leah re-appeared, and I returned the clipboard to her. She scanned the information, nodded, and tucked the sheet into a manila folder with Shadow's name on it. Then she smiled.

"Shadow is resting in the back. Dr. Pullman will see you now."

I collected the bags and Leah escorted me through a door into an examination room. Dr. Pullman and Dr. Griffin sat in the two available chairs. They quieted as I entered the room. The blonde woman's expression held smug satisfaction. Dr. Pullman glowered at me.

I moved next to the exam table with my backpack slung over my shoulder so it hid Dr. Griffin's purse. Dr. Pullman's anger simmered in his expression, only I wasn't sure which of the stupid things I had done caused his annoyance: meddling in Tobin's death or harming Shadow.

Dr. Pullman cleared his throat and stood. His lips stretched into a single, tight line. The man was more than irritated—he was flat out angry. My knees buckled, and I leaned into the steel table.

"Claudia told me everything," he said, glaring at me. "I never thought you were capable ... After I vouched for you. Sarah, how could you have hit this sweet animal?"

"WHAT?" I shot daggers of hate in Dr. Griffin's direction. "I have never, ever hit my dog. She has never missed a meal or gone thirsty because of an empty water bowl."

Dr. Pullman shook his head. His jaw jutted forward and his scowl deepened.

"Claudia has offered to take in Shadow," Dr. Pullman continued in a stiff voice. "If you agree to let her take Shadow home, I won't bring in animal services. Did you know animal cruelty is a misdemeanor at a minimum and a six-month jail sentence? If Shadow had died, the charges could have escalated to a felony."

Conniving witch thought she had figured out a way to steal my dog. Good thing I had something to make her recant her lies.

"I don't know what she told you," I said, my voice trembling with outrage, "but she's ... mistaken."

Knowing how smitten Dr. Pullman was with her, I didn't dare call her a liar. I shrugged the backpack off my shoulder, revealing Dr. Griffin's purse. I thrust the bag at her. The woman's blue eyes widened.

"I'm afraid the contents spilled," I said. "You better check and make sure everything's there."

She clawed through her belongings while I took quick short breaths to ease my temper. I had to appear as if I were in control. Dr. Pullman must be convinced that I hadn't intentionally harmed Shadow, but I couldn't make his girlfriend look like a villain, even though she was.

"I know Dr. Griffin is quite fond of my dog," I said. "She might have overreacted a bit and misinterpreted what happened."

The woman squirmed. She had scoffed when I threatened to tell Dr. Pullman what she did to her high school boyfriend, but now that I held proof, she didn't look at me. Instead, she ogled my backpack. She knew what I had all right, but she was wrong to presume where she would find it.

"Well...no," she said.

I faced Dr. Pullman. If Dr. Griffin hadn't mentioned my use of Shadow's ghost-seeing ability, I might have a chance of swaying his opinion. My father used to say most people can tell when a person is telling the truth.

"Let me explain what really happened," I said. "Shadow was acting strange on the drive home from school. She's been posing as a living model in art class. I calmed her down, but when Dr. Griffin showed up, she went into a barking frenzy. I was so concerned that I didn't even open the door. Dr. Griffin was at the end of the driveway when my girl collapsed. I immediately asked for help. I imagine Dr. Griffin presumed the worst when she saw Shadow's condition. You didn't see me hit Shadow, right?"

Claudia shook her head.

"We drove straight here," I added. "That is the honest truth."

Dr. Pullman turned to Claudia, "Is this what happened?"

I glared at the woman, daring her to contradict me. Her gaze flitted to my bag then back to Dr. Pullman. She shifted in her seat.

"Well, um ... yes," she said. "Perhaps, I did overreact. Shadow is such a special dog, I guess I ... I let my emotions get the best of me."

Dr. Pullman studied his girlfriend with a furrowed brow. She wouldn't meet his gaze. Hah! I could tell he believed me.

"Well, then," Dr. Pullman said, "I'm glad we got that straightened out. Maybe we'll get lucky, and the lab reports will help us find a cause for Shadow's relapse. The brain is a complicated organ, and it's sometimes hard to pinpoint a problem. Maybe the stress of sitting still too long triggered the seizure. She did have head trauma earlier this year. At any rate, I think it best that Shadow not return to your art classroom."

"No problem. We're finished with the assignment. But even if we weren't, Shadow isn't going back there."

"Great," he said. "And I apologize for being so cross. Now, do you want to see Shadow?"

"Yes. Oh, yes, please."

"She's resting comfortably. We'll keep her under observation for the rest of the night, but she's stable, and I don't anticipate any problems. Don't worry. She'll be well cared for. There's no reason you can't celebrate Halloween."

He led me into a dimly lit room. To my surprise, Shadow had the deluxe suite—a penned enclosure with her own doggie bed.

I stepped inside the gated area and patted my sleeping dog. Her chest moved in a steady rise and fall. She looked peaceful.

Dr. Pullman glanced at his watch. "I'm off the clock."

Uh-oh. Was he going to boot me out? I wasn't ready to leave Shadow.

"May I stay for a little while?" I said, giving him the big, puppy-dog eyes that had always swayed my father.

Dr. Pullman pursed his lips. "Well, I guess you can stay until Leah leaves—she has a half-hour left on her shift."

"No," Claudia said. "Sarah needs to drive me to her house. I left my car there."

She thought the ornament was in the car. Well, I wasn't driving her anywhere.

"I need to stay with Shadow. I'll pay for a taxi," I said.

"No need for that," Dr. Pullman said. "I'll take Claudia back to your house."

I smiled my thanks at Dr. Pullman. Maybe Dr. Griffin could convince him during the drive to stay with her tonight and let Kyle enjoy Halloween without a chaperone.

Dr. Griffin smiled a Cheshire-cat grin. I suspected she planned to decline his offer. I should have known she wasn't going to let the hood ornament go without a fight.

"Thanks, Mark, but on second thought, I'll just wait for Sarah. I'm missing a packet of Kleenex from my purse."

"Don't be silly, Claudia. We need to talk. I'm sure Sarah will lend you her keys to check under the seat for it."

"Sure," I said. "My keys are in my backpack. Help yourself."

Dr. Griffin's eyebrows crunched together. She was probably trying to figure out where else I might have stashed the ornament. She couldn't exactly trash my car while Dr. Pullman stood watch. Once they got to my house, he would probably wait until she drove off in her car, so she wouldn't be able to linger and wait for me to get home. For the first time today, things were definitely going my way.

CHAPTER TWENTY-FIVE

Alice: "I wonder if I've been changed in the night."

The last thing I expected was for Paul to call me. I had just stepped through my front door when Paul's name flashed on caller ID. I answered with my heart drumming like a misfiring engine.

"Hello?" I said.

"U-nit," he said.

I hadn't heard him use his M.T. Anderson dialect since we had met at Starbucks. I chuckled. Leave it to Paul to find a way to make me laugh after all the stress I had endured this afternoon.

"It's way skip that you called," I said, smiling.

"Yeah?"

He sounded happy, like he was grinning.

"Yeah," I said. "I missed you in art class today."

"Cutting class was stupid. I couldn't face watching you sit next to Kyle. But I had to come clean with my mom when I got home. Even if the school didn't phone her, I would have told her. But then she backed me into a corner with her why-would-I-cut-class questions, so I told her the whole story. That's when I realized you had invited me to go with you guys, and you wouldn't have done it if you thought of Kyle as your boyfriend. So... is the invitation still open? Can I hang out with you and Kyle tonight?"

I hesitated. I suspected Kyle would be annoyed by Paul's presence. I hadn't given Kyle any reason to believe I had feelings for Paul. But I couldn't tell Paul he couldn't come. Crap. No matter what, somebody would get hurt.

And what did I want? Kyle or Paul? I couldn't say for sure.

"Sarah?"

"U-nit, I just walked in the house," I said, dropping my keys on the table to emphasize the point. "Hang on a sec."

I put the phone against my chest. I liked Paul. I liked his integrity. I liked his sense of humor. But Kyle had those dimples. He was talented and smart. I couldn't choose. Not tonight. I had been on an emotional roller coaster today. But maybe I didn't have to. If Kyle and I were going as part of a big group, would it matter if Paul hung out with us?

"Sorry," I said. "I just got back from taking Shadow to the emergency clinic. I guess I'm still shook up."

"Oh my gosh. Is she okay?"

"Yes," I said.

"Thank goodness. She's such a nice dog. What happened?"

"She collapsed after school. They're keeping her overnight, but she'll be fine."

"Wow," Paul said. "All the more reason you should go out. Otherwise, you'll sit around and worry. Everyone gathers at Broderick and Fulton," he said. "I'll catch up to you and Kyle there, okay?"

"You're right," I said. "I do need to get out of the house. I have to warn you though, Dr. Pullman, Kyle's uncle, is going to chaperone us."

"Really? Well, I don't care. As long as I've got a pretty girl by my side."

"You're out of luck there. A sheet and two eyeholes will be alongside you. The creature from the black lagoon could be underneath for all you know. What are you coming as?"

"Guess."

"Football player?"

"Nope."

I imagined him in tight-fitted black clothing, his biceps adding contours to the drab color. A headlamp banded to his hardhat and a coiled rope around his shoulder would complete the outfit. The thought of his taut muscles gave me goose bumps.

"Spelunker?"

"Nope."

"You'll never guess. I enlarged your mitosis and meiosis diagrams and I pasted them on two poster boards. I'll wear them like those guys that walk around advertising stuff.

I'll be the only reproducing cell costume in the history of Halloween."

"You wouldn't."

"It's a done deal. But don't worry, your secret is safe. I blacked out the words and I won't let anyone know what those football drawings mean. People will just think I'm a playbook."

I laughed, tipping my head back. Had I ever even chuckled in Kyle's presence? Dad's Relationship Rule #8 advised avoiding anyone who had no sense of humor. I suddenly wished I had Paul all to myself tonight.

"Well, you'll be easy to find," I said. "See you tonight."

"Glad Shadow's okay," he said before signing off.

If I had left it alone like Dad and everyone else had told me to, Shadow wouldn't be at the vet clinic. I closed my eyes. I reminded myself she would be fine.

I was done meddling. It had brought me nothing but grief and fear and almost killed Shadow. Maybe now my dad and the jack-o'-lantern figure would leave me alone. Maybe Mrs. Warzueski was better off living with the hope that her boy was still alive. Even Kyle would have benefitted if I had let the past stay in the past. Absolutely nothing good had come of my decision to pursue the mystery surrounding the little boy. But if all went well next week, Shadow and I would be settled into our life together in this house.

I glanced at the clock. I had to cook Mr. O'Shawnessy's dinner tonight then I could dress for trick or treating. Margaret decided to stay and help her grandfather pass out candy, so I didn't have to feel guilty leaving him home alone. I had made a deal that I would be nicer to her, and I intended to keep it. I planned to cook her favorite meal: sausage and mashed potatoes. Then I would bake a Halloween-inspired cake, decorating the frosting with black and orange sprinkles.

Halloween would be over tomorrow. Shadow would come home. I could devote my attention to Paul. I hoped for Kyle's sake that after tonight, his mom would give him more freedom for the rest of his senior year.

* * *

True to my word, I acted friendly toward Margaret during dinner—even though she described my ghost costume as primitive and told me the sheet turned my hazel eyes the color of mop water. I chipped in and helped her with the dishes though it wasn't my chore. I stayed civil as she ridiculed me for being a candy-grubber. When she told me that my ass, which was already huge, would be ginormous once I ate all those treats, I shrugged and laughed. Shadow had been spared, so I hadn't reacted to her snide remarks. No more snakes placed in her bed. In just one day, I had changed.

At 7:45, the last dish had been hand-dried and put away, so I hurried away to collect my sheet and a belt to secure the costume around my waist, find a flashlight and a pillowcase for the candy, and head to my car. I wasn't surprised to hear the snap, crackle of my father's arrival as I reached my Civic. Warm air gripped my shoulders as though he intended to physically restrain me.

I glanced up and down the street. I wanted to tell my father to chill, but I didn't want anyone to think I was talking to myself. A dad and a toddler batman headed toward Mrs. Bellweather's house and were out of earshot. Otherwise, the street was empty.

"Give it a rest, Dad," I hissed.

To my surprise, the warmth disappeared. I climbed into the driver seat, wondering why my father had conceded so easily. I had my answer the moment I twisted the key in the ignition. The engine failed to turn over.

I popped the car hood and saw the problem immediately. Someone—my father no doubt—had disconnected the battery cable. Too bad he had taught me how to fix this as well as a flat tire. I got the tools out of the trunk knowing the delay would make me late. I texted Paul and Kyle about the delay. Score one for Dear Old Dad.

Once my car was functional, I double-checked the directions on my phone, surprised to discover Kyle had suggested a meeting spot three blocks from where I was to meet Paul. I assumed that was because parking would be a challenge.

I crept through the neighborhood trick or treaters. A group of teens clustered at Fulton, but if Paul was there, I didn't see him. The new housing development spread out at the base of a hillside so my car's nose tipped up in a climb as I headed to the meeting point with Kyle.

At the second block, a cluster of partially-constructed homes stretched down the street. I didn't think I had the wrong street. Maybe he had chosen to meet here to avoid being seen arriving with Dr. Pullman.

I turned left onto Fremont. The houses under construction on this street were just framed structures without roofs. Without streetlights, the wooden posts glowed white in the moonlight like rib bones in an elephant graveyard.

Kyle's car was parked curbside a few houses away, but not Dr. Pullman's. Maybe they had driven together, or Kyle's ploy to ditch him had worked. Or maybe Dr. Griffin had enticed Dr. Pullman to keep their dinner date. Either way, I was relieved not to have the vet ruining our Halloween.

I parked behind Kyle's car and cut the engine. A stack of two-by-fours and cinder blocks were stored at the curb. Dad's warm touch on my wrist caught me by surprise. Had he been in the car the whole time? Where his previous contacts had been insistent, this action was a steady tug. His touch held more of a pleading feel.

I had reservations about getting out of the car. Why wasn't Kyle standing outside waiting for me? I rolled down the window to get a better view since the interior had fogged. He must have seen my car lights approach so where was he? And why had he suggested meeting three blocks away from the group on a deserted street? Something didn't feel right.

Dad's tug became persistent.

"Okay, okay, Dad," I said. "Let me text Kyle that I'll meet him at Fulton where the other kids are."

I whipped off the message and started the car. Kyle's face appeared next to the driver's side of the car. He must have been hiding behind the pile of boards. I almost screamed.

"Surprise," he said.

He was dressed in black, his wavy red hair slicked into submission. He held a Mickey Mouse mask and a white pillowcase. He placed the mask over his face then pulled it off laughing.

"Get it? I'm a loose rodent. What do you think? I wanted to come as a rat, but this was the closest costume I could find."

It took me a moment to collect myself. Kyle seemed oblivious to my reaction to his stunt. Calmer now, I had to admit, his outfit was clever, even kinda funny. I turned off the car.

"It's perfect," I said with a smile.

Kyle put his arms in the air like a football referee signaling a touchdown. "I knew you'd like it!"

I felt foolish for wanting to flee. Dad was overreacting as usual. My father's warm hand exuded more pressure as I took the key from the ignition, but I pulled my wrist from his grasp. Kyle was just a kid who wanted to have fun.

"Let's find the others, shall we?" I said.

I stepped from the car, glancing up and down the street. Still no sign of Dr. Pullman.

"How'd you lose your chaperone?"

"It was easy." Kyle grinned. "His girlfriend talked him into coming to her house for dinner and meeting us later."

Well, well. Dr. Griffin had convinced him. I turned to head up the street and Kyle caught my hand. His touch was warm and gentle, but I pulled away, feeling disloyal to Paul.

"Let me get my costume on."

I pulled the sheet over my head, adjusted the eyeholes, and belted the waist.

"All set," I said.

"Let's take the short cut," he said. "We're already late."

Kyle pointed at a dirt trail between two of the partially constructed houses. The narrow trail plunging down slope looked foreboding. Several large oak trees on either side of the trailhead blocked the moonlight.

"I don't know. It's so dark."

Kyle pulled an object out of his pillowcase. He clicked on the flashlight and put the glowing light under his chin. His smile accentuated his dimples. The trail would get us there sooner, and I had a flashlight, too. Even though I had let Paul know about my car trouble, he must be wondering where I was. I collected my pillowcase and light from the back seat.

"Lead the way," I said.

CHAPTER TWENTY-SIX

Duchess: "You're thinking about something, my dear, and that makes you forget to talk."

I swept my flashlight back and forth. The blackberry bushes along both sides of the path became impenetrable so there was no way to step off the cleared path. Was this a deer trail the developer had kept in place as a wildlife corridor? The descent was even worse than I expected. Dr. Griffin had said I didn't live in a rabbit hole, but as I followed Kyle down the steep path, that is exactly what it felt like.

It was a slow descent and ten minutes later we must have only traveled halfway to the gathering spot where I hoped Paul and the others would be waiting. I wished I had suggested that we drive to the meeting location. It would have been faster by car.

The trail leveled then widened around a boulder, but the trees drooped into the opening, which forced us to crouch. Kyle progressed about ten feet ahead. He stood tall, suggesting less overstory. Beyond him though, his flashlight lit a narrower path.

I clutched my pillowcase to my chest and hunched over to avoid the canopy. The car keys inside in the bag poked into my stomach, and when I straightened slightly, the overhead branches snagged my costume, wrenching the eyeholes to the side so I could no longer see.

"Kyle, hang on a sec," I said, grappling with the sheet.

I groped forward and wrestled the branches until I could stand straight. I continued on to the wider area where I had last seen Kyle and could stand tall then stopped to adjust my costume.

I had cinched the sheet tightly around my waist with a belt, wanting to look slim for Paul. Now, I couldn't adjust the eyeholes without loosening the buckle. I heard a rustle close in front of me, which I assumed to be Kyle, but a branch also snapped behind me. There weren't bears in the area? Was someone following us or in front of us? My sense of direction was all screwed up. Why hadn't I waited to put on my costume?

My fingers trembled as the seconds ticked by, and I couldn't see. At last I disengaged the belt buckle and adjusted the eyeholes. I flashed the light ahead expecting to see Kyle. My breath caught. Before me, stood the jack-o'-lantern killer.

Oh god. Oh god. Blood curdled in my chest feeling cold and thick. My breath came in uneven hitches. I wanted to turn and run but my feet felt cemented in the leaf litter.

"Kyle?" I called.

Where had he disappeared to? The carved pumpkin mask had horizontal tear-drop eyes that tapered in the direction of the temples and a tiny triangle nose. The mouth had dozens of jagged incisors.

The killer towered over me by at least six inches—too tall to be Kyle. I searched behind me for him, but only dense branches crowded the trail. I couldn't pull in air as though all the oxygen had disappeared.

A shiver worked through me. I hadn't heard any kind of struggle. Maybe the killer had murdered him in one swift blow. Oh, Holy Mother. Had Mrs. Warzueski's worst nightmare just come true? Was she to lose a second son to violence on the seventh anniversary of Tobin's disappearance?

I wanted to be brave, but I was just plain scared. If he had taken out Kyle so soundlessly and in a matter of seconds, then he could do the same to me. Kyle. Oh, Kyle. My mind churned, but I couldn't speak. Finally, I gasped and found the words.

"Wha-at d-d-did you d-d-do to Kyle?" I said stuttering, taking a step backward.

"I'm right behind you," Kyle said.

I whirled around. I heard a click. The glow of his flashlight illuminated his feet. Kyle stood only a few feet away. Why hadn't he answered when I called? Had he squeezed past me while I was tangled in the costume, turned off his flashlight to hide, but decided not to abandon me? What was going on?

"Let's get out of here," I said, giving him a shove.

Kyle held his ground, blocking my escape. "Can't."

What? I heard the word, but it took a moment for his meaning to sink in. The rendezvous spot had been Kyle's idea—a remote area under construction where we would have to walk down this path and where they could dispose of my body—the same way Tobin's remains had been buried at the high school when it underwent renovation. Kyle was in on this.

"No." I had meant to shout it, but the word came out as a whisper.

Kyle shrugged and placed the Mickey Mouse mask over his face as if by lurking behind a costume, he wouldn't be responsible for whatever happened next. The Disney character now seemed sinister with those elongated eyes that reached toward his eyebrows and an open-mouthed grin that revealed Mickey's tongue.

I tried to maneuver around Kyle, but he grasped my upper arm with his free hand and wouldn't let me pass. My head swiveled left then right. Bushes on both sides of the trail blocked my escape. The jack-o'-lantern killer hadn't budged and his tall frame filled the trail in the opposite direction. I was trapped between the two of them.

My breath came in short spurts. My heart reverberated in my chest as if it might come loose. The sheet clung to my brow where I had begun to sweat. What were they going to do to me?

Why would Kyle want to hurt me? Why had he agreed to help the killer? I should have heeded my dad's warning and driven away when I had the chance.

The killer took a step closer into the widened area of the trail, leaving just enough space for me to slip by him and escape down the narrow path. I lunged forward, counting on the killer's limited view through his eyeholes. But I hadn't counted on Kyle grabbing my sheet. When he did, I fell into the jack-o'-lantern killer, latched onto the giant orange orb, and ripped the mask off.

I blinked twice taking in the pocked face and sandy brown hair. Dr. Pullman stood before me. Was he involved in Tobin's death? Had he killed his nephew? I remembered the stuffed pumpkin toy Tobin had held then threw away then wanted back, all the while crying.

"Why?" My voice sounded husky and strange.

Dr. Pullman shook his head from side to side.

"You couldn't leave it alone," Kyle said.

My fingers grew numb and lost their grip. The jack-o'-lantern mask tumbled to the ground. I scrambled backward, putting distance between myself and the man who I had thought of as my friend.

"Help!" I screamed. "Somebody help!"

Kyle clamped a hand over my mouth. In the distance, the excited shrieks of children and teens goofing off emanated from the neighborhood at the base of the hill. No one would have paid attention to my pleas for help.

"Now what, Uncle Mark?" Kyle said. "You were just supposed to scare her. She wasn't supposed to know it was you."

Dr. Pullman ran his hand through his hair. "Shut up, just shut up. Let me think."

The edge in his voice scared me. The man's eyes darted around as if he might find answers in the bushes. Or maybe he was looking for a hiding spot to stash my body. I dropped my pillowcase and flashlight as I thrashed and managed to twist my face so I could breathe though I couldn't escape Kyle's grip..

"Look," I said, putting my free hand up and patting air. "I just want to go home and pass out Halloween candy. I won't say anything. Okay?"

"Yeah." Kyle said. "We should let her go."

I sidled closer to Kyle, hoping to position myself to squeeze by him while he and Dr. Pullman debated my fate. Kyle countered my move, blocking any hope of escape. Despite his words, it seemed Kyle intended to follow his uncle's instructions.

"Once and for all," Dr. Pullman shouted, "would you SHUT UP? If you hadn't shoved your little brother and made him hit his head on the curb, we wouldn't be in this mess."

Shoved him? The events of Tobin's final night unfurled before my eyes. Dr. Pullman had volunteered to take the kids trick or treating. Mrs. Warzueski had pinned the emergency phone number on Tobin, worrying he might get lost, never once imagining she needed to protect her toddler from her older son. As the night wore on, maybe Tobin slowed Kyle down. The frustration built up. Perhaps Tobin attached himself to Kyle's leg or maybe Tobin said something that irritated Kyle, and Kyle pushed him away. The little boy fell, hit his head on the curb, and just like that, Tobin was dead. Even if it didn't quite happen that way, the result was the same: the toddler's body was buried at the high school.

"Me?" Kyle took a step toward his uncle, jabbing his finger at him. "I was just a little kid. You decided to cover it up and make me lie. Well, I'm not going along with hurting anyone else. You may have thought you were sparing my mother, but she has suffered all these years not knowing."

"Great, just great, Kyle." Dr. Pullman clenched and unclenched his fists. "Why couldn't you keep your mouth shut? Now, you've made it impossible to let Sarah go. I will not let you hurt my sister.

"Hurt my mom? You're the one who planted Toby's costume in a dumpster to throw the police off track. That sent her over the edge for weeks."

"You think she's suffered wondering what happened to Tobin? Finding out her eldest son killed her baby boy would destroy her."

Kyle flinched and pulled off his mask. His lower lip trembled.

Dr. Pullman pointed a finger at Kyle. "Not to mention what the truth would mean for me. I don't think I could survive prison."

Dr. Pullman pulled a knife out of his back pocket and unfolded the blade.

"Jesus," Kyle gasped.

I started to shake. I never really believed Dr. Pullman capable of murder. A mosaic of emotions descended. Fear, anger, disgust.

The serrated edge of the hunter's knife gleamed in the glow of the flashlight. My knees gave out. I could have sworn I heard the crunch of leaves beyond Dr. Pullman as I fell. Maybe raccoons were fleeing the scene.

"Get her keys and move her car," Dr. Pullman said in a deadpan tone. "Take it across the bridge and leave it near the bus station downtown. I'll come pick you up when I'm done here."

"No," I squeaked, scrambling to my feet. "I won't tell anyone. There's no need to do this. Besides, I told Paul I was meeting Kyle. He's waiting. If I disappear, who do you think the cops are going to come after?"

"She's right, Uncle. We can't do this."

"Do as I say, Kyle. You never met up with her. She told you she planned to skip town, because I warned her I would turn her in to the authorities for felony animal abuse. She doesn't have family who will come searching. Nobody cares about her. End of story. We don't have a choice. If we don't get rid of her, I'll go to jail and so will you. Is that what you want?"

My breath caught. Dr. Pullman's cold voice held resolve. He meant to murder me. He really meant it. My hands and feet shook as if I were having an epilepsy fit.

"Don't Kyle," I pleaded. "He won't kill me in front of you."

But my red-headed classmate took the pillowcase that held my keys then turned and ran in the direction we had come. I inched backward, but Dr. Pullman rushed forward and caught my arm.

"Claudia told me everything. About Shadow. About how you know where Tobin's remains are," he said. "And Kyle told me how Shadow kept investigating the corner of the classroom where I buried Tobin on the eve of the foundation being laid. I am sorry, Sarah. But I know how to use a knife. I'll make this as quick and painless as possible.

"You're wrong that no one cares if I disappear. Shadow would miss me. And there are people too. Mr. O'Shawnessy. My caseworker at social services. You can't just pretend I never existed."

I thought about Paul too, but I didn't want to mention him.

"We're going to have to take a short walk," Pullman said as if I hadn't spoken, "to the unfinished house beyond this brush. Your grave has already been dug."

My grave? This was premeditated. He had never intended to just scare me. He had put on a show for Kyle, but his cover up had been planned. Is that why Claudia discouraged me from meeting Kyle? Had she regretted that she had said too much, and so she had been trying to protect me but when I didn't listen, she let Dr. Pullman convince her to go along with his scheme?

I tried to wrench my arm from his grasp, but he held tight. My father had been hovering every time I got near Kyle. Now that my life depended on his help, Dad wasn't here.

"Da-ddy," I screamed.

No crackle of air, no warm touch. Nothing. Why had he left me to fend for myself? Had he decided he wanted me to join him on the other side?

"Shut up," Pullman said. "I'd rather not do this the hard way."

He grabbed my hair. The pain barely registered against my panic. I dug my heels into the leaf litter, the smell of decaying leaves filling my nose. My arms paddled the air, but gravity was on Pullman's side. The man muscled me a few feet up the slope.

"Help," I screamed, louder this time. "Somebody—"

Branches snapped. Something large charged in our direction. Then I saw crumpled white poster board twisting and flailing in a ghostly onslaught.

Paul. I knew those muscular biceps. His wide chest pummeled through the brush. He barreled toward us, his face set in a cloud of fury.

"Get your hands off her," Paul yelled as he slammed into Pullman.

The knife slipped from Pullman's hand—and I did what Dad would have wanted me to do if he had been there—snatched it up, rolling out of the way as the two men scuffled. Within moments, Paul had wrestled Pullman's arms behind his back, but the man continued to struggle. I handed the knife to Paul, and he put the blade against the man's neck.

After a moment, Pullman's shoulders shuddered, and he stopped resisting. His body seemed to melt to the ground, as if he wished for his own burial.

Paul, that giant, lovable guy, smiled at me. Pullman had been wrong. Someone did care about me. I retrieved my flashlight and whipped my cell phone out of my pocket to dial 911. After I explained the situation and described our location, I turned to Paul.

"How did you find me?" I said, muting the phone, but staying on the line with the operator.

"I saw you drive by and turn left then I waited forever. When the other kids started knocking on doors, I jogged up the hill until I found your car. That's when I saw the trail and figured I had missed you, so I raced to where we were supposed to meet. When you weren't there, I followed the path until I heard voices. I was about to call out when you screamed."

"After all this time," Dr. Pullman said, "Why did you have to start snooping around? Why?"

Why? I had wanted to help. I never meant to hurt anyone. Yet, I put myself, and Paul, and even Kyle in danger.

In the distance, police sirens wailed.

CHAPTER TWENTY~SEVEN

Alice: "Who in the world am I?"

I directed my flashlight onto the prostrate form of Dr. Pullman lying face down in the leaves. Paul straddled the veterinarian's back, keeping the edge of the knife pressed to Pullman's neck. My hero gazed up at me from his crouched position, his face a mixture of shock, pride, and fear. Neither of us imagined that our evening of trick or treating would end with Paul holding a blade to a man's throat. Pullman remained still. Was he afraid of knives or waiting for Paul to drop his guard?

Suddenly I felt too warm and confined by the ghost costume. I crept forward and balanced the battery-end of the flashlight on the ground so that the light radiated out into the clearing then backed away to strip off my ghost outfit. Without the bedsheet, I felt vulnerable, exposed. My hands shook. I clutched my cell phone as if it were a rope that prevented me from toppling down a cliff.

Even as I admired Paul's courage, I couldn't help but berate myself for being a coward. I remained safely out of reach of Pullman. I couldn't even rally myself to retrieve the flashlight. I wished the police would get here.

The 911 operator squawked on my cell phone. "Are you okay?"

"Yes," I replied in a wobbly voice. I had already explained that Dr. Pullman had drawn a knife to kill me, but that he was now being held by Paul.

"Is your attacker still restrained?"

"Yes."

"Stay on the line. The police are about three minutes out," the 911 dispatcher said.

Three more minutes? Could Paul keep Pullman restrained that long? Paul was such a kind person, he probably wouldn't be able to hurt the man, even if it meant letting him get away.

Pullman bucked, but Paul countered the weight shift.

"Don't make me hurt you," Paul said.

Sweat dripped from Paul's face. He looked at me with pleading eyes.

"Please tell them to hurry," I said into the phone.

Would I ever stop shaking? I wished I were at my guardian's house drinking a cup of warm cow's juice. Even sitting in the same room with Margaret right now wouldn't be so bad.

The distinctive chimes of a text's arrival emanated from Dr. Pullman's pocket. The man bucked as if trying to dislodge Paul from his back, but Paul kept his balance kneeling on the man and the steady pressure of the knife at Pullman's throat. Dr. Pullman once again quieted.

The text was probably Kyle confirming my car was at the bus station and asking when Pullman was coming to get him. But what if it was the emergency clinic calling about a change in Shadow's condition? I had to check. But I didn't trust my legs so I sank to the ground. On trembling knees, I crept forward and tapped Paul's leg. He shifted so I could snag the device then I skittered backwards.

The text wasn't from Kyle. It was from Dr. Griffin. It read, *where r u?*

Had Pullman arranged to meet her for dinner after he "took care" of me? Was she to be his alibi? Well, let her wonder. Just then another text arrived.

Mark? R u ok?

What a piece of work. He doesn't reply for a minute and she assumes he's fallen off a cliff. I was contemplating sending a snarky response saying that he would let her know after he finished kissing his new girlfriend, when the phone chimed again. I stared at the words.

Did she get away? Should I fill in the hole?

A river of ice water cascaded down my spine. She was a co-conspirator. I imagined Dr. Griffin standing in the center of a partially constructed home with a shovel at the ready. Only moments ago my heart had threatened to pound its way out of my chest now it became still and heavy as a stone.

"What is it?" Paul asked.

I shook my head. I couldn't answer. It was as if a vacuum had sucked all the air out of my lungs. The stress of the night had been bad enough, but to know that three people, two of whom I had trusted, had decided I was as disposable as trash rocked my core. My eyes grew moist and tears threatened to spill.

Dr. Pullman had been my key witness at my emancipation hearing. But after tonight, he would be charged with attempted murder. My chances of independence were gone. And then there was Dr. Griffin. What judge would allow a teen to live alone when news got out that a lunatic had invaded her home? I could handle Margaret tonight or even a few more weeks, but for nine more months? And what would become of Shadow? I let myself and my dog down once again. I was an eternity away from living my life the way I planned.

"Sarah? Are you okay?" Paul repeated.

I couldn't tell him about Dr. Griffin now. He needed to stay focused on keeping the man underneath him restrained. I also didn't want to tip off Dr. Pullman about the text. Paul's look of concern only made me feel worse.

Mr. O'Shawnessy thought girls shouldn't date until they were eighteen. Margaret had broken that rule, lying that she was out with girlfriends. I hadn't cared about his strict rules. But my situation had changed. Would I ever have a Friday night out with Paul? And how would I deal with Margaret's jealousy? There would be hell to pay.

"I'll explain later," I said, my voice cracking with emotion.

The phone chimed again.

Mark? U r scaring me. Tell me what 2 do.

I pondered whether to instruct Dr. Griffin to fill in the hole or ignore her. Shoveling dirt would keep her busy until the police arrived, but would she bolt at the sound of them crashing through the brush? She must know she would be in trouble if they caught Dr. Pullman. The phone chirped again.

Should I take Shadow back?

Shadow? She had my dog? Dr. Pullman must have released him to her care. If Dr. Griffin were busy tossing soil into my intended grave, then she couldn't run off with my dog.

I typed one handed. *Plan failed. All OK. Fill in hole.*

"Who are you texting?" I looked up to see Claudia's boyfriend roll his head to the side, and his eyes squinting at me against the brightness of the flashlight between us. His expression was one of determination. "Is that Kyle? Leave him out of this. I forced him to go along with my plans. He never wanted to do this."

I believed that. Kyle had been very young when Tobin died and been put in an impossible situation. He had lived a lie for so long that he probably believed he had no choice. But Kyle was still an accomplice.

"Yes," I said. "It was Kyle. My car is in place."

The police sirens grew loud then quieted. Voices drifted through the trees. Pullman didn't struggle, but maybe he was luring Paul into complacency.

"This was all my doing, okay?" Despite the darkness, Pullman's eyes again sought mine. "Tell the cops about my scheme to kill you; tell them I'm a psychopath, but don't bring up the past. It would ruin Kyle's future and destroy my sister."

I remembered Kyle's mother's haunted expression. If Kyle were charged with conspiracy to commit murder, he would be locked up. She was bound to lose her second son over this. But how much had Paul heard? Even if I withheld some information, Paul wouldn't lie.

"Sarah, the police are heading up the trail," the operator's voice announced on my cell.

I swallowed hard. Just a few more minutes and this would be over. Branches snapped in the distance. The sweep of flashlights promised the imminent arrival of help. I pocketed Pullman's cell phone, gathered my courage, and retrieved the flashlight. I aimed the light toward Dr. Pullman.

At that moment, Pullman arched his back throwing Paul off balance. It happened so fast. Paul was on his back with Pullman standing above, straddling him. The knife was now poised in both of Pullman's hands ready to drive the weapon into Paul's belly.

"No," I screamed.

Branches snapped behind me—the wrong direction for the police. Dr. Griffin? My shoulders tensed expecting to be tackled. My body turned in slow motion. Not Dr. Griffin. In the dim light, the white gleam of canine teeth. I knew coyotes occupied these hills, but this animal was too big. Could it be a rogue wolf? My arms came up to protect myself from attack. But at the moment of impact I recognized the red coat, the pointed ears. Shadow stormed by me and body slammed into Dr. Pullman, knocking him over.

Paul scrambled for the knife that had fallen to the ground. Shadow grasped Pullman's arm and growled. My brave dog held tight until Paul once again held Pullman at knifepoint. To my relief, Pullman closed his eyes and rested his head on the ground. The crack of snapping branches suggested the police were close.

"Hurry. Up here," I called out.

A moment later, the cops charged onto the scene. A yellow halo of light flashed in my eyes before landing on Paul and Dr. Pullman.

I recognized the first police officer running toward us with his gun drawn. His picture had been in the newspaper article about Tobin. The man had aged, but the bulky form and handlebar mustache of Officer Mathers were unmistakable.

"Good work, son," he said pointing his weapon on Pullman. "Drop the knife and step away. We've got this."

Paul dropped the knife and jumped out of the way. Mather's partner pulled him backward.

"Now call off the dog," he said.

I squatted down. Shadow had to be confused. She liked Dr. Pullman.

"Hey, girl," I crooned. "Hey, Shadow. Come."

My obedient girl released her grip and bounded into my arms. She sniffed then kissed me, then sniffed again to make sure I was okay.

Mathers' flashlight swept the clearing before landing on Pullman.

"Hands behind your back," Mathers said.

Pullman did as instructed, and Mathers snapped handcuffs around his wrists.

"Are either of you hurt?" the cop said to Paul.

"No," Paul and I said together.

Pullman was jerked to his feet while Mathers recited the Miranda rights. Paul stumbled into my arms, his body quaking. He had put on such a strong front.

"You did good," I whispered in his ear.

He pulled back to look at me. Paul's face was in shadow, but his eyes connected with mine and pierced straight into me.

"You two sure you are all right?" Mathers asked, flashing a light in our direction.

"Yes," Paul and I said in unison for the second time, and we both laughed with relief.

I squeezed Paul's hand. A corner of his costume—a crumpled mess of poster board—poked into my side. I stepped back, wanting to make sure he was really okay. My drawings were distorted and smeared with dirt, but not blood. He appeared unharmed.

"You should have dressed as a superhero," I said then blushed.

"I'll be Superman, if you'll be Lois Lane," he said with a grin.

Mathers barked orders into a walkie-talkie. Two other cops showed up. One photographed the knife. The other, of considerable brawn, restrained Pullman. Still another placed yellow police tape along the shrubbery. In the cramped space, Paul leaned down as if to kiss me.

"Sarah, you still there?" yelled the 911 operator through the phone.

Paul jumped backward. I shook my head. Would we ever have our first kiss?

"Yes," I said, bringing the phone to my ear. "The police are here. Thank you for staying on the line with me."

"Okay, Sarah," she said. "I'm signing off now. Glad you're safe."

Safe? Was I? With Dr. Griffin still at large?

"We'll need to take you in to the station to get your statements," Mathers said.

"Wait," I said.

I retrieved Dr. Griffin's texts from Pullman's phone and showed Mathers. I explained how she was filling in my intended grave at this very moment somewhere in the housing development up near where Kyle had parked.

"Where is Claudia Griffin?" Mathers demanded of Pullman.

Pullman pressed his lips together and looked away. I wasn't surprised that he wouldn't give her up. Mathers ordered two of the officers to stop processing the scene and comb the area for Griffin. As they sprinted up the trail, he radioed for a helicopter.

"She has to be close," I said. "She had taken Shadow and somehow my dog escaped."

"Let's clear the area," Mathers said.

The burly officer escorted Pullman downhill followed by me, Paul and finally Mathers.

* * *

Flashing red lights created an eerie glow inside the cruiser. Someone draped a blanket over my shoulders, and I snuggled into it. Shadow sat in the seat between Paul and me. Dr. Pullman was carted off in another car. Mathers told us that Pullman lawyered up and would be taken straight to booking, leaving Mathers to bring us to the station.

Mathers rode shotgun. The partition between us and the front seat was open and the detective jotted down our names. But once the investigator recognized Paul to be the high school football quarterback, all the detective wanted to talk about was the game. I might have suspected he was only trying to distract Paul, except it soon became clear that the cop was totally into the high school football scene. Throughout the drive, he praised Paul's performance, asked about the competition for sectionals, and offered suggestions on strategy. He even complimented Paul on his Halloween costume after Paul explained it was a playbook. A sly grin formed on Paul's face at that point, and I joined him in smiling at our secret.

The drive was shorter than expected. When we entered the city building, Mathers turned to me and pointed to the chairs that lined the precinct's walls.

"Take a seat," he said. "Since you were the intended victim, your statement and interview will take much longer so I'm going to clear Paul first. Shadow can stay with you."

I nodded, sinking onto the cold, plastic seat. I pulled the blanket tighter around my shoulders.

Mathers and Paul entered a room at the far end of the corridor, discussing a play called a Pro Right X-Crash 32 Sweep. I suspected the detective interviewed Paul so they could keep talking football. I welcomed the delay. I could check Shadow over, and I would also have time to collect myself and decide how much information to offer up.

I ran my hands along Shadow's muscular body. She rewarded me with a slurp of her tongue. Her eyes were bright and curious. She appeared to be fine. She arched her regal neck then sat, turning her attention to the hub of activity around her.

The room held a dozen or so tired-looking metal desks, many stacked high with manila folders. A tall woman in a miniskirt, black mesh stockings, and stiletto heels screamed obscenities that this was her Halloween costume, and how dare they charge her with prostitution. I slumped in the chair, too tired to be amused. Just then, two cops entered the building, sandwiching Dr. Griffin between them.

"Shadow," Dr. Griffin exclaimed. "That's my dog.

I jumped up at once, squatting down to pull Shadow close. Her brown, intelligent eyes found mine, and she woofed in excitement. Her docked tail whipped back and forth.

"Get that creature away from my dog," Dr. Griffin screeched, pointing at me.

"She's mine," I said. "I have her veterinary records to prove it."

Shadow's tongue caught my cheek. I don't know what I would have done if Dr. Griffin had run off with her. My dog wiggled, and whined, and tried to crawl into my lap. I burst out laughing.

"Looks to me like that's this young lady's dog," an officer said to Dr. Griffin. "And you can't keep a dog in a jail cell, now can you?"

"I'll be out of here just as soon as my lawyer gets here," Dr. Griffin said with a smirk.

Strong words from someone with wrists locked in handcuffs. When the officer attempted to guide her away, she resisted. As she passed, she clenched and unclenched her restrained, rat-bone hands. Dirt coated her red-polished nails and mud splattered the black material of her witch costume.

"You should think about Monday," she hissed. "You can still have it all, Sarah. The fairy tale ending. I haven't done anything wrong. I don't even know why I'm here."

One of the cops rolled his eyes and shoved her down the corridor and through a doorway. Dr. Griffin must not know they confiscated Pullman's phone. Nothing she said now would matter.

No sooner had Witchy Woman disappeared when Kyle's mother stormed through the front entrance.

"Please," Mrs. Warzueski screamed to no one in particular. "Somebody help. My boy has gone missing."

Her hair was a mess. Her eyes darted around the room. She looked insane.

A female police officer rushed to her side, guiding her to a dented, gray desk and asking her to calm down. Dr. Pullman had been right about one thing. Losing Kyle would send her over the edge. Mrs. Warzueski burst into tears.

Shadow rested her head on my knee and whined. She hadn't liked this woman at my house when she rekeyed my locks, but now she seemed distraught by the woman's grief. She nudged my leg with her nose.

I didn't know what to do. Should I tell her Kyle might be at the bus station? But then would I have to explain why I suspected Kyle would be there? I was torn. Kyle hadn't known of Pullman's intention to kill me. He thought the man only wanted to scare me. Part of me wanted to protect Kyle. Then again, he left me alone with Pullman after discovering his uncle's true intention. What if I held my tongue and Kyle told them that I knew where he was all along? I would be caught withholding information. What would that do to my credibility if I needed to testify against Dr. Pullman?

"My son," Mrs. Warzueski wailed. "He won't answer his phone. He's dead, isn't he?"

She scanned the room as if looking for Kyle's body. When her eyes landed on me, she pointed a finger at me.

"You," she screamed. "What did you do to my son?"

I remembered Paul's question, "Who are you?" I thought about his refusal to lie, how he gave me credit for changing his life. His goodness and his moral character showed just how far I had drifted from the person my father wanted me to be. He would follow Relationship Rule #5: Always be honest.

"He's fine," I said to her. I directed my next words the woman officer. "You may find him at the bus station, but you better send a policeman in plain clothes. Kyle's liable to run otherwise."

"He's running away from home?" Kyle's mother grasped the cop's arm. "You have to stop him."

"What do you know about this?" the officer said to me.

"It's a long story," I said. "But you should send someone to pick him up right away."

"Please," Mrs. Warzueski begged.

The officer nodded and spoke into her radio. Down the hall, a door creaked open and Paul and Mathers emerged.

"Hey," Paul said.

He grinned and sauntered over, dropping to his knees and scratching my dog behind the ears. Shadow twisted her head and licked Paul's hand.

"Paul?" Mrs. Warzueski said then snuffled, wiping away tears. "What are you doing here? Do you know why Kyle's running away?"

"What?" Paul's brow crinkled.

"She says Kyle's at the bus station," Mrs. Warzueski said. "The police went to go get him."

"Oh, good." He reached out, grabbed my hand, and gave it a squeeze. "Mrs. Warzueski, Kyle's fine. He wasn't running away," he said.

"But—"

The woman police officer took Kyle's mom by the elbow and led her toward a room.

The detective who had questioned Paul slapped him on the back.

"Your turn to wait in the seats. Your mother has been contacted and she'll be here soon."

Paul nodded. Mathers studied Shadow while he twirled the end of his moustache with his thumb and index finger. Then he shrugged.

"Hey, Mathers," the policewoman said as she and Kyle's mother passed. "I need to talk to that girl."

"You'll get your chance," Mathers said.

He waved at me to stand. "Follow me, Miss Whitman. You can bring the dog with you. I'll try to keep this brief. I talked with your social worker, Mrs. Wright, so she knows where you are."

I had given Mathers her number instead of Mr. O'Shawnessy's to spare the old man. The press were already all over the story. But maybe the TV would be off and he wouldn't see the news while drinking his warm cow juice tonight.

Shadow's nails clicked on the linoleum as we entered the rectangular interview room. It contained a long conference table, six chairs, a blue pen and a yellow notepad. Shadow tipped her nose back in response to the smell of stale coffee and sweat.

Mathers gestured to a side seat closest to the paper. After I settled into the chair, he took the seat across from me. Shadow positioned herself next to my chair and leaned her body against my leg.

"Quite an evening you've had, Miss Whitman," he said. "Can you tell me how you came to be on that remote trail tonight?"

This was the moment I dreaded. No matter what I said, it would hurt Mrs. Warzueski. She was as much a victim as Tobin. I wished I had listened to Paul and my father and left the mystery surrounding Kyle's stepbrother alone.

I ran my fingers through Shadow's sleek fur, plucking out a few granules of soil then took a deep breath.

Mathers listened to my whole, crazy story from the time I arrived, and found Kyle dressed as Mickey Mouse, until Mathers restrained Pullman and brought him into custody. The detective scratched his head.

"And why did Dr. Pullman think you figured out where Tobin's remains were buried?" he asked.

I wrung my hands. How could I explain without describing Shadow's ability? Bringing up ghosts could ruin the case against Dr. Pullman. I was so nervous that I started babbling.

"I had picked missing children for my senior project and got interested in Tobin's disappearance. His mom saw a flyer about Tobin on my table. Then today, I told Dr. Griffin, Pullman's girlfriend, about how Shadow kept investigating one corner of the art classroom. Kyle observed my dog's behavior firsthand. He must have told Dr. Pullman who must have worried Shadow's obsession with the corner of the classroom would somehow lead to Tobin's body being discovered. He must have thought I'd—"

"I'm afraid you've lost me," Mathers said.

I took a deep breath and tried again.

"Mrs. Durgette, my art teacher, asked me to bring Shadow in to be a model for our current drawing project. In the classroom today, Shadow kept getting up and sniffing this one corner of the room." My nerves got the best of me and I started rambling again. "I remember Kyle giving me a funny look. Maybe he said something to his uncle. And I told Dr. Griffin, too."

I stopped myself. This wasn't going well. What if I screwed up and Dr. Pullman walked?

"Before you arrived at the clearing," I said, "Dr. Pullman admitted burying his nephew at the high school."

Mathers stroked his chin. "Is Shadow a rescue?"

I nodded.

"You know, our county is the training center for cadaver dogs. I seem to recall an experimental program where the force adopted puppies from the shelter to train them. Only one dog out of dozens worked out. The others were re-homed. Perhaps Shadow was one of those dogs."

According to Dr. Griffin, Shadow had descended from a litter that had been part her research studies into the paranormal. Given my dog's ghost-seeing abilities, that seemed more likely. But I wasn't about to contradict the officer.

"Well, she already knew a lot of commands when I got her. That makes sense."

I was so thankful that Mathers brought up this explanation.

Mathers nodded. "Yes, Paul heard that part of the conversation. But we need more evidence. What do you think about running a test? What if I brought in two chunks of cement from the evidence room, one with bones embedded and one without? If Shadow shows interest in the one with the bones, I'll have Principal Huntsman meet us at the school tonight. He's a golfing buddy, so he'll let me into the school after hours. What do you say? Can we see what Shadow does?"

I didn't have much hope that Shadow would pick the bone-in cement. As far as I knew, she only reacted to ghosts, but I nodded.

Mathers disappeared and returned a few minutes later with two chunks of concrete and a video camera. He set the blocks about six feet apart on the floor. Shadow's ears perked up. She whined and clawed at my leg then strained at her leash to get closer to the objects. Maybe a ghost hovered near the cemented bone. Perhaps this would work.

"Okay, if I record this?" Mathers said.

I nodded. He raised the camera, pushed a button and a red light appeared.

"Go ahead and drop Shadow's leash," he said.

Shadow didn't hesitate. She headed straight for the block furthest from her. She sniffed and whined. Mathers grinned. Shadow must have picked the right one. Mathers pressed a button and lowered the camera.

"We did walk Bones, our German Shepherd cadaver dog, through the high school construction zone when Tobin first went missing. Bones was twelve years old and on the cusp of retirement. Now that I think about it, there were plenty of distracting smells like freshly painted walls and new carpet. The old guy might have missed the scent. Our current canine in the cadaver unit is a bloodhound. He's top notch. If both dogs show interest in the same area of the room, on top of Pullman's confession to you, we'll have a strong case for intrusive work. You game?"

I was so proud of Shadow. She could be instrumental in ensuring Dr. Pullman stayed behind bars for a long time. I patted my dog on the head and nodded.

"This is huge." Mathers grinned. "But I still don't quite understand how Claudia Griffin plays into this?"

I chose my words with care. I had no problem ratting out Claudia, but the hood ornament was my insurance policy.

"Dr. Pullman is her boyfriend," I said. "She's a veterinarian, too. She's obsessed with my dog. She's tried to steal her from me before. Just like tonight, I left Shadow at the vet clinic where Pullman works, and the next thing I know, Griffin has her."

"Well, she does have an interesting history," Mathers said. "First, the woman's high school boyfriend died on their prom night about ten years ago. Then Griffin's parents were in a horrible car crash. And now she's involved in this? That woman attracts trouble. I swear there's more to her story from her high school days and her parent's car wreck."

He knew about David's death? I had another decision to make: give up the hood ornament or not? This had been my means to keep Dr. Griffin in line. What if her lawyer bailed her out of jail? I would need the silver eagle for protection. But Mathers suspected her. The silver eagle might keep her in prison for a very long time. The right thing to do was to turn the object over to the police. I couldn't keep this secret anymore. Not if I were to step into the person that Paul and my father had seen in me. I had done a poor job of living up to their expectations thus far. I had already made one tough choice by calling Mrs. Wright and not trying to cover up this mess. A first step to live up to their vision. Now, I had a second opportunity to prove myself.

"Uh ... I think I can help you with that, too."

I explained that last spring Dr. Griffin confessed how she had used the hood ornament to kill David on her prom night and that it had fallen from her purse and that I had hidden it. I explained where to find the object under the gnome with a basset hound face at the vet clinic. Mathers grilled me on details.

When he was satisfied that this crazy story could be true, he got on his radio. He had a Cheshire-cat grin. Would a promotion be forthcoming for solving multiple cold cases in one night?

Mathers disappeared. When he returned, he brought a soda and a second pad and pen and told me to write up both stories. He stood watching me, as if trying to figure out if he should tell me something. I fingered the pen and met his gaze.

"We picked up, Kyle," he said. "It was just like you said. Your car was parked in the bus station lot. So far he's cooperating."

I hoped they would take into account his age and the circumstances. I hoped college, not jail time, was in his future. But mostly I hoped his mother would survive the shock of the truth.

"This can't have been easy," Mathers added, "but you did the right thing. Your social worker told me about your hearing on Monday and how much it means to you to live with Shadow."

I pulled my dog close. She was a victim of this mess, too. By telling all, by giving up the hood ornament, I had probably sacrificed any chance at gaining emancipation. I would still have to leave Shadow alone each night. I had failed my girl.

"You know, you have handled yourself with dignity and honesty. You are a remarkable young woman and mature beyond your years. Judge Heart and I know each other. I'll make a call on your behalf on Monday."

I looked up. With the endorsement of a police officer, how could the Dragoness deny my petition? My eyes filled.

"Did you hear that?" I said to Shadow. "I might get to come home soon."

Mathers smiled, a kind, fatherly smile. "Don't get all goopy-eyed on me now. We have unfinished business."

I could hardly contain my joy. The detective explained that the high school principal agreed to grant the police access to the art classroom and let the dogs sniff around. Huntsman would meet them at the school in about an hour. He said a uniformed cop would come by in a moment in case I needed anything, and then Mathers left to retrieve the hood ornament.

My father would be proud of my decisions tonight. I longed to feel the warmth of him by my side. I had been awful to him, pushing him away. Oh that sweet connection we had when his spirit melded with my mind. He had said I needed to do something for him. I had been so self-absorbed that I hadn't even thought about what I could do to help him.

I closed my eyes and called for my father. Seconds later, the familiar snap and crackle of air announced Dad's arrival. He must have been close by this whole night. I leaned into his hug. I thought about how much I've changed since he died. I thought about how he had tried to prepare me for life with his gift of the relationship rules and how I found solutions in them.

Always be honest had been the relationship rule I had broken the most. To cover up my embarrassment, I lied to Kyle about going to see my dad. I lied to Dr. Griffin when I said Kyle was my boyfriend. I lied by omission to poor Mrs. Bellweather about her dead rat. I lied to Margaret about the snake in her bed. But most of all, I lied to myself. I fooled myself into thinking that the most important thing to me was my independence, and I had been willing to twist the truth at the expense of others to make it happen. This was not the kind of person Dad raised me to be.

Dad had asked me for help but I hadn't bothered to figure out what he needed. After all, how does a living person help a dead one? He had told me to let go. What if he hadn't been talking about Tobin? Wasn't it the longing of those left behind that prevented ghosts from crossing over? I understood that Dad wanted me to let *him* go. He hadn't intervened when Dr. Pullman tried to drag me away, because he wanted to show me that I didn't need him anymore. I silently thanked him for my life, for his love, and for believing in me. My chest swelled and I sat tall. For the first time since Dad's death, I knew I would find my way without him.

"Okay," I said aloud to the empty room. "Thanks for everything, Dad. I'm going to be okay. You can move on now."

The warmth of my father's embrace receded. I slipped off the chair turning to the one creature I loved as much as my dad. Shadow pressed the flat of her head into my forehead. I looped my arms around the slope of her bowed neck wishing I could melt into her. Together we would get through the challenges that lay ahead because the love we shared was infinite.

EPILOGUE

*'... you will one day see a brighter dawn than
this ...' Lewis Carroll.*

I set my last moving box on my guardian's kitchen table, waiting for Paul to return from next door. Mr. O'Shawnessy's lips puckered into a pout. I walked to the couch where he sat in the living room and planted a kiss on his wrinkled forehead.

"Don't look so sad," I said. "It's not like you won't see me anymore. The court ordered me to check in with you daily until I turn eighteen, remember?"

"Aye, lass," he said with a sigh.

I didn't think supervision was necessary given that the court set bail for both Pullman and Griffin so high they weren't getting out anytime soon. Tobin's remains were recovered just where Shadow and the bloodhound indicated, and the hood ornament sealed Dr. Griffin's fate. Juvenile court ordered Kyle to perform community service and attend joint therapy with his mother. He apologized and had been so sincere that I believed Pullman had tricked him into following Pullman's plan but didn't know how to get untangled. He had never intended to hurt me. Mrs. Durgette testified for me, and Mathers' call to the judge had probably tipped the scales. The birth certificate became a nonissue. I burst into tears when I learned I could live with Shadow again.

"Oh," my guardian said. "I almost forgot. Officer Mathers gave me this to give to ye. He found it when Dr. Griffin's things were catalogued. Said he knew it had to be yers."

He handed me a gold key attached to a key chain decorated with the head of a silver Doberman. It was the spare key that I had kept under the rock. I was happy to have the keychain back, but the key was useless. I wonder what she had been plotting? Well, it didn't matter anymore. I had purchased a lockbox with a number pad and my spare key would be out of her reach from now on.

"Thanks," I said.

Paul trudged into the house, eyed the carton, then smiled. "That the last one?"

"Yep," I said. "But then I need you to bring in the box labeled books from my garage next door into my living room."

Mr. O'Shawnessy frowned. My guardian had forbidden Paul and me to be inside my house alone.

"Don't worry," I said. "I'll stay with you."

This forced Paul to schlep my stuff next door by himself. But he said he didn't mind. I hadn't wanted the old man to feel compelled to chaperone us next door.

"Ye remember me words. I can see how smitten he is with ye."

I smiled.

"Don't worry," I said.

"Where did you want these books again?" Paul asked.

Mr. O'Shawnessy squinted as though I were an opponent he was trying to read. Then he sighed.

"Ye bring me the egg timer and ye've got five minutes to show yer beau where it needs moved."

"Thanks," I said.

After I handed the plastic timer to him, I sprinted out the door and across the driveway into my home. Not my house but my home. Shadow barked an indignant woof at being relegated to the backyard so she wouldn't slip out the open front door. I found Paul standing by the dining room table. I linked my arm through his and guided him into the garage.

"He's timing us," I said. "Five minutes."

I pointed out the box that I wanted brought in the house. After Margaret had found the card with Dad's relationship rules, I had stashed it away in his all-time favorite book. Paul plunked the box onto the floor next to a half-empty bookshelf in my living room. He grinned at me.

"We have four more minutes," he said.

I elbowed him. "Enough time, Romeo, to get the packing tape off."

Paul squatted next to the box. His muscles flexed as he ripped the clear adhesive off the box. I thought about how we had sat together under the old walnut tree at lunch today, shunned by Margaret, her worker bees, and even most of the football team. However, toward the end of the break, a few of her wannabes and a few of Paul's teammates had moved to sit with us. Margaret had fumed, but what else was new?

Paul folded the flaps back and right there on the top was exactly what I had hoped to find: my father's childhood copy of *Alice's Adventures in Wonderland*.

"That's what I wanted," I said, stooping over Paul's shoulder to take the book.

My hand brushed his shoulder and I blushed because of what he might have interpreted from my words along with my touch. The heat radiating from his body warmed me. My fingers trembled, and I dropped the book. The binding splayed, and my face flushed as I realized what fell to the floor.

"Hey." Paul picked up the card "What's this?"

"Something my dad gave me before he died."

I hadn't intended to share the list with him, but I made no attempt to take it away. Instead, I dropped to my knees and leaned close to read the list along with him.

Twelve Relationship Rules

Rule #1: *A successful relationship needs to have balance. Balance of power, balance of respect, and balance of compassion.*

Rule #2: *Be generous.*

Rule #3: *Nobody loves a drama queen. Even if they say they do.*

Rule #4: *Act interested. Be interesting.*

Rule #5: *Always be honest.*

Rule #6: *Never make a promise you don't intend to keep.*

Rule #7: *Run like the wind from possessive guys.*

Rule #8: *Avoid anyone who has no sense of humor.*

Rule #9: *Treat others the way you want to be treated.*

Rule #10: *Never pretend to be something that you're not.*

Rule #11: *Never forsake safety. Keep a cell phone on you, meet dates in public places, and never, ever, get high or drunk on a date.*

Rule #12: *Love is infinite.*

I stopped at Rule #4: *Act interested, Be interesting.* This wasn't necessary for young lovers enamored with each other when everything the other person did seemed endearing. The rule applied to people who had gotten through puppy love, but still wanted to be together. I hoped Paul and I reached that seasoned stage.

"Wow," Paul said. "These are amazing."

"Wait," I said. "Didn't Margaret tell the whole school about these rules after she found them in my backpack? Remember when she was laughing hysterically that lunch period? It was over these."

"No," he said.

"Why did she say she was laughing?"

"She never said. I told her to quit being a mean girl. She rushed off to fix her makeup and then lunch was over. The topic never came up again."

He defended me? I thought about how just a few short days ago I labeled him a dumb jock. But he could be a poster child for Dad's relationship rules. He followed Rule #2: Be generous. He lived by Rule #5: Always be honest. I doubted he had violated Rule #6: Never make a promise you didn't intend to keep.

We both practiced Rule #9 when we went to tell Mrs. Bellweather what really happened to Mansfield-the-rat. Paul insisted on us staying a while longer with the old woman, when I rose to leave. And so we lingered and let the old lady reminisce about her pet between her bouts of tears.

Dad's Relationship Rule #1 required both parties to cooperate. Together we would discover the truth in that rule: A successful relationship needs to have balance.

Balance of power, balance of respect, and balance of compassion.

"Your dad wrote these for you?" he said.

I nodded. Pride welled in my chest that he recognized the goodness in my father. My fingertips lingered on his hand when I took the paper. Electricity charged the space between us.

"I think I would have liked your father," Paul whispered, tucking an errant strand of my hair behind my ear

Because we both squatted on the floor, the couch blocked Mr. O'Shawnessy's view of us if the old man watched out his door. Paul's gaze held mine. I did not look away. I wanted him to see me, really see me.

His lips, soft and gentle, found mine. He tasted of coffee and nutmeg. I brought my hand to his face and pulled him close, shutting my eyes. I didn't ever want to let go.

Shadow barked, jarring me out of my trance. I could almost feel Mr. O'Shawnessy's disapproval wafting from next door, so I stood and pulled Paul to his feet.

"We'd better go," I whispered, "before Mr. O'Shawnessy comes charging over on his walker."

"I've got practice till late tonight, a ton of homework, and I have to start my college apps. Lunch tomorrow?" he said.

I answered with my smile.

I walked Paul to the front door, waving at Mr. O'Shawnessy who watched us from his front window. As soon as Paul drove off, Margaret pulled up in her car. She glowered at me, but I turned away, and shut my front door. I would honor my oath to be nice to her that I had made in exchange for Shadow's life. It would be easy now that I lived next door.

I let Shadow inside the house, picked up Dad's book, and collapsed onto the couch. My dog crawled into my lap as I flipped through the tale of Alice's adventures. The last few pages held an 1876 Easter letter from Lewis Carroll addressed to his young readers. In it, he reflected on the range of emotions that children experience as they grow. The tone of the letter reassured me. I ruffled Shadow's fur as I read Carroll's thoughts in a final paragraph: *"Surely your gladness need not be the less for the thought that you will one day see a brighter dawn than this..."*

Because of Paul, I had lived through Halloween night and had not ended up under the foundation of a new house. It was surreal—what had started as an adventure had morphed into a nightmare. Mr. Carroll had been right though. I had woken from that awful dream to a brighter dawn.

Shadow woofed. I hugged her, careful to keep my fingers away from her eyes. I didn't need to view the world from her perspective anymore. My ghost-viewing days were over. I had found a fairy tale ending. Just like Mr. Carroll described in his letter, tomorrow I would wake up in my own bed to *a new and glorious day.*

AFTERWORD

Ruby, a red Doberman with a distinctive ridge on her snout, came into my life in 2017 when she became the icon for my newly launched, dog-rescue column in San Francisco East Bay's local arts and entertainment newspaper, *The Diablo Gazette*. With her characteristic zipper nose, this celebrity girl captured my heart and she and owner, Charles Lindsey, have taught me a lot about this often-maligned breed.

While many people equate the breed with their roles as guard dogs, the reality is that reputable breeders of American Doberman pinschers have been working to enhance their gentler side. These days, individuals belonging to this affectionate and highly intelligent breed are often nicknamed "velcro dogs" because they don't like to be separated from their owners. They are perfectly suited as search and rescue or therapy dogs.

Hollywood has been responsible for vilifying Dobermans. John Walter notes the portrayal of the breed as vicious in his Doberman Planet blog https://www.dobermanplanet.com/famous-dobermans-in-movies-and-television/, "Famous Dobermans in Movies and Television: The Complete List", the breed is often portrayed as vicious. In the 2009 Disney movie, *Up*, Alpha the Doberman, spends a great deal of time baring his teeth.

1978 wasn't a good year for the breed. They appeared in the iconic film, *Halloween*. Worse, the 1978 American horror flick, *Dracula's Dog*, depicts a Doberman on a killing spree in a national forest. The breed also appears in these well-known movies: *Father of the Bride*, *The Other*, *First Blood*, and *Flags of our Fathers* to name a few. A comprehensive list of movies that include everything from cameos to major roles including foreign films can be found at http://www.reeldogs.com/doberman-pinscher/. The best example of the breed's softer nature is the 1946 movie, *It Shouldn't Happen to a Dog*, where Rodney the Doberman is portrayed correctly as intelligent, loyal, and lovable.

Ruby is a tribute to the gentle side of her breed. She is a smart, mellow Doberman pincher with a knack for attracting attention, largely due to a combination of her owner's photographic skills and her regal appearance. Ruby's long head, cropped and erect ears, and sleek, muscular body are indicative of her breed. Her ability to shine under the lens has made her wildly popular on social media with over 139,000 followers (and growing) on Instagram.

If you are now smitten with the Doberman breed and are considering adopting or purchasing a dog, as with any pet, examine your lifestyle. Are you able to train and exercise your dog? Do you have space for a large dog? How much time do you spend away from home? If purchasing a puppy is your preference, please go through a reputable breeder. Dilated cardiomyopathy (DCM) is a common and lethal genetic defect that is perpetuated by backyard breeding. It also can be tragic for Doberman owners who prematurely lose their beloved pets. The extra money spent on a well-bred Doberman is worth it. Whether you have a Doberman or appreciate all dog breeds, I hope you find joy in reading about Shadow's adventures in *Between Shadow's Eyes* and *From Shadow's Perspective*. Sign up for announcements on future novel releases at www.jillhedgecock.com.

Dear readers, if you enjoyed *From Shadow's Perspective,* please go to my website www.jillhedgecock.com to sign up to receive news on the release date of future novels. Please also consider posting a review on www.goodreads.com and Amazon.

Many thanks!

Book Club Questions and Discussion Guide

1. How do you feel about the idea of a pet rat? Are you afraid of snakes? Were you surprised that Sarah wasn't squeamish about handling these types of animals?

2. Have you ever judged people based on a first impression then changed your mind the way Sarah did with Paul?

3. At any time in the story did you think Sarah should stop investigating the identity and the cause of death of the ghost boy?

4. Sarah grapples with feelings about Kyle and Paul. Do you think Sarah made the right choice? Have you ever been conflicted about choosing between multiple boyfriends/girlfriends?

5. If you could add one or more relationship rules to Dad's list what would they be?

6. Do you think Sarah should have told Mr. O'Shawnessy what Margaret did to her computer?

7. Did reading the book make you want to consider the Doberman breed as your next pet?

8. Should Sarah have immediately alerted the police to Tobin's possible burial spot?

9. Have you ever been afraid of someone in a Halloween costume?

10. Were you surprised when you learned the identity of Tobin's killer?

* * *

I LOVE book clubs. I am happy to Skype into your meeting (or visit in person if possible).

Contact me through my website to coordinate:

www.jillhedgecock.com

ACKNOWLEDGEMENTS

From Shadow's Perspective was written while my agent at Red Fox Literary, Karen Grencik, shopped *Between Shadow's Eyes*. Throughout the writing journey, the talented members of my critique group remained by my side. Elisabeth Tuck is the best editor a novelist could hope for. Despite her efforts, I still manage to make mistakes and assume full responsibility for any lingering errors. Some of the *Alice in Wonderland* quotes do have those grammatical issues that were not corrected. Cheryl Spanos brought insight into the special considerations of YA plots. Fran Cain has an uncanny knack to sniff out logic flaws. David George is great at all things weather, Susan Berman has a flare for improving romance scenes, and Melanie Denman lends her gift for plotting.

Much gratitude goes to Charles Lindsey for allowing his dog, Ruby, to grace the cover of this book. A big thank you to John Walter for his enthusiasm for the Doberman breed and my novels. Many thanks to my supportive family, my husband Eric, daughters Kelly and Lindsay, and sister, Sue. Lastly, I hope my prose has done justice to the many dogs that have enriched my life.

The path to publication for my Shadow books was a long one. I'm grateful to my Shush and Write group for the scheduled time and tea and snacks that fueled my creativity and to Marianne Lonsdale, Janine Kovac, and Colleen Gonzalez for including me in Write On Mama's writing retreats in the picturesque Santa Cruz mountains. These scheduled writing times whether on a weekday evening or during a quiet weekend away provided both a supportive community and productive writing time.

Dear readers, if you loved *From Shadow's Perspective*, please go to my website (www.jillhedgecock.com), and sign up for news on upcoming novels.

About the Author

Jill Hedgecock is an award-winning and internationally-published author. She is an avid animal lover, with a special love of all things canine. Ruby, the Doberman featured on the book cover, is the mascot for Hedgecock's dog rescue column in the *Diablo Gazette*. Her debut novel, *Rhino in the Room*, was a Solo Medalist Winner for New Apple's Book Awards for Excellence. She lives in California with her husband and three rescue dogs. Visit www.jillhedgecock.com to learn more.

If you enjoyed the book, please consider posting a review on www.goodreads.com and other platforms such as Amazon.

Many thanks!

Also by Jill Hedgecock

Novels

Rhino in the Room, 2018 Solo New Apple Medalist Award

Between Shadow's Eyes

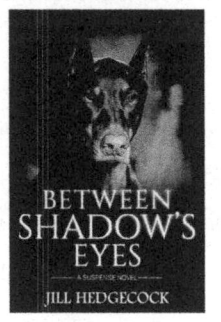

Short Stories

"A Year and a Day" in *What Doesn't Kill You: An Anthology of YA Short Fiction*

The Red Book: The Final Word on Sasquatch

Made in the USA
Las Vegas, NV
16 July 2022

51720986R00213